NORMAN'S COUSIN & OTHER WRITINGS

RON SINGER

Author's Note

These writings reflect a half-century of my life in New York City. The period has been divided between Brooklyn (1974-95) and Manhattan (1995-the present). The book's arrangement is roughly chronological, which means that two long, paired stories, *Buying a Car* and *Selling a Car*, are separated. Aside from *Voir, Dear*, a radio play, and *Carla*, a libretto, the contents are all stories. In the sense that it is a retrospective collection of my work, *Norman's Cousin & Other Writings* forms a trilogy with *The Promised End* (Unsolicited Press, 2019) and *Gravy* (Unsolicited Press, 2020).

To Leo and Zoe, the beloved carriers of my family genes.

CONTENTS

Buying a Car

Brooklyn, Queens & Long Island, June 1975

--1--

The ideal person to buy a used car from would be your mother. Who else is so generous and kind, so single-mindedly devoted to your good fortune, so instinctively concerned that your nurture be sufficient? Realistically, it is of course unlikely that you would have occasion to buy a used car from your own mother. What I mean to say is that maternal qualities in the seller are the surest signs of a reliable used car. In addition, the transaction itself should have the feeling of "family business." The car should seem like a hand-me-down. You are getting it because "Mother" wants something a little bigger or smaller, a little newer or more luxurious. Also, the financial element ought not to obtrude. Since the seller isn't really your mother, you do have to pay, of course, but the price should be painlessly low, low enough to be thought of as a little something toward her new car. The idea is that you, the son, are working now, so you should pull your own weight, or, at least, seem to. Far from wanting to haggle over the price, you should feel like saying, "Thanks, Mom." If a third party is present during the transaction, be careful not to smile about the price.

Here is a case where my car-buying theory was vindicated. Last year, an Auto Mechanics teacher at the school where I worked bought a used VW Square Back after checking it out very carefully. Two months later, it threw a rod. When I asked him how he could have been so wrong, he explained, "There are things in a car you just can't see."

Exactly.

But, I asked, did he evaluate the seller?

"He was just a guy."

Don't get me wrong. I'm as practical as the next person. I've looked over the *Consumer Reports* frequency-of-repair charts. I know the signs --the color of the water in the radiator, the amount of wear on the brake pedal and on the inside driver's side door handle. And I know the tricks --the odometer that changes one mile every time the car goes a mile-and-a-half, the STP temporarily hiding oil leaks. But I don't think these types of "evidence" are of more than marginal usefulness. As the Auto Mechanics teacher learned, vital signs are often undetectable. A good faker can fool most people. Also, cars are not statistics, but individuals: the *C.R.* charts represent only a minor probability with regard to any particular car.

My own idea of "data" is the twitch of an eyelid and the momentary tightening of the mouth when a seller is confronted with a cleverly pointed question. On the psychological level, buyer and seller are, at least potentially, more evenly matched than on the technical level. Especially if you use my "mother rule," you won't often be fooled. Most of us carry around too vivid memories of our nurture to confuse a pretender with a real mother figure.

Naturally, the reader is free to believe my theory or to laugh it to scorn. This story will show how I came to develop the theory and to apply it. The reader can judge for himself. To anticipate, I was using it when I made up my mind to buy Mrs. Arnold (Ellen) Meltzer's car over the phone. (Of course, I went to see it afterwards, but I had been sold over the phone.) It was a '67 Square Back for $525, which isn't a terrific price. Of course, she said many things that convinced me of her suitability to sell me a car, but, if I had to choose one utterance that was the clincher, it was this:

"Oh, you sound like such a nice young man. I hope you and your wife decide to buy it. It's a good car." Fate had issued its decree. You see, I could imagine my mother saying those words.

The reader should understand that I had been looking for weeks when I called Mrs. Meltzer. My wife and I had been out of New York for about ten years, and back in the city for less than one. We had been wondering when the sky would fall. Since one gets such a bad idea of New York from hearsay and from out-of-town newspapers, we had returned to the city full of fears.

As we had discovered, there was a degree of truth to all the horror stories: New York was dirty, on the verge of bankruptcy, crazy and crime-ridden. Yet nothing had happened to us. Instead, the city seemed to lift our mood, to surprise us pleasantly. For one thing, we had been rather surprised by its charm. This was partly a function of our having grown up enough to be able to appreciate charm. As a teenager, I hadn't been big on charm.

It was now June of 1975. Buying a car was necessary because, as we were told, one needed to get away from Brooklyn during the summer in order to survive another year. The Fourth of July seemed a good time to be out of town, as was suggested by the bombardment that had already started in the schoolyard behind our house. Since my own school was already shut down for summer vacation, I had ample time for wild-goose chases. My wife, currently teaching Art two days a week at a neighborhood primary school, became the junior partner in the car-buying enterprise. Besides, she did not share my obsession, which, in retrospect, was obviously based upon my (inferior) gender. For perhaps the same reason, the firecrackers bothered me more than they did her.

The purchase of a used car loomed in my mind as the litmus test of the city's livability. I had heard about the dirty tricks of people selling used cars in New York. For instance, an attractive car would be advertised, and, when you came to look at it, you would be mugged for the purchase money, perhaps forced to sign a check or money order, and then held captive while someone went to cash it. Since many people now carried cash so that they could just ride off with the car, rather than trust the seller with a deposit, it was often even easier for the thieves. (In 1975, credit cards were not yet available to low-income people like us.) Even if these horrors went unrealized, as I suspected they would, this would be a chance for me to rub up against the notoriously abrasive New Yorker, to be indecently vulnerable to some of the world's consummate insulters.

By the time I called Ellen Meltzer, as I have said, I had already been looking for weeks. Since I had no car in which to look for a car, I began by limiting my search to Brooklyn, the borough in which we lived. Early the first Thursday (June 5th), I bought a copy of *Buy Lines* and called about a VW and a Plymouth. The VW turned out to be near our house, and it sounded good, so I made an appointment to see it at three that afternoon. Then, I called about the Plymouth, and got directions and some reassuring murmurs. I said I'd be there in about an hour. Not that I thought I'd buy these first cars --I was just using them to get my feet wet.

The Plymouth was located in a place called Seagate. I had never been there, but I learned from the seller that Seagate is near Coney Island, which I'd been taken to many times as a child. The train from my house to Coney Island is an elevated, and it twisted, squawked and squealed along over the dull western side of Brooklyn. As it stopped and went, stopped and went, above the rows of houses, something began to dawn on me. He had said it was a Plymouth, but what *kind* of Plymouth? My first mistake had been made, and I was annoyed. An exasperatingly stupid, naive and nervous person had carelessly been delegated to make the call on behalf of the car-sharper now going in person to examine the "Plymouth." We'd have to get rid of that guy.

Finally, we reached the end of the line, and I climbed down to the street. What a shock! This wasn't at all what I remembered. I was terrified, it was too much. Even though I was only carrying about six dollars, I feared robbery. (At this stage, in the unlikely event that I might actually want to buy the car, my plan was to give the seller a verbal assurance, and a check for the deposit.) Instinctively, I reached for my wallet.

To my eye, the population of Coney Island now consisted entirely of pimps, whores, muggers, addicts, pickpockets, the insane and physically disabled, the unsavory elderly, and the dotty poor. Everyone was too fat or too thin. Complexions were uniformly bad. Neither a muscle nor a calm face was in evidence. It was a hot day, but people were wearing everything from woolen overcoats to bare chests. It was all corn on the cob, tattoos, green fingernails, sweat, pimples, and euphoria or stupor. I was in the Anti-Suburb. Trash danced wantonly across my feet, thirty or forty people appeared to be giving me the eye. One man had an earring in one ear. Across from the bus stop where I stood, the roller coaster occasionally clattered, and, at the hot dog stand, a few people stood around waiting for something to happen -- almost no one was eating a hot dog.

To establish contact with another person, I asked a sick-looking old man in a big black suit whether the Seagate bus stopped here.

"Urgghung," he replied, and I thanked him. That was better.

Soon the bus came. I sat across from the driver. We moved west through Coney Island, first past the rides and games, parallel to the boardwalk, through the stretched-out, scattered amusements. Then, we turned right and crept up a long narrow road full of shops, many boarded up or with broken or gated windows. No one got on or off. Old *Vote for Beame* signs and graffiti (*Mungo Biz*) appeared on walls, some dingy, some multi-colored. Garbage covered the gutter and sidewalks. There was almost no one on the street, two or three strays at most. One would have thought it was Sunday, the few open shops were so dark, the customers so sparse.

Now the bus turned left into a narrower street and sped up, slamming and jouncing between rows of young Black and Spanish men in undershirts. We were in the "residential" section of Coney Island. Wine bottles, laughter, "Mother Fucker," the almost uniform wildness of the streets, occasionally punctuated by the despairing or stolid wooden-Indian face of a silent old Jew or Italian who had apparently been left behind on moving day. Past a housing project we went. A few people got on or off. Kids screamed along on banana bikes or skateboards. A paper-faced old woman peeked out at the bus from behind first-floor curtains.

Coney Island! It had changed from the exciting, satisfying scene of goodies and rides I remembered from childhood into a schlock phantasmagoria. It was high camp, something only a junkie could call "fun."

Finally, the bus rounded another corner, jerked to a stop, and we were there. Seagate, the last stop. What an incredible difference! Adjacent as it was to Coney Island, Seagate impressed me as simply a different unreality. It looked as if it had been marooned by social change or shifting tides. Strange, indeed!

Here at the end of Brooklyn, a few feet beyond the hellhole, Coney Island, with the Atlantic on the other side, you see a little white arch. You can drive through, or walk around, this arch, which has a booth in its right leg manned by armed guards with walky-talkies. Young, sleek, tough guards, too, not seedy old dozers. These are pros. Since I clearly belong, they don't even bother me.

And, then, quiet tree-lined streets. The houses are all small and mostly very neat; I believe the residents would describe them as "modest." Boats stand in many of the driveways --also "modest."

Seagate might be a waxwork exhibit of "Suburbia" in a cheap Coney Island boardwalk museum. Some of the houses need a little paint, but most are very smart. The styles imitate imitations, Southern California, mostly: the white, awninged, stucco bungalow with shrubs in front and a small lawn with flowers. No kids' toys outside, and no trash or garbage. High little standards this neighborhood must have. Somehow holding on. The residents are probably paying through the nose to go on living the old life in the now screwed-up city. Why? Loyalty? Insufficient funds to move? Mass psychosis (a shock syndrome)? Who knows?

I find myself wondering how they get out. Do they save up for a semi-annual helicopter trip to Radio City Music Hall? Do they all go out together, armed with tire irons and garden trowels, edging through Coney Island hidden behind moving shrubs? There are no dogs barking, I notice, surely odd in a place like this. The Seagaters, as I learn later, all own huge German Shepherds whose vocal cords have been severed by municipal ordinance.

By inquiring at a local market, I discover that the Seagaters use a lot of toilet paper, but hardly any plain white. They are reported to have the highest incidence of backyard barbecues of any community within the New York City limits. If Coney Island is a junkie's dream, Seagate has been dreamed into life by a Borscht Belt comedian.

There have been three dissertations in Cultural Anthropology, six in Sociology, about the "Gaters." One hundred percent of the women are housewives. The teenagers, after graduating from Seagate High, ride in little electric carts through secret tunnels under the streets to Brooklyn College. There, wide-eyed, they learn that beyond the waters there are other lands, lands with names like "Manhattan," "New Jersey," "Xanadu."

To return to the matter at hand, I was unsure, on first perusal, but I thought that Seagate might be a good place to buy a used car. It would depend on whether old-fashioned moral standards had been kept up along with the old-fashioned lawns and streets. A safe, but guarded, place. Could the inhabitants be trusted? The reader may note that, even then, I was thinking more in terms of sellers than of cars.

For four blocks, I walked down Seagate Avenue behind a blond teenager, who betrayed no fear that she was being stalked. House after house, I passed, the differences between them insignificant. Then, from afar, I spotted an old Plymouth. Huge and black, it looked like a Fury. A growing half-knowledge became a panicky certainty as I saw that I was nearing the right house number. It *was* the Fury! As I got close, I noticed all the signs of a car I didn't want. I was looking at an old piece of junk. Rust along the bottom edge. One bald, and one balding, tire at curbside. I was immobilized between the hope that there might be a nice little Valiant in the garage and the desire to flee this pig of a car and this unreal neighborhood (although, admittedly, Seagate and Coney Island were the most interesting places I'd seen in months).

Then, I noticed the house. Clearly, it matched the car. What was a dump like this doing in Seagate? Superficially, it might have been like the other houses --a white Southern California bungalow, square pillars on either side of the red brick porch steps, geraniums in boxes beside the steps. But it was really nothing like the rest.

The stucco needed paint, many of the bricks were chipped or loose, and one was missing altogether. There were small tears in the front screen door, and one corner was ripped out from the frame. The lawn was balding and full of crabgrass. Lying on its side in the driveway was a broken yellow-and-red hobbyhorse with wheels. This last object (surely a symbol) I only half-registered, for, just as I was looking at the junk-strewn driveway, a man came out on to the porch and started down the steps toward me.

Like the car and house, he was shabby. Car and man: overweight. Car, house and man: all in need of a scraping, a washing, and a new coat. Actually, the man was in his undershirt. He was middle-aged and lethargic. My eye caught a hand-written sign tacked to one side of the screen door: "Everything is FOR SALE." Worse and worse! I thought of walking right past the house, but I had stared for too long, and my eye had been caught. I wish now that I had had the presence of mind to ask if "Elmer Putzbush" lived there.

Instead, "I called about the Plymouth."

A sweep of his hand toward the tank. Of course! As we walked to the curb together, I realized that gas now cost 59.9 cents a gallon --at the discount stations. And what was this? No plates on the car?

"Fury I," I read on the side.

"Uh, does it need any repairs?"

"Nope, not even an oil change."

"Can we go for a ride?"

"Uh, okay, but, uh, just around the block. It has no plates."

I got behind the wheel and started her up. The engine sounded all right, but the car handled like the Queen Mary: the corner turn was like navigating a narrow channel in rough weather. We circled the block and pulled back into the same parking space --a big one, luckily. I noticed there were no oil spills in the parking space.

"How's parking around here, pretty tight?"

"Not too bad. Well, how do you like her? Runs pretty good, doesn't she?"

Leaving the engine on, we had a look under the hood together. Even with the hood up, the car ran pretty quietly, but the engine was shaking heavily.

"How many miles did you say she has on her?"

"Oh, about fifty-eight thousand." A lie?

"Not bad. What year was she, again, a '67?"

"68."

"Uh, actually, it's a little big for me. Uh, does she get good mileage?"

By now, I was stalling, searching for an exit line. He'd been looking down the whole time, hands shoved into pockets.

"Yeah, pretty good. About ... oh... I'd say maybe eighteen in the city."

Alas, my faith had been further shaken. Impossible.

"Uh, six or eight cylinder?"

"Oh ... uh ... eight."

He had hesitated because he realized a lie would be detected immediately, but he was also wondering if I realized that an eight never gets eighteen in the city.

"Uh, how come she doesn't have any plates?" My certainty that I'd smelled this guy out was making me more confident. He smiled.

"Uh, well, I, uh, bought it for my daughter a few weeks ago, but she says it's too big for her. That's why I'm selling it, she can't park it."

He smiled again, "man to man," thinking he was being clever. But I hoisted him with his own petard.

"Yeah, well, you know, that *is* a problem. My wife would probably have the same problem as your daughter." I planned my exit. "You know, she's strictly a Volks driver, we've always had Volks's. Too bad." He thought hard for three seconds.

"Oh? What kind of car were you interested in? It said in *Buy Lines* that it was a Plymouth, didn't it?" This caught me unprepared; I'm not good at unexpected turns. I fell back on the truth.

"Well, actually, uh, I, uh, was more interested in a Valiant --you know, a six. I should have told you that over the phone, I guess."

"A Valiant? Well, you know, as a matter of fact, a friend of mine does have a nice Valiant for sale. A six, too." A cheap shot out of the blue. "Real clean. I think he'd let it go for a song." The clincher. This guy was definitely a swindler.

"Well, at least I didn't buy it," I feebly consoled myself.

Three hours wasted. Well, I was learning. Find out *exactly* what kind of car it is: the model, how many doors, deluxe or regular. It occurs to me to ask why all his stuff is for sale. Is his house for sale? His grandmother?

"Oh, no," he replies, "just trying to clear some of the junk out of the yard."

When he says this, I feel somewhat reassured, so I buy the car, after all. (He's asking $575, but I get it for $550.) I drive the black Fury out past the guards. Two blocks later, it starts to go, "clunk clunk." So I crawl back, clunking, to 126 Seagate Avenue, only to find a vacant lot where the house had been. On a tree beside the curb is a big sign:

"Sold! Everything. Yeah, the house and granny, too! Ha, ha, sucker!"

Even the trash and broken hobbyhorse are gone.

In reality, what I said was, "Well, I don't have any more time now, uh, I mean, uh, for your friend's, uh, Valiant. Listen, I'll call you if I'm interested. Thanks a lot." I left him standing by the car, thinking about something or other. He had already plunged into his own world. His hands were still in his pockets, and his body was curled into what looked like a shrug. I noticed all this as I waved to him over my shoulder.

I hurried back down the street, out the gates, again unnoticed. Returning to the bus stop (the end of the line, and the first stop toward Coney Island), I waited for a minute or two, agitated. Then I went back to the booth and asked a guard when the bus was due. He told me. There was time for a phone call. I hurried to a booth half a block away and called my wife. (Little did I know it, but this was to be the first of many such calls.)

"Hi, it was a bomb. I think the guy's a used car dealer or a fence or something. It was huge, and, when I told him I didn't want it, he said his friend has a smaller one --a Valiant-- cheap. And the car had no plates. He said he got it for his daughter, but it's too big for her. I got away by saying it would be too big for you, too."

"He sounds awful. Couldn't you have found out it was big over the phone?" Good point.

"Well ... it's hard to think of everything. I guess I should have, though. I'm learning ... I'm going to have to be careful. In a way, I'm glad I met such a dumb crook first. Maybe this will make me harder to cheat."

"Wel-ll ... I guess." Silence. "Are you coming back now?"

"Oh, uh, hmm. Oh, hey, you should see Coney Island! I hardly recognized it, it's turned into a bad slum."

"Oh, yeah? Be careful."

"I only have a few dollars. I won't resist if I get mugged --unless the mugger is tiny and unarmed." Big shot now, experienced car buyer. "Hey, want to go see the Square Back in Brooklyn Heights with me? Remember? The second guy I called? It sounded better than this one."

"Okay, but how do I get there. I want to take a shower first."

"Perfect. By the time you take a shower and get over there, I'll be there. I'll meet you at the guy's place. It's --have you got a pen?"

"Uh ... yeah."

"One-four-seven Henry Street. You know where Henry is. Just take the Fifth Avenue bus, and then walk into the Heights. I'm not sure, but I think the number should be pretty close to Atlantic. Let's see, I'll meet you there at ... uh ... " My watch said one-thirty. "What did we tell the guy ... three? Okay?" I felt that I was managing the arrangements with my wife quite well. Unreasonably, this made me feel more like a competent car buyer.

"Okay. But are you sure you can make it in time? It's one-thirty."

"I think so. If I'm not there, just start looking the car over. Ask some questions. I won't be long." A pause.

"I'm afraid. Is it safe?"

"Oh, yeah, that neighborhood is fine during the day. Just don't go inside the house. Don't worry, it ... oops! There's the bus, see you later. Bye."

"Okay, bye." She blew me a parting kiss over the phone.

I ran and caught the bus. The driver and I sat for a few minutes, then headed back to Coney Island. I wondered momentarily if my wife would really meet me in Brooklyn Heights. Of course, she would!

I went down to the Turkish feast,

the people they was eatin' like a wild beast,

I'm going back, back to Coney Isle.

I realized that song had been in my mind for hours.

The return trip was bound to be less shocking, since we went over the same ground, except backwards: the project and the kids, the drinking and shouting in the streets, the old person here and there, the scarred walls and dead shops, the street alongside the boardwalk. Very soon, I was back at the Coney Island subway stop.

It was only 2:15, so I decided there was time for a quick look at the boardwalk. Actually, I "decided" while I was waiting to cross the street at a long light: I just changed my mind about waiting for the light to change. I suppose, too, that having completed my babtism-by-garbage, my fear and shock were giving way to curiosity. Teachers, they say, are curious people. Oh --I haven't mentioned yet that I'm an English teacher. I work for the *SMILE* program at City University: *Support for Minorities in Literacy in English.* The summer vacation had already begun, which is why I was able to spend these days car-hunting.

At any rate, I turned around and walked up one of the narrow streets that led to the foot of the ramp and then disappeared under the boardwalk. I wondered what could be going on under there now, since, even when I was a child, the place had been associated in my mind with sin. As I passed the hot dog booth, the loungers eyed me idly. The corn-on-the-cob seller momentarily raised his eyes from the pot of steaming water, but he quickly saw that I was a non-customer and lowered his glance again. Up on the boardwalk, I went faster. A warm wind was blowing. Two pretty Spanish girls looked me over as I approached their booth, a little round one set out by itself in the middle of the boardwalk.

"Hey, Sport," said one, with a smile and a beckoning finger, "come over here. Let us tell your fortune."

But I hurried past, waving a "no."

"No, thanks, not today," I mumbled to myself.

I hurried on to the next street, feeling exhilarated and flustered, only half-taking in the ocean, the people on the benches, and the food and game booths. The boardwalk seemed to have changed less than the rest of Coney Island, except that there was very little business now, whereas I remembered crowds. For the first week in June, I thought, the place seemed dead, and I guessed that the tawdriness of the area had scared away most of the customers.

Still hurrying, I took the next street down off the boardwalk, but, halfway back to the subway, I was stopped by the sight of an automatic baseball pitch. A few guys were testing their skills. The fast pitch was as impossibly fast as I remembered it: I could no more hit it now than

I had been able to as a teenager. The slow pitch was more tempting: I had always been able to make contact with that one. Why not! Go ahead, be a sport, only a quarter. No, I wouldn't do it, I wouldn't spend the money. It was time to go, anyway.

Back on the main drag. Hot dog at Nathan's? Can't Coney Island tempt me to anything? There's a Nathan's near my house now, and the one I had there wasn't very good. Getting late, anyway, save the money, supposed to be here looking for a car, not fooling around. Be good!

In my subway car on the way back, there were only three young Black couples and me. The girls had cotton candy, and one wore a jaunty Coney Island hat. All six teenagers were brightly dressed. The boys looked sullen and tired, and the girls were chattering to each other.

"Didn't we have a good time!" all three girls seemed to be saying. They were a sisterhood for mutual cheering, and they acted their parts with a certain satisfied self-consciousness, as if their behavior were a convention they were expected to observe: All right, it's nice this way. The boys, on the other hand, were cool dudes. In their sullenness, they took in the girls' good feeling like people trying to hide their pleasure at being praised.

Suppose that a polite and friendly, middle-class Black reporter from the *News* asked them, "And how did you gentlemen enjoy your day at Coney Island?"

They might answer something like, "Coney Island, man? It's all right, not bad, it pass the time. The ladies dig it, so you see, man, it's cool with us."

It seemed strange to me that they were going home so early. Actually, maybe they were going someplace else, making a day of it. Or they had run out of money, or had used up Coney Island.

A few other people, Black and white, joined us as we headed for downtown Brooklyn. More than one of the whites looked a little startled to see six Black teenagers in the nearly empty car. One white --me-- didn't count. Then, when another white got on, and another Black, two didn't count.

The merrymakers got off at DeKalb Avenue and, unsure myself of where to get off, I chose Court Street, which I knew was somewhere in Brooklyn Heights. It turned out that this station was actually on the other side of the Heights from Henry Street. It was almost three by now, so I had to hurry.

Since this account is already long, and I realize that not every reader is all that interested in the minutiae of car-buying, I'll skip the Brooklyn Heights episode. Obviously, my wife and I took a pass on that car, a VW Square Back offered by another liar. That first day of car hunting left me less sure I could find what I wanted if I limited my search to Brooklyn. So the next day (Friday), I called a cousin of my wife's, who had often said we could use his car, and arranged to borrow it the following Thursday.

Buying a car turned out to be not at all easy. In fact, the next three weeks were a farce. To borrow my wife's cousin's car (which I wound up doing three times), I had to take two subways and a bus to his wife's office, where I would collect the keys, a map showing where the car happened to be parked that day, and a letter authorizing me to use it. (I kept giving this letter back to them, in hopes that each time I borrowed the car would be the last.) I would then take a second, long bus ride to the car, and begin the day's search. Returning at six or seven, I would park near their house, give them back the keys and letter (they would be home by then), recount the day's misfortunes over dinner, and, finally, take the bus and subway home, usually arriving by ten or eleven. If not for these kind relatives, the search would have been even more trying. They loaned, fed and sympathized, all with a free good will.

During those weeks, I went all over the city and suburbs: in the borrowed car, by bus, subway and taxi. I also walked a lot. Once, I took the Staten Island Ferry and a bus. (I'll skip that one, too.) Another time, I spent $1.65 for a ride on the Long Island Railroad. I was met at the station (as if I were a commuter) by a high school kid driving the car I had come to look at. My reaction to seeing the kid pull up in the car was, "At least it got him here." (I'll come back to this one.)

I visited all sorts of places: a garment factory in Bay Ridge, Brooklyn; a commune in a row house on Staten Island; several middle-class apartments in Brooklyn and Queens; a pee-stained hallway in a Brooklyn ghetto; a split-level house way out on Long Island, with two Cadillacs and a boat in the driveway. ("My" car, a '67 Valiant without plates, was parked around the corner in another driveway.)

I toyed with, and then discarded, the theory that had first occurred to me in Seagate, that neighborhoods mattered. Various brands emerged as favorites, especially Volvos, Darts and Valiants, all from 1965 to 1968, which was the newest we could afford. I soured on VW's and became indifferent to others.

Little by little, I got into the habit of watching people carefully, and I developed a repertoire of what seemed to me to be probing questions. I did not buy a car from: a tough, thirty-year old Italian (whose car shook too much), a Puerto Rican gypsy-cab driver (whose car, the cab, was dying), a Puerto Rican housewife (car sold before I arrived), a teenage Arab who installed shag carpet (the Valiant without plates), an elderly perfect gentleman (whose son had sold the car before I got there), and several others.

I had one ten-minute phone conversation with a man whose accent was so thick that all I could make out was his address and his claim about the car --"shebeeoooteeefooool." I couldn't even guess which continent this man came from, and I didn't go see that car, because I hadn't been able to learn anything about it, and because it was far from my home.

In the ensuing three weeks, the boom of the firecrackers grew louder and more constant, putting pressure on us to buy so we could escape by the Fourth of July. Each Thursday, I would get *Buy Lines*, and for most of the weekend, I would go all over the city and suburbs in pursuit of a decent $500 car. Of course, the reasons I always failed to come home with a car were miscellaneous, but, after the first two weeks, I began to see a(nother) pattern.

In almost every case in which a car was not bought, the breakdown of negotiations in some way involved a failure of trust. When a car started clunking or smoking, of course, or when the seller was simply greedy, there was no question of trust, or the lack thereof. But most cases were not so obvious. If the seller was a bull-shitter, rather than a liar, the interaction might prove not unpleasant. But there were several instances when the lack of trust was serious, and these reached crisis proportions during the third weekend. It was then that I met Mrs. Meltzer, and my "mother" theory crystallized.

That weekend was a busy one. On Thursday, I called several likely sellers and saw three or four cars that I either didn't like or couldn't afford. I also set up three viewings for Friday, one each in Staten Island, Brooklyn, and Forest Hills, Queens. To give away the ending, what eventually happened was that, during the third weekend, I saw a good car. And, before the end of that weekend, I bought a different one.

One of the cars I had noted in that week's *Buy Lines* was a '67 Square Back. It sounded good, but I didn't like the model much, and there were lingering associations with the liar in Brooklyn Heights. The last car was a '66 Dart. It, too, sounded good, but it was listed as "N" --Nassau-- so how would I get there? Another expensive, time-consuming wild goose chase? Another begging phone call to my wife's cousin (which, by then, we had vowed against)? What the hell! I called the Dart.

A young voice answered. It was the seller, a high-school kid who worked on the car, himself. It was a good car, he said, nothing needed to be done on it. $525. 56,000 (on the low side). I got directions and said I'd call again the next day if I could find a way to get there. "The car might be gone." That was why I would call again. To his surprise, I gave him my name and number and asked for his name (in reaction to a previous experience).

I was keyed up to see more cars, but there didn't seem to be any left to see. If this was to be the weekend when I finally got a car --and enough was enough, I was getting sick of the whole thing. So I called the VW.

This, as the reader may have anticipated, was Mrs. Arnold (Ellen) Meltzer (although it is important to realize that I didn't learn her name until I reached her house). Perhaps because she sounded so much like my mother, I feel that I can report our conversation almost verbatim. From her first few words, she soothed my wounds.

"Hello?"

"Yes, hello. I'm calling about your VW Square Back. Is it still for sale?"

"Well, yes, it is. A girl looked at it yesterday, but she didn't say if she wanted it. Uh, some other people have called, too, but no one else has come to see it."

"Uh, could you tell me a little about the car? For instance, what repairs would it need? I'm planning a long trip, so I 'm looking for a car that's in really good shape."

"Uh, let's see. Well, the only thing that's wrong with it is that it doesn't always start. Once in a while, it has to be pushed before it will start. That's kind of a nuisance, especially if my husband isn't here."

"Oh, that wouldn't matter to me. I would be the one driving it, mostly, so I could push it. My wife doesn't drive much. And we live on a hill. Uh, how often does that happen?"

"Well, not very often, uh, I'm not sure. Once a month, maybe? Or once every six weeks?" She was asking me. "Just a minute ... ('Arnie --Arnie-- how often do we have that trouble getting the car started?') ('Oh, I don't know, once every five, six weeks, maybe less.') "My husband says, every five or six weeks."

"Oh, that doesn't sound so bad. What about the other things? Brakes? How's the engine? If you can push it, it's a standard shift, right?"

"Stand...? Oh, right, it has a clutch and a shift. Oh, it's a very good car except for the problem with the starting. I think you'd like it."

"Has it ever been in an accident?"

"Oh, no, never."

"Do you mind if I ask why you're selling it?"

"Oh, no, not at all. No, that's a good question. You see, it was my son's. He lived in Georgia, but now he's back in the city, so he doesn't need a car. I'm using it temporarily, because my car was in an accident. I, uh, had a VW bug, and, uh ... I've always liked them. This car is really too big for me. I'm going to get another bug."

"Oh, yeah? That's funny. We've always had bugs, too, but now we want something bigger, like a Square Back."

"That's a coincidence, isn't it?"

"Yes, uh, let's see. Has the car been kept up carefully?"

"Very. I have all the bills. I take it to the dealer for tune-ups and repairs."

"Repairs'? Like what?"

"Oh, uh, let's see. The brakes were fixed last month. Things like that. I had a new turn signal put on, then, too."

"How long have you had the car?"

"Oh, about three months now. It's a nice car, but I'd rather have a bug."

"Uh, let's see. What was I going to ask next? Oh, yeah, what did you have done on the brakes?"

"Umm, I'm not sure, let's see. They squeaked. Uh ... the linings, maybe? Does that sound right?"

"Oh, yeah, that would be possible. How's the body? Any bad dents?"

"Oh, no, none. We have a garage. My son took good care of the car when he had it, too. He lived in the country."

"I see. What was the mileage, again, 54?"

"That's right. A little below 54, actually." She paused, then abruptly said, "You sound like such a nice young man. It's a good car. I hope you and your wife decide to buy it." Then, she added, half-jokingly, "I think fate meant for you to have it."

"Oh, uh, thanks, it's nice of you to say that, it does sound like a good car. Would we be able to see it today?"

"Today? Oh. I'm not sure, hold on." ('Arnie ... can they come see it today? Is Bob coming over? Do we have to go out?') His reply was inaudible. "Hello? Yes, you can come over. But could you make it tonight? We have to go into the city this afternoon ... oh, but there's supposed to be a storm tonight. Do you have a car to come in?"

"Well, no, we don't. Can we come by subway? Where do you live?"

Arrangements were made. They lived in Maspeth, Queens, and getting there would mean a long subway ride and a bus. But, since the car sounded so good, I arranged for us to arrive around 7:30. For some reason, we just assumed my wife was coming, too, although, after the first day, she had not accompanied me on any of my car-buying adventures.

We ate breakfast, during which I told her about the woman and the car, keeping my excitement in check, in light of recent disappointments. The rest of the day we spent working. She is an artist and paints in our big front room, and I have a small study where I do my work for school and write scholarly articles so I can get promoted. The day passed pleasantly.

After an early supper, we started out. It was about six, and it was only drizzling when we left, so we took just one umbrella. By the time we came up out of the subway in Queens, it was pouring. The streets glistened. Most people had taken shelter, and those who hadn't were moving forward in that tense, hopeless skitter city people use when it rains hard. It wasn't clear where the bus stopped and, when I asked a dispatcher, I learned that, to reach the address we wanted, we would have to take not one, but two, buses, with a longish wait in-between. It was gray, getting darker, we were already a little wet, and the buses would have cost $1.40, so we decided to splurge on a cab. I darted out with the umbrella several times before I could find a driver who knew where the address was, a circumstance that still puzzles me. The trip was proving difficult. Inside the cab, we were quite cozy, but most of my pleasure was stolen by the frequent jumps of the meter.

"Do you think we'll like it?" my wife asked.

"I bet we buy it." We smiled.

By the time we arrived at the indicated corner, the fare, including tip, was $2. Not bad, after all. We got out and scurried toward a big building to look for the address. This was the building. But, as we entered the outer lobby, I had a sinking feeling: I realized that I knew neither the name of the seller nor her apartment number. Mrs. Meltzer had neglected to mention her name, and I had just assumed she lived in a private house: she must have sounded like a homeowner. My wife stood waiting for me to ring the buzzer, but none of the names on the list of residents stood out as belonging to the woman I had spoken to. I grimaced and broke the news.

"Do you know what? Something stupid has happened." And I explained.

"Oh, God! You mean she didn't tell you? Why didn't you ask? We've come all the way out here and wasted all this time and money? Oh, no!"

I was thinking fast. "Look, I have an idea. I'll go find a phone and call her again."

She considered this. "But where will you find a phone around here? I didn't see any phone booths or stores or anything."

Actually, I had just realized that, myself, and had already thought of another feeble idea. "Maybe, I could ring someone's bell and ask to use their phone."

Before she could reply, the front door sprang open and a tall, mustached man in a very wet raincoat came in, shaking himself like a dog. He had no umbrella, and he looked miserable as he stood there fishing for his keys.

"Some night," he remarked.

"Say, maybe you could help us," I said, without thinking. "I've done the stupidest thing. You won't believe it. We came here to look at a car that's for sale, but I didn't get the seller's name or apartment number. Do you happen to know a lady in this building who's selling a '67 Square Back? Uh, let's see, her husband's first name is 'Arnie.' I know this is stupid, but..."

He had been listening curiously, and replied immediately. "Oh, yeah, sure. Ellen Meltzer. You're in luck. She mentioned the other day that she was selling her car. Come on in."

Amazed --I, by my luck, and my wife (I suppose) by my quick wits, we followed him into the lobby. It was a nice building. I noticed an announcement for an *Owners' Meeting* and realized I had been right, that Mrs. Meltzer was not a renter, after all. This may also have explained why our helper knew about the car: a building where everyone knew everyone else's business.

Without saying anything else, he led us to the back of the lobby and up a flight of stairs to 2E. He rang the bell, and a slender, simply dressed woman with gray, curly hair and black-rimmed glasses opened the door.

"Ellen, you forgot to tell these people your name or apartment number. Lucky I came by."

"Oh, how stupid of me! Thanks, Harry." Harry smiled at us, and left, waving off further thanks as he headed for the comfort of his own apartment. Mrs. Meltzer smiled warmly. "Come in. I'm so sorry about that. Ar-nie? The couple is here about the car."

He came out: medium height, fat, bald, tee shirt, baggy pants, slippers, a pleasant-looking man. We wiped our feet vigorously on the doormat, left the umbrella in the hall, and stepped over the threshold.

"Arnie Meltzer," he said, extending a hand.

"I'm Ellen Meltzer," said Ellen Meltzer, smiling.

"Bob Green. My wife, Ruth."

"Very nice to meet you, Mr. Green, Mrs. Green," said Mrs. Meltzer politely. "Come in and sit down."

Ruth and I sat next to each other on the couch, Mr. Meltzer sank into an old papa's chair, and Mrs. M. sat down on a mama-sized wing chair. The room surprised me. I had expected Flatbush Rococo, but this place was simple and nice. The prints might not have been to my taste, but the room as a whole felt comfortable and pleasant, not at all jarring or distracting.

"Were the directions all right? I hope you didn't get too wet," Mrs. Meltzer said, after we had all settled into our seats and smiled for a moment. She seemed just the way she had sounded on the phone: slightly scatterbrained, but kind and sensible. She probably talked too much and annoyed her phlegmatic husband, but she looked perfect to buy a car from. Mr. Meltzer, pleasant and placid, sat and listened to the conversation. Mr. and Mrs. Jack Sprat, a common New York combination.

"Oh, the trip was okay," I said. "'It turned out we would have had to take two buses from the subway, so we came by cab. But it didn't cost much more than the buses would have." I was being frank, because I felt comfortable.

Mrs. Meltzer's reply was concerned, but not defensive. "Oh, I'm sorry. I guess I forgot. It's been a while since I took the bus." She smiled a bit anxiously. "Anyway, one of us will certainly drive you back to the station afterwards." She did not treat us like strangers. I liked her more and more.

And so did Ruth, who said, "That's really nice of you."

"How long did it take you to get here?" asked Arnie.

I looked at my watch. "Let's see. We left around six, so about an hour and a half. We made pretty good connections. "He nodded, an agreeable man. No third degree, no anxious follow-up questions. "Well," I suggested, "let's talk about the car."

"Right," said Mrs. Meltzer, standing up. "Here, I brought the bills in so you could look at them.

She produced an official VW owner's folder stuffed with white and yellow bills. I pulled the sheaf out. Some of the bills had the imprint of a dealer in Athens, Georgia, some, of a dealer on Northern Boulevard, here in Queens.

"Wow, you really *have* taken care of this car!"

There were bills not only for frequent tune-ups and oil changes, but small ones for light switches and lenses, medium ones for touching up a fender and for a new battery and some electrical stuff, and the biggest, which was for the brake linings. Nothing major, nothing suggestive of pathology. Several said, "Check out starting system," and "Starting system okay."

Mrs. M. had characterized the one problem accurately: it was a mystery. Apparently, both she and her son, "Mr. R. Meltzer," had been lucky in their mechanics, since they had never been charged for something that had never been fixed. I held the bills out to Ruth, as if I were passing a box of chocolates or a family album.

"No, thanks," she said, smiling.

By now, we all were smiling, especially Arnie. "She babies it."

"Well, let's go have a look," I suggested.

Mrs. Meltzer rose and smoothed her hair. "Are you coming, Arn?"

"No, Dear, I think I'll stay here. Selling the car is your idea, remember? So why don't you go ahead and show it to them, yourself?" He said this matter-of-factly, without malice or sarcasm.

"Okay. We'll come up again afterward, to have some coffee or a drink or something, so don't say good-bye yet."

As the three of us headed out, Arnie had already put on black-rimmed glasses like his wife's. Hoisting his feet onto an ottoman and reaching for a book, he wore that air of hurried contentment that can imply a return to a first-rate mystery novel. We took the umbrella and walked down the stairs. Outside, the rain had let up enough for us just to hurry, instead of bothering with the umbrella.

"It's right across the street." Mrs. Meltzer pointed to a big, low cement structure behind a little strip of grass with a few young trees on it. We crossed the empty street and went in, Mrs. M. unlocking the door, then pulling it down behind us.

The interior of the garage was large and well lit. Our voices echoed. There were broad strips of blue foam rubber tied to most of the pillars beside the smallish parking spaces. (Evidently the car owners had grown tired of denting their fenders in their own garage.) With

Mrs. Meltzer leading the way, we walked about two-thirds of the way down one of the aisles. I peered ahead, searching for the car.

"Here it is," said Mrs. Meltzer.

It was the navy blue we both like, and very clean. Simultaneously, I said, "What a nice car!" and Ruth said, "Oh, it looks nice."

Mrs. Meltzer nodded and handed me the keys. She had become tense. "Here, you drive," she said quickly. "But, please, be *very* careful. I'm still afraid from my accident."

Ruth caught her anxiety and reassured her. "Don't worry, Mrs. Meltzer. Bob is a wonderful driver. You'll feel safe with him."

I felt proud. We all got in, Ruth in the back, and the car started right up. Mrs. M. put her seat belt on. I followed suit. No one said anything. The car seemed excellent, making that reliable ticking sound. I turned on the lights, tried the wipers, let out the emergency brake, and played a little with the gear stick. Then, very slowly, I let out the clutch, giving her a lot of gas, and inched back into the aisle. There was no sign of stalling. Mrs. Meltzer was perched on the edge of her seat. In the mirror, I could see Ruth, who looked placid and slightly prim, as she does when she is relaxed and enjoying something I am doing. Life meant for Ruth to have a skillful chauffeur.

"Runs great," I remarked, as I started slowly forward.

I wanted to do everything possible to put Mrs. Meltzer at ease. She said nothing. There was an electric eye, so we drove right out. Slowly, still, I turned onto the quiet, medium-sized street. Mrs. M. was so tense that she looked distracted and far away. She must have been in an awful accident.

"I'll take it very easy," I said, slowing almost to a stop and peering both ways as we approached the first intersection, even though there were no other cars, no signs, and no traffic light. She remained stiffly upright and silent. I drove ahead for a few more blocks.

"How's the gas mileage?" I asked just to make conversation. I knew it would be good.

"What?" I had startled her. "The mileage? Oh. I don't know. I don't keep track. Arnie says it's pretty good." She spoke fast and then receded into the distance. The car satisfied me completely. It ran like new, the price was fair, the defect, insignificant, and, most important, the seller beyond doubt. We drove around for a few more minutes. At one point, thinking of how to announce that I wanted the car, I hurried past a yellow light, and Mrs. Meltzer gave a little gasp. Glancing over, I saw her gripping the edge of her seat.

Back in the garage, a quick inspection showed the car to be just as good as it had seemed on the test drive. There was nothing at all suspicious. Even hot, the engine ran quietly. It was clean and did not shake. Mrs. M. looked relieved to be back on *terra firma*. There was a brief silence as the three of us gazed at the running motor. More compliments would sound foolish.

Then, in a burst of sympathy, Ruth spoke up. "You must have been in a really bad accident, Mrs. Meltzer."

Mrs. M., although still very tense, looked a little relieved at this opportunity to bring her fears into the open. "It was *very* bad. The car turned over. I was driving alone on a snowy day, and I skidded. Actually, I guess I was lucky. I wasn't even really hurt. But when they pulled me out and I saw the car ... I ... oh, God..." She looked terrified, even now.

"But I don't get it," I said impetuously. "Wouldn't you feel safer in a bigger, heavier car like this one than in another bug?"

"Oh, no, I don't think so, I don't like a big car, I feel like I have more control in a bug. It's so little, I always know ... where the front is. Do you know what I mean?"

"Oh, yes," I agreed. "Sure we do. We always felt that way in our bug. It was like pedaling a tricycle."

Mrs. M. smiled. It was beginning to sound as if she were using us to help her regain her confidence in driving. But hadn't she driven since the accident, which must have been at least three months ago (the last snowfall)?

"Haven't you been driving since the accident?" I asked, trying to sound casual.

"Well, no, to tell the truth. Arnie hasn't been very busy lately, so I've been getting him to chauffeur me around. I don't have to go to that many places, anyway."

"Then why do you want to sell the car?" I asked. "If you're not driving it yet, how do you know you don't like it?"

"Well ... I would really rather have another bug ... I do expect to drive *sometime*." She smiled, looking a bit surprised by her own logic.

"Oh, I see." (I didn't.) "Well, that makes sense." (It didn't.) I looked at Ruth. "Well, honey, what do you say?"

Ruth smiled.

"We'll take it," I announced.

Mrs. M. also smiled, coming out of another reverie. "Oh, that's good. You know, I was hoping you would. If you don't mind my saying something stupid," she said (again), "fate meant for you to have it. Do you believe in that stuff? Anyway," she went on, relieving me of the need to answer, "you're a nice couple. I like you both."

We went back up to the apartment.

"Arn, they want it," she called as we came in.

He put down his book and took off his glasses, but kept his feet up. "That's good, I thought you would," he said mildly. "It's a nice car." We assented, returned to our former seats, and there was a brief pause. Ruth and I, by the way, had agreed to forego the mechanic this time, if the car looked good and the people seemed reliable. I had the money orders in my pocket.

Mrs. M. remarked, "Yes, isn't it a nice car? You know, even though it isn't the right car for me, I *have* gotten to like it... I hope I can find a good used bug." Suddenly, alarmingly, she sounded irresolute, even slightly loath to part with this good car. There was a longer pause. "I think I'll call Robert and tell him the news."

While Mrs. M. spoke to her son on the phone in the foyer, which was right next to the living room, the rest of us made small talk.

"Uh, what do you do, Mr. Green?" asked Mr. Meltzer.

"I work for CUNY. I'm a teacher. I teach English at the Ebbets Field campus of Brooklyn Community College."

"Oh, yeah? Ebbets Field? There's a project there now, isn't there?"

"Right. In fact, the campus occupies the ground floor of one of the buildings in the project."

"You don't say. How is it set up?"

"Well, let's see." I had explained the odd set-up many times. "Each Division has one apartment: Science is 1A, Humanities, 1B, and so on. Then, each Department has one of the rooms in the apartment. For instance, our classes --English-- are held in the master bedroom."

"Are you pulling my leg?" Mr. Meltzer smiled broadly. "The classes are in the bedroom?"

"No, I know it sounds funny, but, you see, we run a very small operation. Of course, we have blackboards and desks in the rooms, not apartment furniture. Myself and one other guy are the whole English Department. We only have about a hundred, maybe a hundred and twenty, students at this campus."

"Where are the offices?"

"Well, the Humanities Office is in the living room of 1B. The general offices --you know, bursar, registrar, those-- are in the lobby. You'd be surprised how well it all works out."

As we talked, I kept hearing snatches of what Mrs. Meltzer was saying to her son. "Yes, they do ... right, definitely ... now, I suppose ... 525 ... I know, that's a problem ... you don't need it for anything, do you? ..." How disquieting! I was also trying not to let Mr. Meltzer know I was eavesdropping. Now that the subject of my campus had been exhausted, we smiled and tried to think of something else to say.

"Uh, what do you do, Mr. Meltzer?" asked Ruth.

"I'm a mover. I have my own truck. I work for artists. You know, I move their pieces to galleries or museums and back to their studios."

"Oh, yeah?" I said. "That sounds interesting. Have you worked for any well-known artists?"

"Well, yes, I guess some of them are pretty well-known. I never worked for Picasso or anyone, but let's see ... which one is the most famous? Have you heard of Rothko? Let's see. Or Phil Baber? Gail Marvijan? Schwartzman? Morris Riley?"

"Oh, uh, yes, I have heard of one or two of those --Rothko, of course. Ruth, you must have heard of them, haven't you? My wife is an artist," I explained.

"Oh, yeah?"

Ruth muttered that she had heard of some of them. "What was Rothko like?" she asked.

"Well, uh, I guess you know he killed himself. A few years ago now. I don't know. He was a nice man, very considerate." Mr. Meltzer shrugged. "Generous. But, the last couple of times I spoke to him, he was very depressed. Let's see, that must have been 1967, '68." There was another pause.

"I heard he became bitter," Ruth said.

Mr. Meltzer considered this for a moment. "Yeah, I guess so. I don't know ... you know, he was a nobody for a very long time, almost his whole career. That might have had something to do with it." Another silence. "Yeah, well, business is bad now," Mr. M. continued.

"Mine. The recession, I guess. The galleries just aren't doing the business."

"I guess people aren't buying paintings," I said.

"That's it," he agreed, looking worried. "I've had to take some regular jobs lately --you know, apartments, homes, furniture. Uh ... and I've moved some crates and stuff for a few factories in Long Island City. But business is slow, very slow."

At this point, Mrs. Meltzer finally returned. I had missed the last part of her conversation. She looked very upset. "Robert says they're having trouble with the opening. The theater's booked for all the dates he wanted. They'll have to reschedule the whole thing." She turned to us and brightened. "My son's a movie director. His second film is just coming out." She went over to a desk in the corner and brought back a promotional sheet for a movie called *The Premonition*, directed by Robert Meltzer. It seemed to be about radical politics on a California campus during the '60's. As Ruth and I looked over the sheet, I vaguely remembered having seen another movie on that subject --a god-awful movie.

"This looks interesting," Ruth said politely. "What was his first one about?"

"Oh, he made that one about three years ago," Mrs. Meltzer replied. "It was kind of an up-to-date Western. You know, a gay sheriff, cattle rustlers who smoke marijuana. You probably never saw it, it didn't get much promotion." That one sounded like Mel Brooks' *Blazing Saddles*.

"It must be fun having a director in the family," I suggested.

"You know, at first we didn't like it at all," Mr. Meltzer recalled. "For one thing, I guess we didn't think Robert had a chance. But now that his second film is coming out, we're proud of him. Especially since lots of his 'sensible' friends are on Unemployment."

"Robert's a very creative guy," his mother boasted. "He has tremendous self-confidence. If he didn't, he would have given up. You know, it's hard for an unknown to get backing for a film. It took him a couple of years just to get the first one financed." She paused. "And this one wasn't so easy, either ... I wish you could meet him, he's an interesting guy." She considered the possibility further. "You know what? This may sound stupid, but if you like, I'll send you tickets for the opening when they get it re-scheduled. Do you think you might want to come?"

Ruth and I looked at each other. "It sounds like fun," she said. "I've never been to a film opening."

"Neither have I. That's really nice of you, Mrs. Meltzer. Thanks. But are you sure there'll be enough tickets?

"Oh, don't worry about that. Robert will have lots of them for us to give to our friends." That was a nice thing to say. Mrs. Meltzer wore a thoughtful expression. She smiled self-deprecatingly. "You know, I just realized ... I hope you don't mind spending your Saturday evening with two dull old people like us. You probably have better things to do. We don't meet many of Robert's friends, so it's rare for us to get a chance like this."

"Oh, no," I assured her, "this has been very nice. Maybe you're more interesting than you think." I meant that; it *was* nice. But I was also getting uneasy about the car, which seemed to have disappeared from the conversation. So I got back to the point. "Oh! What about the car? I can pay you now, if you like. When do you think we could take it?"

Mrs. Meltzer responded to my bluntness with a worried frown. She took her lower lip in her teeth. "Yes, the car ... uh, I guess you want it right away?"

Ruth answered promptly. "As soon as we can. We want to get out of the city early next week, if we can, and we'll have to register it and all that."

Mrs. Meltzer seemed to calculate. "Okay, then, let's see ... the only thing is ... I'll need it to go around in, to look for a new car for myself. Otherwise ... how could I go around?" She had a point.

"I know," I admitted, "that's been a big problem for us." I thought for a moment. "Look, Mrs. Meltzer, how long do you think it will take you to find a car?"

"Gee, I don't really know, I haven't started looking yet. In fact, I haven't even thought about how you buy a car. I guess I'll look in *The Times*. I'll have to make sure I'm getting a good one, though. I don't want to wind up with one that will give me trouble."

"That's true," I admitted, "it *is* hard to find a good used car. You have to be careful." I was boasting, showing off my hard-won knowledge, even though I realized I might also be cooking my own goose. I rolled on. "I've met lots of cheats and seen plenty of bad cars in the three weeks I've been looking. What year are you looking for?"

"Oh, a '73 or '74, I guess. I'm willing to spend up to 1500, but I want a good car."

I thought for a moment. Was Mrs. Meltzer just being annoyingly indecisive, or was the car slipping out of our grasp? I needed to be firm. "Look, Mrs. Meltzer," I said, "it shouldn't be very hard to find a good late-model bug in *The Times* for what you're willing to pay. Suppose we give you a week to find a car before we take this one. If you like, we'll pay you now and pick up the car next weekend." I looked at Ruth. "That'll be okay, won't it, Honey? We've waited this long."

"But it would mean being in the city over the Fourth," she objected. "I thought we didn't want to do that."

"Look, what difference will it make? We don't have any plans to go anywhere in particular. The traffic will be terrible. Anyway, the fireworks are so bad already, how much worse can they get?" I paused. "It'll be worth it to get a car we can rely on." I turned to Mrs. Meltzer. "How about it, Mrs. Meltzer? A week?"

Ruth didn't say anything. Mrs. Meltzer looked at her husband. I had the feeling that each of us was pursuing an independent line of inquiry.

"What do you think, Arnie?"

"Well, Ellen, you know, these people want the car. We should really let them take it now. You shouldn't have advertised it if you weren't ready to sell it. They came all the way out here in the rain."

"But how will I look for my new car?"

"I don't know, dear, that's our problem. By bus and subway, I guess, like they did. Or I could take you around in the truck."

"Oh, you know I'm afraid of the subways, Arnie. And the truck is too big to drive around looking for cars in. People would think we were crazy. Anyway, aren't you doing a job for Prime this week?"

'Oh, yeah, that's right. I forgot about that."

There was a silence. I tried repeating my offer.

"How about a week, Mrs. Meltzer?"

"I don't know what to say." She looked flustered.

"You should agree, Ellen," Arnie urged. "The Greens are being nice about this. They're putting themselves out, as it is." He sounded as if they had gone through scenes like this before.

"How long *do* you think it will take?" I asked, starting to get annoyed.

Mrs. Meltzer considered the question for several seconds. "I'm not really sure ... a month, maybe?" I was stunned. Then, she came up with an even more astounding proposal. "I have an idea. If you'll wait, I'll take $25 off the price. I'll only charge you $500 if you wait until August First."

$25? A $25 reduction? I could hardly believe she had said that.

Finally, Ruth spoke up --decisively, but not unkindly. "You know, Mrs. Meltzer," she said, "I'm getting the idea you don't really want to sell the car. You know, if you don't want to, you shouldn't. I guess it will be okay with us if you change your mind."

"You're very sweet," Mrs. Meltzer said anxiously. "But what about you? You still wouldn't have a car. And I would feel terrible about making you come all the way out here, getting your hopes up, and wasting all your time, all for nothing. And you said you want to go away soon. Won't you be angry with me? It really isn't right."

"Frankly, it *isn't*," Ruth agreed. "But it would be worse if we got the car because you felt you had to sell it. We couldn't enjoy it if we were worrying that you had no car and should have kept this one. If you want to change your mind and not sell it, of course we'll be annoyed, but it won't be the end of the world. We'll get over it."

Mrs. M. smiled and looked at Ruth warmly, as if she were looking at a favorite child. As it happens, this speech of Ruth's was just the kind that produced the greatest love and admiration in her own mother (RIP), with whom she always had a very close relationship. After a few seconds, Mrs. Meltzer turned toward me. Her head lowered, she raised her eyes to meet mine. The posture, both dog-like and maternal, was deeply affecting.

I improvised an idea. "I'll tell you what, Mrs. Meltzer. Suppose you hold on to the car for now, and we don't set any date for the sale. I'll keep looking for another car, and you start looking for yours. If I find one, since I'll probably still prefer yours, I'll call you before I make any deal, to see if you're ready to sell yours. If you find a car first, call me, and I'll buy yours. Does that make sense?"

"It sounds fine," said Mrs. Meltzer, looking relieved. "You're both very nice. Aren't they, Arnie?"

"Uh, huh, they are."

A few minutes later, the visit ended. Arnie said he would drive us to the station, and Mrs. Meltzer made him put on a hat, because of the rain. She repeated her intention to send us an invitation to her son's opening, and, just to make a friendly ending, we reviewed the elaborate calling arrangements.

On our way to the station, the car sounded so good that I ate my heart out. Nevertheless, Arnie, Ruth and I chatted happily enough, as we drove through the wet streets, the wipers moving back and forth in front of us. I was sure Mrs. Meltzer would take a very long time to find a car --assuming she would even try, since she must now be aware of the folly of trading $1,000 plus a good, proven car, for an unknown one. Maybe, this evening had been her ritual for taking to the road again. Who knows? I was pleased that my wife had acted with characteristic generosity and insight. All in all, the evening was not without compensations.

One last observation about the Meltzers: when we reached the station, Arnie parked the car and came in with us, both to see us off and to buy *The Times* (for the car ads). As Ruth and I discovered when we compared notes later that evening, we had independently observed that he had still been wearing his bedroom slippers in the subway station. His wife had provided for his head, but his feet had gotten soaked. Anyway, we shook hands at the turnstile and said sincerely that we hoped we'd meet again, but with no idea (at least on our part) of whether we really would.

As it turns out, we haven't. And, as far as I know, Mrs. Meltzer has not found a car to buy. In our few phone conversations, she's sketched the history of her failure to change cars. First, her sister was supposed to drive a bug up from Florida for her, but the visit was postponed. The cars in the paper are never any good. The Square Back has been acting fine.

"Who's been driving?"

"Oh, Arnie, mostly."

For various reasons (which did not include the lack of a car), we wound up spending the Fourth in the city, after all. It was horrible, but (obviously) we survived. As for Robert's opening, the date was so long in being set that, by the time the invitation arrived, we were finally about to go off to the country, and couldn't change our plans.

Before leaving town, however, we did call Mrs. Meltzer, to apologize, to thank her, to tell her about *our* new car, and to wish her, and her son's movie, good luck. That has been our most recent contact, and I am always meaning to give her another call. Thus did I fail to buy a car from someone very like my own mother...

As to the actual purchase of a car, it happened a few days before the last time I called Mrs. Meltzer. I took the Long Island Railroad out to Nassau and bought that '66 Dart from the kid, who met me at the station and drove me to his house in his mother's '74 Camry (Deluxe).

"One last question: how come your car's still for sale?" I asked, as mildly as possible, as we pulled into the driveway beside the Dart. He shrugged.

But what the hell! I was sick of looking, and he was a nice kid. On the drive over to a nearby garage owned by my landlord's cousin, the car ran well, and the brakes and compression were pronounced satisfactory. I liked the red shag carpet, the blue steering-wheel cover (hiding a crack, as it turned out), and the bright maroon exterior.

So we drove back to the house, and went into the kitchen, where I gave the boy two money orders totaling $500, and a personal check for $25. He was more nervous than I was. This was the first car he had ever sold --or owned. He, a friend, and his mother came back out to see me off. The boys (as agreed) removed the huge rear speakers. I made sure my two receipts and the Title were in order. Everyone said good-bye, and, standing in the driveway, they watched me back slowly onto the street.

Soon I was driving west on the Belt Parkway toward Brooklyn in the light-to-moderate Sunday traffic, with the windows down and the radio on.

A NEW NEIGHBORHOOD

July 1976

Everything about the man approaching me on the sidewalk was askew. Even his small dog seemed to walk on a diagonal. With tiny steps, man and dog stuttered along until they were alongside my car, which I was washing.

"Do it right!" he said. "Don't miss any spots!"

That got my attention. As I nodded, I noticed that he looked like a semi-bum –a homeless person. His blue pants were baggy and stained, and although it was a hot and sunny summer afternoon, he wore a zipped-up tan windbreaker, also stained. But his most notable garment was a checked, woolen porkpie hat, which he also wore askew –at a jaunty angle.

He must have been in his forties or fifties. He needed a shave and a haircut, but looked as if he lacked the "two bits" to get them (actually, about six or eight bits, in this transitional Brooklyn neighborhood). He stood there offering a running commentary on my car-washing skills, his speech halting and slurred. I wondered if he were drunk or had possibly had a stroke.

That evening, across our low boundary fence, my next-door neighbor, a fellow yuppie who worked at a design museum, told me more about the man. "Oh, that was our resident sidewalk superintendent. His name is Jim Fahey." When I asked his age, she shrugged, and replied, "Who knows? Forty? Sixty?"

It turned out that, sometime after being drafted into the Korean War in 1950 or '51, Jin had suffered an injury that resulted in "shellshock." ("PTSD" would not become a formal diagnosis until 1980.) By doing the math, I decided he must now be in his forties.

Drawing upon her supply of block gossip, my neighbor went on to tell me the rest of what she knew about the disabled vet. Jim lived with his mother in a dilapidated house the family had owned for at least two generations, dating back to when the neighborhood had been blue –or no-- collar, and mostly Irish and Italian. His main activities were light shopping, walking the dog, and sidewalk supervision. Since my neighbor ended by informing me that Jim's mother was "at least eighty," I wondered who did the "heavy" shopping. She shrugged.

"Who takes care of whom?" She shrugged again, and, excusing herself, went back into her house to finish cooking her dinner.

Back in my own house, as I heated up some leftovers, I worried about what would become of Jim Fahey when his mom passed away. Recalling the sidewalk encounter, I realized I was now living in a very car-centric neighborhood. Jim had generously tried to school me in an important local skill.

Although I had moved in only a few weeks before, my car already had a history on this block. The first night, someone had removed the "Toyota" logo (leaving the "Corolla"). Since it was by no means a new car, and I had not recently washed it, the missing letters had left dusty ghosts under the rear window.

The next morning, when I complained to Bobby Langford, a massive bus driver who lived across the street in a double house, his face had lit up. "Choir Boy!" he exclaimed. "You'll have it back by tomorrow."

The following morning, the logo was in its place on the car. When I thanked Bobby, he explained. "It was …" (He named the culprit.) "He collects those whatchamacallits."

"But why is he called Choir…?" I started to ask.

"Because he used to sing in the St. Saviors choir. The name stuck because he still looks so innocent. Actually, he's fifteen, sixteen now, a hard-core juvenile delinquent." Clearly, Bobby was a law-and-order man.

The Rented Pet

Brooklyn, 1977

PART ONE

Jerry Kaplan dry-washed the sawdust from his hands and slowly walked toward the front of his shop. Through the open door, he saw cars flashing by in the sun. Jerry's Lumber stands on a wide, gently sloping one-way street which runs down past an expressway entrance, and the traffic on this particular early Saturday morning was moderately heavy, as it normally is there and then. Any minute now, business would start trickling in, and soon Jerry would be selling plywood, wall molding and pine planks, all cut to customers' sixteenth-of-an-inch specifications (which often turned out to be wrong). Perhaps he would even sell the odd board-with-hole-in-the-middle, a board destined for use as part of a home gas dryer window exhaust unit. That board, twenty-eight to thirty-two inches by five inches of one-half-inch plywood, with its difficult to cut, four-inch, round hole, would cost you five dollars.

Jerry stood in the frame of the pulled-up garage door that served as the front entrance to his shop. He looked at nothing for perhaps a minute and then saw coming down the street a woman whom he immediately tagged as "Frustrated Spinster." Among the visible features which inspired this snap judgment were: straight, skinny, stick-like legs somehow dominated by the shins, and encased in black stockings with a bluish tinge; sadly inadequate breasts and chin; a thin plain face marked only by a gash of lipstick so red you could taste it; a shapeless black dress too warm for this June day and too long or short (hem cutting sticks at mid-shin); a small, square, red plastic pocketbook that looked silly; and the absence of an appreciable behind.

Jerry's face formed into a weak smile that would have seemed pitying rather than friendly to anyone who had noticed it, but the woman for whom it was half-intended was looking straight ahead as she pounded her way down the sloping sidewalk toward the avenue which crossed the street some seven or eight buildings beyond the lumber store.

"What's she doing around here?" Jerry wondered, as he turned and walked slowly back into the shop with the idea of heating some water for coffee on the coil in his office. The question occurred to him because that particular few-block area contained only garages, light industry, and retail and wholesale building, plumbing and automotive supply businesses, and none of the bakeries, five-and-tens, grocery stores, supermarkets, and flower, card and clothing shops which such a lady --a working lady from the look of her-- would be likely to visit early on a Saturday morning.

"Huh?" wondered Joe Bassano, Personnel Supervisor of the Addeo Moving Company, which is three doors down from Jerry's Lumber, as he noticed the spinster through a plate glass window. He asked himself the question Jerry had asked some twenty-five seconds earlier, and then quickly forced his mind back to the business at hand, which was showing a new crew "the ropes."

"Uh, men, as I was saying," he continued, preoccupied, "legs is the sine qua non of our profession." The three of the seven novices who happened to be paying attention stared at Bassano oddly, but he did not notice, because he was once again looking out the window. By then the woman had passed, however --swallowed by the street.

Less than a minute later she made a right turn onto the avenue, caught her breath and went into a store the interior of which was hidden from the street by door and window Venetian blinds. The characters on the dusty plate glass door read:

2   1   8   4

AARF

GUARD DOG'S

FOR SALE

AND

TRAINED!

Had the lumberman or the moving man learned that it was the guard dog store which had been the woman's destination, he would have nodded an "Ah Ha," surmising without hesitation that she wanted a dog to guard her apartment while she was away at work during the day. He would have deduced, furthermore, that the general deterioration of this neighborhood, or even a particular break-in, had prompted her desire to purchase a guard dog. But, assuming Jerry or Joe had somehow learned where the woman was headed, and assuming further that he had gone on to guess her intention, the guess would in fact have been mistaken. For it was not fear of crime which brought the pale thin woman to the guard dog store.

At the sound of the door opening, the fat unshaven proprietor looked up from the tabloid that was spread out upon his counter. Seeing the woman, he managed to supress his surprise by telling himself with lightning speed: "It takes all kinds."

"Good morning," she said with a smile which asked, not unpersuasively, that he like her.

"Morn'," he replied, closing the paper and standing up.

53

She recited her lead question quickly and matter-of-factly, before irresolution could misword it or falsify the intended tone. "Do you rent dogs --or do you just train and sell them?"

The silence which followed seemed fairly long to the woman, but to the owner of the guard dog store it was but a moment, during which he experienced a "brainstorm" that set in motion rapid calculations as to the slow state of business, possible risks to dog and woman, feasible prices, and the insurance question.

"What did you have in mind?" he asked.

The woman clutched her purse and worked her lips. "Well, you see," she said in a businesslike manner, "I live here in the neighborhood, and I ... uh ... would like to rent a dog one day a week."

The proprietor watched her carefully as she spoke, as a guard dog would a person who has reached the very edge of the guarded area. Making a preliminary assessment that this was neither a madwoman nor a pervert or a criminal, he allowed his natural curiosity to assert itself, tempered of course by caution and by tact.

"Uh huh, I see. But what do you want a dog for? You got some valuables you have to move once a week or something? Is that it?"

"No, not exactly." Sensing the onset of amenability, she became precise --even prim-- for she was that type of woman whose formality increases, at least in certain situations, with familiarity. "You see, I would enjoy having a pet as a companion. Living alone as I do, I thought that a dog might . . cheer things up a bit."

The phrase dropped to the counter like spilled milk. They both eyed it for a second, then tacitly --and kindly, on his part-- agreed to ignore it, as if it were an old stain made long ago by some forgotten party.

"But you see," she continued, "living alone as I do, and going to business --I'm a bookkeeper-- I would be unable to care properly for a pet, or at least for the type of pet which I have in mind --a dog. It would be too cruel to the animal."

This made sense, and the proprietor of the guard dog store, now openly curious, sympathetic and enthusiastic, began nodding his head in vigorous agreement. In fact, a scenario was flashing through his head in which he and she would exchange the weekly dog loan for a weekly review of the store's books (scanty though the entries would prove in these hypothetical "books"). His imagination darted forward to the third Saturday morning and to their two heads, his round and bald, hers pale with dark, lankly hanging hair, bending together over the books, which were spread out on the counter.

"I see your point," he said quietly.

"Yes? Good. I tried a pet shop but . . ."

"Oh, I know they'd never do it," he interrupted. "No percentage. It was smart of you to think of coming to a guard dog store. I don't see where else you'd have a chance of getting a part-time dog." He smiled at his phrase, and she too moved the corners of her lips back. "I think we can fix you up."

"Now, as to the time." She had this all worked out. "I would prefer to pick the dog up late Saturday afternoons, if possible. Say -- four-ish? That way I could finish my marketing, straighten up the apartment, and so on, before calling for ... it. Ideally, the dog might be returned Sunday evening, but if you don't come in on Sunday I would be prepared to . . ."

"No, no, that ain't necessary," he chuckled. "Course I'm in on Sundays. The dogs got to eat and so on, don't they? Like a hospital, sort of. I'm here all the time. I stay in the back. These dogs are too valuable to be left alone for long."

She frowned. "Yes, I thought of that. Isn't there a problem, since they are valuable, of my renting . . ."

Again he interrupted, this time holding up a courtly hand. "That's what we're here for, ain't it? Anyways, I ain't about to rent you no Elka von Elkland or Foofy Schaefer --them's famous Shepherds."

She nodded, and just at that moment a huge, square brown head poked through the doorway behind the counter. Neither barking, nor baring his teeth, or even pricking up his ears, the big dog sized up the situation instantly and stood absolutely still in the doorway, ready to respond to his owner's least command.

"And who's this?" the woman asked politely.

"Oh, this is Buzzy. He's my own personal dog."

"Oh? My, he's big! A Great Dane, isn't he?"

"That's right." The proprietor turned and eyed the big dog affectionately. "Ain't it, boy?"

The dog's eyes sparkled, but he did not move.

"I don't think I should rent a Dane," the woman remarked matter-of-factly. "My place is far too small." Something occurred to her for the first time. "Why aren't the dogs barking?" she asked.

"Oh, their kennels are way out back. It ain't good to get them all excited every time someone comes in the store."

"But can't they hear us? I thought dogs had very keen hearing."

"True enough. But these are *trained* dogs," he said proudly. "Just go back in their area and enter the guarded territory by yourself, and you'll hear them do some barking!"

He smiled. His muted cruelty was not lost on her. She smiled, too, letting him have his little joke.

Then suddenly her smile began to widen. Quickly, it grew and grew until it had become a genuine beam. The dog owner was surprised. He knew that she could not be smiling like this at his little pleasantry, and he wondered what she was thinking, but he was too polite to ask. In fact, the lady was experiencing what can only be called an epiphany.

It was a drizzly Saturday night, in her imagination, and from below came the sounds of the teen-age stoop loiterers laughing and talking. She saw herself in a robe, lying on a couch reading a magazine which rested on her knees, and eating a very red apple. Beside the couch, stretched out on the rug, was a large handsome German Shepherd. Its big paws pointed forward and its mouth was stretched into what appeared a serene smile. From time to time a white hand would absently reach down to touch the fluffy head.

"What about a Shepherd?" she asked, returning from her vision refreshed and easy. "Would that be a suitable type for me?"

"Just the thing. Reliable, friendly, tough --oh, I forgot, that wouldn't matter in this case-- er, and smart enough to remember you even though he, uh, would only be staying with you the once a week."

"Do you have a suitable dog on hand?"

He did have a suitable one on hand, and terms were reached easily. The dog would be rented every Saturday to Sunday evening -- or Monday morning, at no extra charge-- for a minimum of three months. The fee would be twelve dollars a week, a deposit of one-hundred dollars would be required. Fee and deposit were low, the proprietor explained, because the dog was old --fourteen-- and while his ferocity and other faculties had in fact remained unimpaired, his grizzled appearance and calm demeanor might be perceived as flaws by the general run of (uninformed) customer.

"I like the idea of an older dog," she assured him.

A check was written for $124, identification was offered and refused, and a handshake sealed the bargain. The owner excused himself, walked back to the kennel area and returned a few minutes later with the Shepherd, whose name was Rex, on a slip chain. When he first saw the woman, Rex was alert, but absolutely silent. She had been instructed to make no move toward the proprietor, the dog or the door of the shop.

A half-hour of recognition and obedience training ensued. For the first ten minutes, Rex was repeatedly led out and brought back in to the waiting woman --whose name was Mildred Schapp-- by the proprietor, Eddie Mays. Eddie would bring Rex right up to Mildred Schapp and let him sniff her. After several repetitions he had her start to talk to the approaching dog, and finally she was told to stroke the grizzled head. As the ten minutes ended, Eddie had Mildred offer the dog a biscuit, which was sniffed perfunctorily, then snapped in half and chewed down.

Next the chain was removed and Rex was left "on guard" in the shop. At first Mildred Schapp and Eddie Mays would go out into the street and come back in together. Rex was alert and growling the first four or five times, then simply alert.

Now came the acid test. Once again Mildred exited, closing the door behind her as she had been doing all along. This time, however, Eddie did not accompany her. Instead, he left Rex alone --lying down in the store -on guard- while he himself went into the back. As Mildred opened the door, Rex leapt to attention. Stiff-legged, ears pointed, the alert dog growled menacingly.

"Hello, Rex," Mildred said. Following instructions, she was careful to speak in a voice that was neither frightened nor falsely sugary. Slowly, then, she extended her hand, palm upwards, and carefully, even more slowly, sniffing constantly, the dog inched toward the hand. A breath away, he stopped, sniffed some more, and then flopped right down at Mildred's feet.

Feeling a surge of friendship, but careful still to move with all deliberativeness, she reached down and once again stroked the noble head, softly saying "Good Dog" as she did so. At that moment Eddie came running in from the back, laughing jubilantly. As for Rex, he lay where he was and smiled.

"Perfect, perfect," Eddie said, bending to slap the dog's side and tossing him another biscuit." All finished. You did it perfect, nice going. That's all there is to it, he knows you now."

"See you at four?" She smiled with pride.

"Right."

Mildred left, Rex was chained and led back to his kennel, and five minutes later Eddie Mays was once again resting his elbows on the counter and bending over the newspaper.

PART TWO

Just as people do, dogs come and go. Despite their deserved reputation for fidelity, and despite the stories one hears of dogs that gracefully age alongside their masters, sometimes reaching the equivalent of ninety or more, there are other dogs whose unsuitability becomes apparent almost as soon as one emerges from the shop with them; dogs that meet sudden, violent death; dogs that go berserk and have to be "put away." From time to time one even hears with alarm of a dog's suddenly turning vicious and attacking his own master, biting and rending.

The terms of Mildred Schapp's rental of Rex made the relationship both exciting and frighteningly insubstantial. She became more animated, and her change was sharp enough for even a casual observer like Jerry Kaplan to notice. Jerry would see the woman on her way down the sloping street every Saturday afternoon, and he might think, "There's that skinny broad again. Seems happpy today, wonder if she's getting some!" Or, depending on his mood, "There goes that skinny creep. Looks scared shitless, as usual."

For several weeks Jerry never saw Mildred with Rex. Thus he neither knew about the dog nor understood Mildred's fear and joy, or had any chance to see the qualities that emerged when she took Rex's leash: the sweetness, tranquility and childlike excitement.

The cause of Jerry's ignorance was simple: Mildred and Rex never took the sloping street home. Even though it was longer, they took the avenue on which the guard dog establishment stood, proceeding towards the neighborhood's commercial and residential section several blocks ahead. This was the section with the bookstores and toy stores, the cleaners and fruit stores, the section crowded with shoppers and loungers, and with uniformed guards who watched impassively over great piles of inexpensive goods. Mildred's motive for taking the longer way home was simple: pride in displaying Rex.

When they reached her apartment building, Mildred would sometimes decide they should walk three more blocks to a small park. When they got there, she would sit down on a favorite shaded bench with Rex at her feet, half in and half out of the sunlight. Thus would she dream away an hour, or so, until it became necessary to think about supper.

The summer days lengthened and Mildred enjoyed the time. She took pleasure in the sound of Rex's nails tapping along her linoleumed hallway, and she would watch with tender love the grizzled head bending over the new red bowl filled with the special food she bought. Perhaps the greatest pleasure was her unconscious awareness of the big dog resting in the next room, never bored, never angry or sad, while she went about the housework. Mildred's routine became threaded with joy, a cloth of gold.

Late in July came a terrific heat wave, and one Saturday when it reached its apogee, Mildred broke with habit. The result was that Jerry Kaplan, the lumberman, finally got to see her with Rex.

As usual, she picked up her rented pet just after three-thirty. Since the afternoon showed no signs of cooling off, it was not a day for extra walking. She would retrace her steps and get Rex home, where he could have a bowl of water and they could sit at, and under, the bridge table across from the window which caught the breeze.

Thus it happened that, having given Eddie Mays the weekly check and having suffered his quip about "dog days," Mildred emerged with Rex and turned left, instead of right. She rounded the corner and, despite the heat, strode with her usual briskness up the long slope, which veered slightly to the left in a way that would reduce their walk by perhaps a quarter of a mile.

Arriving at Jerry's Lumber just as the proprietor and a customer were carrying a load of two-by-fours to a station wagon at the curb, Mildred and Rex stopped to let the men pass. The lumberman muttered his thanks, looked over his shoulder and, seeing the dog with the woman, did a double take.

Then, as he helped the customer tie the boards to the roof of the car, Jerry kept glancing after Mildred and Rex. He saw them cross the avenue at the top of the block and continue straight ahead.

Today Mildred was wearing her coolest dress, the sleeveless red rayon, and Jerry could follow its bright color beside the more muted form of the dog as the pair moved on, growing smaller and smaller.

In a minute the customer drove off and Jerry succumbed to impulse. Rushing back into the shop, he switched off the power for the machines. Then he snatched checks and paper money from the cash drawer, threw them in the safe, slammed the door and twirled the lock. Still hurrying, he set the alarm and secured windows and back door. Finally, he flipped the lights and ran out the front, garage door, pulling it down behind him. He stopped, then, and absent-mindedly jiggled the locked handle of the door while he stared in the direction the dog and woman had taken. Then he smiled, gave a tug at the waist of his overalls, and strode up the hill.

"It's okay, I made plenty today. Anyways, it's too hot to work all day. Who is that?" he wondered. "She never had no dog before. Where'd she get him, anyhow, AARF's? I got to see where she takes him."

This unlikely fascination with the old maid and her dog was born of boredom and a slow, summer sexual itch. And why shouldn't Jerry Kaplan take a little walk? His time was his own. "This is going to be a special Saturday. For once I ain't winding up at McGonegal's half-plastered on quarter beers."

But the sun was hot on his bare arms, and he must not push his bulk uphill too fast on a day like this. He was glad he was wearing his peaked cap. He felt sure he could maintain a pace slightly faster than that of the woman and dog, but less sure of what he would do when he caught up with them. Jerry peered ahead and only hoped they would not turn a corner before he could spot them again.

The air was stiflingly moist and still. Arriving at her building, Mildred saw with despair that a crowd of teenagers covered the stoop, drinking beer and swaying to very loud radio music. So she abandoned her plans of home and, without even pausing, crossed the street and proceeded the three blocks to the park, where she sat down on her favorite, shaded bench. For several minutes, she sat perfectly still, trying to cool off, while Rex lay in front of her, tongue out and sides heaving.

Then she heard the flick of a switch. Almost directly across the path from their bench, no more than fifteen feet away, stood a young man of unprepossessing appearance. He was tall, pale, towheaded and bony, and wore shiny brown pants and a dirty sleeveless undershirt. His shoulders were pink and freckled from the sun. He stared glassy-eyed at Mildred and at Rex, who had begun to growl and strain at the leash. Mildred sat up straight. She was very, very annoyed, for on the ground to the young man's right was a huge radio, which he had just turned on at full volume. The young man's head rolled on his neck. In his left hand he clutched a long object wrapped in a dish towel. The radio was tuned to the news station, and to each item the young man added a commentary.

"That's right," he said. "Bilk the taxpayer, John Q. Public. Give it to him good." He even had a remark about the weather. "Sure it's going to be cooler tonight. Sure it is."

Having restrained Rex for several minutes while they listened to this mad cacophony, Mildred finally stood up and said pointedly, "This is not pleasant. Not. At. All. Let's go home, Rex."

As they started to move, the young man quickly unwound the towel and let it drop to the ground, revealing a long rusty butcher knife. Using both hands, he raised it slowly to the level of his own forehead, smiled conspiratorially, and appeared to aim the point directly down at Rex. All the while, the editorials continued.

"Homeowners, who else? Sure, give them the dough, anything to keep the homeowners from moving out of the city."

Mildred stared at the knife. Her mouth and the pale hand which had been clenched around Rex's leash both fell open. At the very moment Rex was flashing through the air at the young man's throat, a heavy, vaguely familiar figure in cap, T-shirt and overalls rushed into the park and up the path.

Jerry's presence may be credited to his determination and to the keen sense of intuition found in certain easygoing fat men. Sweating and panting, but trusting at any moment to regain sight of woman and dog, he had continued undaunted up the hill. On such a day, he had surmised, the park must be her destination. But where were they?

More than once had Kaplan nearly turned on his heel, more than once had he almost wavered and gone back down to McGonegal's. But time and again he persevered, until finally he reached the park entrance --only to see the violent confrontation unfolding some eighty feet in front of him.

Reacting perhaps one-fifth as fast as the dog, the lumberman rushed forward, shouting, "Hey! You! No! Hold it!" As Jerry moved toward the fray, Rex tore large pieces of skin from the assailant's neck and cheek, and began to savage the rest of his face. The knife dealt the big dog a superficial shoulder wound, and the combatants fell locked to the ground with Rex on top and the young man slowly drawing back his arm for a second thrust. All the while he kept muttering, as the radio emitted news and commercials.

During the first moments of the fight, Mildred Schapp had been paralyzed with fear, but now, recovering, she rushed across the path and kicked hard at the young man's drawn-up shins. "Let that dog alone, you pervert! Stop that!"

The knife was poised, but before it could descend Kaplan was on the scene. Grabbing the man's wrist in both hands, he slowly forced the weapon back down toward the ground. By now Rex had the assailant by the throat. Unfortunately, Eddie Mays had neglected to teach Mildred how to call Rex off once he attacked, and the madman's throat might well have been ripped out were it not for the fact that Jerry's friend and neighbor, Joe Bassano, the personnel supervisor, had once introduced Jerry to the huge Doberman who guarded the moving vans. Fascinated by this ferocious monster, Jerry had asked and been told how the creature was signaled to attack and stop. With great presence of mind, he now recalled the instructions and shouted them to Mildred: "Lady! Lady! Tell him, 'Down, Boy!' Quick, tell him! Quick! Quick!"

"What? Oh! Down, Rex!" Mildred ordered crisply. With reluctant obedience the big dog backed off a few feet, sat down and watched alertly, panting, blood trickling from his left shoulder, mouth opened in what looked like a compassionate smile. By this time, Jerry had plopped with a grunt on to the fallen assailant's chest, and he pressed one knee on to the man's knife hand, which began to open. In another moment the knife was in Jerry's hand, the point between the young man's eyes.

A frail old man walking a tiny dog at the far end of the park had seen the fight break out and hurried to an emergency call box on the corner. Now, across the grass ran this old man, his tiny dog on a slender red leash, and with them, a policeman, groping for his handcuffs. Very soon the assailant's hands were secured behind his back, the policeman was radioing for an ambulance, the flushed old man was smiling at the couple, and the dogs were circling and sniffing. The little dog tried to lick Rex's wounds, but was unsuccessful because of their relative heights and because Rex kept turning away the injured shoulder.

It was Mildred Schapp who finally thought to reach down and turn the radio off. As the news stopped, so did the editorials. Immediately, the young man began to groan and gnash his teeth.

"Drugs?" Kaplan asked the policeman.

"What else?"

Minutes later the ambulance arrived. The attendants kindly dressed the wound of the heroic dog as well as those of the attacker, who was locked into the back of the vehicle. Mildred was advised to take Rex to a vet for a tetanus shot and was told how to dress the wound without causing undue pain. After writing down brief statements from the three human witnesses, the policeman commended them and the dog, drove his car into the park and, red light blinking, followed the ambulance off. The old man accepted Mildred and Jerry's hearty thanks, tipped his hat, and pulled the little dog off in the direction from which they had come.

Mildred and Jerry looked at each other in silence. Jerry smiled at the thin woman.

"You know," he said, "I seen you go by my place --the lumber place-- and I wondered why you had this dog with you. But I ain't wondering no more. Some dog, ain't he! Did you see him fly at the guy? Heck, these days a single lady ain't even safe in the daytime."

Mildred smiled and looked at her feet. "Well, actually, I don't keep Rex for protec. . . ." She broke off because she had just noticed a piece of filthy notepaper where the assailant had fallen. Folded into quarters, it was covered with dark heavy pencil scrawl and smeared with blood, though whether its owner's or the dog's no one could have said.

"And what's this?" As she picked up and unfolded the sheet, Jerry came close so that he, too, could see. A single sentence, scribbled over and over in apparent furious haste, completely covered both sides of the paper:

DEATH TO EVERY GODANN FUCKING DOG IN NEW YOUR CITY

"How do you like that!" Jerry exclaimed. "A dog hater!" And I thought . . ."

"What a horrible person!" Mildred stooped to stroke Rex's grizzled head.

After a moment, Jerry blurted out a question: "Say, you think maybe I should see you home?"

"Oh, I don't see . . . ." She changed her mind. "Well, actually, that would be kind of you, sir. I am shaken, and I imagine that, er, Rex is, too. Although he obviously has more presence of mind than I do." They smiled and left the park in the direction of her home.

The trio strolled along, Rex nearest the curb, Mildred in the middle. She and Jerry conversed happily, going over the incident and speculating about the young man. They prolonged the walk with a detour to a drug store, where Mildred bought a bottle of antiseptic. By the time they reached her building, there was no fresh blood on Rex's dressing.

By then the man and woman had become quite interested in one another. The trauma had torn away Mildred Schapp's reserve. Even in her wild and joyful state, as she answered Jerry's questions, Mildred spoke with precision. But she spoke more.

For some minutes the sky had been darkening and, as they stood at her stoop, both thinking about what they wanted to happen next, a wind came up, promising rain and perhaps relief. The stoop-loiterers had dispersed, so they were alone. Mildred blushed and Jerry, moved, extended a hand. But at that moment a honking car sped by, and Mildred turned to watch it. Jerry felt chastened and, contemplating the inadequate form in the bright dress, he sensed that a liaison with such a woman would not be a winning proposition. It would require, at the least, torrents of insincere rhetoric and preliminary alcoholic priming. And afterwards? God knew what would be required, then.

So it was down to McGonegal's, where he would wind up with "a package on," after all, and where, if he could find a way to tell his friends what had happened without exciting their ridicule, some of them might actually enjoy the little story. And why should there be a problem? "Can't a guy knock off early on such a hot day," he asked himself a second time, "and go for a little walk?"

As for Mildred Schapp, all at once she felt pressed for time. She knew she must hurry upstairs to call a vet and a cab. Eddie Mays, too, would have to be informed. It was about to rain and she was anxious to get started. If the arrangements were made promptly, Mildred calculated, and then medical attention, dinner and dishes seen to, there might still be an hour for her to lie on the couch and read, in the company of her dear rented pet.

PART THREE

"All right, then. Yes. Well, what more can I say? Goodbye."

Mildred Schapp laid the receiver in its cradle and sat for a moment, her lips pursed, her red fingernails drumming on the black plastic. Then she took a deep breath, let it out with a whoosh and stood up. "How tiresome!" Her high-heeled shoes tapped on the linoleum floor and she began unscrewing an earring as she made her way to the bedroom to change back into her "around the house" clothes.

Bad news. It had been Eddie, calling to tell her not to come for Rex today. He was glad he had reached her in time to save her the walk down to the store. Apologizing several times, he explained that he had just signed a long-term lease for Rex. A man he knew slightly had come in asking to rent a dog with seeing-eye experience for a blind friend until the first of the year. Six weeks. Since Rex was the only eligible dog, could she do without him for that long?

Eddie did not say as much, but Mildred supposed he needed the extra dollars and, being herself the equivalent of a gentleman, she did not try to hold him to the informal agreement they had relied on from the start. Eddie's expressions of gratitude were so lengthy that she, too, was grateful when he finally said goodbye.

In a few minutes Mildred emerged from the bedroom wearing gray rayon slacks and a blue sweatshirt. Sighing once more, she went to the refrigerator and looked in at its contents in the same way she might have watched a television set that happened to be on when she was at a relative's house for a holiday meal. She closed the door, shook her head briskly to clear off incipient melancholy and, returning to the couch, picked up the phone and dialed a well-known number.

"Is that you, Jerome? The saw? Right."

She waited while Jerry Kaplan went to the work area to turn it off. When he was back she said, "Eddie called. No Rex," and explained.

"Ah, what a shame," Kaplan replied. "Look, I'll be closing up around four. Shall I?"

At four, having completed the marketing, the laundry and the vacuuming, Mildred was once again wearing her dress, stockings, and so forth, as she waited on the couch for the consoling Mr. Kaplan. Ten minutes later, it was he who sat on the couch, neat and scrubbed in his clean overalls and white shirt, alert with pleasure as he watched Mildred cross the kitchenette and pause at the doorway to the bedroom.

Looking back over her shoulder, she smiled coyly. Then she bent at the knees and, still watching him, she grabbed with both hands the hem of the black dress and slowly wriggled it up to waist level. The surprisingly white globes of a small backside glowed at Jerry.

"Hah! hah! hah!" gasped Kaplan. He was hunched over on the very edge of the couch, his face bright red, his hands clasped tightly. "Finally!" he shouted, leaping to his feet.

"Hurry!" said Mildred. "I can't wait." And she disappeared around the corner into the bedroom.

An hour later, when they were sitting up in bed holding hands, with the covers pulled to their chins, the phone rang again.

"Ha!" said Mildred. "This is what I call an eventful day." And Jerry got another nice look at the glowing behind as she hurried to the closet for the silk peignoir she had bought a week after the incident in the park. Three months, and then the shock of losing Rex, it had taken the couple to bring the events of that hot August day to fruition.

For several minutes Mildred talked on the telephone while Jerry leaned against the upturned pillow, hands folded behind his head, trying lazily to guess, first, who it was and, then, what was being discussed.

"Yes," he heard, "mm hmm. Same price? Well, perhaps. That's right, you still have it from the first time. Mm hmm. I think we --em, that is, I-- can. Yes, plenty. One more thing: you do understand that I reserve the right of refusal on sight. Yes, of course. But that may turn out to be months, mayn't it, Mr. Mays? Certainly. Until then."

"Did you hear enough to guess, Jerome?" She stood in the doorway wearing a small, bright smile. The orange parrots on her bright green robe stared cross-eyed at each other from breast to breast.

"Good news," he said. "Say, do we have time for a little more you-know-what first?"

She shook her head up and down. "His name is 'Caesar', isn't that nice?" A chasm yawned between the parrots.

She was sure Caesar would be very nice. While Jerry waited in the apartment --the silly boy needed a "cat nap"-- Mildred Schapp pounded down the sloping sidewalk just as she had on that first memorable Saturday and so many times since. The lumber mill was closed --oh, she knew where that one was! -- but from behind the moving company headquarters came a loud, low growl, and she guessed it might be Jerry's nice friend, Mr. Bassano, teaching a new man how to work the complicated gears on one of the enormous orange trucks.

As soon as she saw the dog, Mildred knew that, yes, Caesar would do very well, indeed. Heeding Kaplan's advice to avoid mental comparisons, Mildred took to the new dog instantly. And the feeling was mutual. For Caesar, a black and tan part-Collie bitch, and a reclaimed stray who still limped from the time she had been hit by a large rusty car with no muffler, unfailingly knew and appreciated kindness.

"Female? 'Caesar'?"

Mays shrugged. "A kid named her. What do kids know?"

Since Caesar was not a watchdog, there was no need for any but the most perfunctory get-acquainted session, but Mildred liked the idea of keeping Kaplan waiting, so instead of hurrying home she stayed to chat.

"Hmm, well, I suppose it's too late to change the name now."

"Why bother? Oh, but she's a real smart one," Mays beamed. "Yup, unusual. You know what one of the kids brung her in told me? See, last winter they was feeding her on their block, out on the street, and one day when it got too cold she opened the door to one of the apartment houses all by herself. With her paws. And a kid found her there in the vestibule when he come home from school. Ain't that a cute story?"

"Do you suppose it really happened?" asked Mildred.

"Ah, hey! Christmas is almost here, Mrs. Schapp, ain't it?"

"What has that got to do with it, Mr. Mays?"

"Well, Santa Claus is coming, and elves, and all them reindeer, right? And little kids never lie, neither, right?" He winked and, seeing his meaning, she laughed. "Just the weekends, like with Rex? Wouldn't want her full-time now, would you?"

"Just the weekends, I'm afraid."

Terms, too, were the same. At this time of the approaching holiday season, and today in particular, Mildred would not quarrel over a few pennies, although she realized that Caesar should come cheaper, lacking, as she did, Rex's specialized education. What Caesar did have, Eddie explained, was extensive life-experience. And that, too, could come in handy.

"Sophistry, sir!" she exclaimed.

"Who?"

"Never mind. Dog to be returned tomorrow evening, as usual?"

"Agreed. Want me to write it all up for you, Mrs. Schapp?"

She did want that, so Eddie wrote it up. Then they shook hands, and she left with the dog on a new red leash which he provided free of charge because she had been such a good sport about Rex.

For Jerry, a widower, and Mildred, who had "seen" few men over the years, this was a holiday season worth the name. She cooked good meals, and they ate them with wine. They spent time at the movies and, locked together in her excellent old bed, they saw each Saturday become a Sunday. Then, on cold bright Sunday mornings, they would walk hand in hand down the street which ran alongside the expressway, while trucks bounced past like skipping children.

"Anybody home?" Jerry would call to the pulled-down garage door of his shop, and they would continue all the way to the harbor, where they gazed across the decks of the boats from South America at the skyline of the city. Sometimes they stayed so long that just before leaving they could see the large orange sun peering through the timbers of the burnt warehouse on the wharf.

"It looks like a big face in jail," Jerry once remarked.

When they reached her house again, he would make up his mind whether to spend another hour or two with her at table and in bed, or to hurry back down the hill to catch the subway home, where he would gather his dirty clothes and trudge off to the laundromat.

"Why do you always wait until the last minute to decide?" asked Mildred on the fourth Sunday night, as they stood hugging in her vestibule. "Are you trying to excite me, Jerome? You don't have to, you know."

"Oh, no, that's not it," he explained. A car horn sounded. "Nah, I just like the suspense myself. Of not knowing 'til the last minute. Actually, I think I will stay a little longer tonight."

"Good." The keys had been in her hand while they were talking, and she quickly unlocked the inner door.

Christmas arrived. Gifts were exchanged, dinner eaten, and they continued. Since they had agreed to spend only weekends and holidays together, at least until they knew each other better, almost all of Mildred Schapp and Jerry Kaplan's good times were shared with, witnessed by, or enjoyed in proximity to the good Caesar. As for the dog herself, the second of Mildred's rented pets, the times were possibly as happy as they were for the human pair. As Mildred and Jerry walked hand in hand down the hill, Caesar would limp easily after on the leash, looking up with her perpetual expression of playful, loving expectation. When they strolled she would stroll, and when they trudged back up she would limp at a pace which pulled the leash neither forward nor back. Then Caesar's head would be lowered, in harmony with the tranquil evening mood of Jerry and Mildred.

On Christmas Day, after controlling her frenzy at the smells for what seemed an eternity, Caesar feasted on a ham bone. Later she lay outside the closed bedroom door and listened to the breathing, jangling and laughter, herself panting from the big meal, her pink tongue lolling, and on her face what looked to be a wise, happy smile. Seeing this expression, a human observer would have been sure Caesar had no premonitory regrets about returning to the quiet pen the next morning. For, like Rex, Caesar was patient and mature --she was almost eleven--and the kindly Eddie Mays never let too much time elapse between visits to the kennels, during which visits every animal was assured of at least some individual attention. Thus, for the dog whom Jerry Kaplan affectionately called "Julia," life was rich.

Rich, perhaps, but uneven in its gifts.

"I wonder," said Mildred, "how Rex is making out with that blind person." It was eleven o'clock on the night of December 29th, and Mildred was sitting on the couch eating an apple while Jerry, in an armchair with his feet up on the poof, read the paper. That he was there on a weekday, and that he wore new brown vinyl slippers bought specifically for use at Mildred's apartment, suggested the couple had entered a second, more domestic stage.

"Hmm," he said, looking over the edge of the paper. "That's right. The blind guy must be making a bundle."

"Yes, I imagine he is. I do hope he's treating Rex well."

"Don't worry, honey. Didn't you say Mays knew the guy or something? Anyhow," Jerry smiled, "Rex can take pretty good care of himself, can't he? Remember?"

She, too, smiled. "How could I ever forget?"

Of course there are limits to the ability of any of us to take care of ourselves, and at that moment Rex lay on his side on a damp, almost deserted subway platform. The body of the grizzled Shepherd was rigid, his brow furrowed. Blood ran from several bullet wounds and the dog whined softly, but he neither grimaced nor flinched from the careful hand with which the kneeling blind man stroked his face. Except for a bump on his forehead, suffered when the muggers threw him to the platform, the blind man was himself unhurt. Before knocking him down, they had ripped from his coat pocket the paper bag containing the day's proceeds, some thirty-seven dollars.

"Rex, oh, Rex," said the man. "I'm so sorry. I was greedy. We stayed out too late. I'm so sorry."

Meanwhile, after hearing shots and then ducking from sight as the two men ran past, the token vendor wasted no time before calling the police. Five minutes later eight officers raced down the steps to the platform, their footsteps echoing, their equipment clanking and jingling.

"Which way they go?" shouted the sergeant, a tall fat man with auburn hair.

"You okay? What'd they look like?" asked a cop with drawn revolver.

"Good Christ!" exclaimed a third. "The guy's blind."

"Look! the fuckers shot his dog."

"Eddie Mays," said the blind man weakly. "The dog's hurt, get Eddie Mays." And he managed to give them clear, concise directions to the guard dog store, although for all his presence of mind he was unable to recall Eddie's phone number.

So for several hours on this cold, clear night the noisy daytime bustle of the holiday season was prolonged.

Since morning, people had been eating, drinking, laughing, pushing, returning unwanted presents and selecting new ones. Some had even stood with their children in front of the display windows, belatedly keeping a promise they had hoped would be forgotten. Then, just when this activity was subsiding --when the bus lines were growing shorter and the bright filthy subway trains carried fewer passengers as they inched or raced through the tunnels-- there was a burst of noise in one of the stations. Harsh commands. A man pleaded, a dog barked. Harsher commands. Four gunshots echoed down the tunnel. The noises became blurred: yelping, laughter, running footsteps. After that, silence, broken only by the urgent voice of the token vendor on the phone. Then, very soon, squad cars raced into this neighborhood, their sirens and red lights piercing the night sky.

Noise and movement accelerate: sirens, flashing lights, screeching tires. Men rap at a door, lights go on and a startled Eddie Mays appears, dressed in sweater and baggy slacks, still clutching the paperback he has been reading. He listens to the news, runs inside for his coat, then leaves with the police. Car doors slam, people shout. Typewriters clack, statements are signed, cold red hands are rubbed and blown upon. Cigarettes are lit, then either forgotten or smoked and stubbed out. The interrogations are tedious, the expressions of regret awkward and formulaic. For hours the squad cars swarm relentlessly over the area. The search is thorough: block by block, building by building. But the perpetrators have long since disappeared into . . . cars? buses? the sanctuary of apartments? And with no single witness to the crime who can both see and speak, arrests seem improbable.

As soon as the police give him a minute, Eddie Mays telephones to one Dr. Matt Brunn, the vet used by AARF. He tells him the news: a dog has been shot. Luckily this old man and his wife are still up watching the late movie, and now he dresses quickly, grabs his bag, and is driven by squad car to the subway station. Meanwhile Mays is back at the guard dog store, making hasty preparations to receive the wounded animal.

"Good Lord," says the vet when he sees who it is. "Not again!" And the doctor, a medium-sized, dignified old man with straight white hair and clear-rimmed plastic glasses, stands for a moment shaking his head and staring down at Rex, who still lies on the dirty platform. Then the vet rouses himself, sedates the dog and, hastily examining the blind man's forehead, declares him to be in no danger. So the man, Charles Miller by name, is driven home in the squad car that brought the doctor. Considerately, the young officer drives right up to Miller's door, helps him out, walks him up the two flights and refuses to leave until Miller's aged mother, herself nearly blind, has been convinced that her son is safe and basically unharmed.

Meanwhile, the old vet supervises the wounded animal's transportation. A city ambulance carries Rex to the guard dog store, where he is placed on a long table beneath an unshaded bulb in a room directly behind the one in which he first met, and was rented by, Mildred Schapp. While the doctor washes his hands, Eddie slips away to telephone Jerry and Mildred, asking that they "come by to lend a little moral support." The couple bundle into warm clothes and rush down the hill.

By the time they arrive, it is well after midnight and finally quiet. The police having just left, the ministrations of the vet are carried out in silence, except for an occasional whispered remark, or a low groan from the drugged patient. As Dr. Brunn works on into the night, the onlookers stand across the table from him, Mildred and Jerry holding hands, Jerry reaching over once or twice to squeeze Mays's shoulder. All three witnesses wear pained expressions as the old man cleanses, stitches and bandages the sedated dog's wounds. Fortunately, none of the four bullets has struck muscle, bone or organ, but there is a great deal of blood.

"Will he need a transfusion?" asks Mildred.

"Nope," says the doctor, wrapping a paw. "Red meat should do the trick. Going to be some big butcher bills, eh, Ed?" he adds with a wink at Jerry and Mildred.

"Lucky I kept up the insurance," Mays rejoins. "With what your bill's going to be."

It was one-thirty when the old vet finally sighed, straightened up and said, "As usual, Rex will be all right."

Once the others had finished expressing their relief and gratitude, there was little left to say or do. A taxi was called, which the vet shared with the couple, and soon Kaplan was brushing his teeth while Mildred Schapp got into her nightgown. Meanwhile, in his living room, Dr. Brunn quietly undressed down to his underwear. Then he crept trembling into the dark bedroom and slipped into bed without waking his wife.

As for Eddie Mays, he carried the still unconscious Rex to the small room used as an infirmary. He lowered the dog onto a thin mattress in a large basket and covered him with a worn pink blanket. Relying on the vet's assurance that Rex would sleep until morning, Mays returned wearily to his own room where, without undressing or even turning on the light, he sank into the armchair next to the bed. On the rug on the other side of the bed, peacefully asleep and completely forgotten, lay Buzzy, the Great Dane, Mays's own "personal dog."

For more than an hour, Eddie sat in the dark, going over the night's events, picturing the confrontation and recalling the aftermath. Then, he thought back to the incident in the park the previous August and to other, earlier events which had also involved Rex. As he sat in thought, from time to time Eddie would smile, sigh, shake his head or drum his fingers on the soft round arms of the chair. At last, after three, his round head slumped down on to his chest and Eddie Mays's memories turned to dreams.

PART FOUR

Often injured, slow to heal: this time Rex's convalescence took three months. Still, thanks to his eager spirit and strong constitution, and thanks also to the expert care of Eddie Mays and Dr. Brunn, the dog's torn body once again knit up. By late March, few signs of the subway attack remained: a slight limp in the right hind leg, the tendon of which had been grazed by a bullet, and four new scars, which the dog wore as unselfconsciously as many Generals and Admirals wear their ribbons and medals.

These months were also marked by other developments in the small circle of which Rex was center. Increasingly taken with the brave Shepherd, Jerry Kaplan volunteered to aid in his rehabilitation by playing with, and walking him. To this end, Kaplan was seconded twice daily from the lumber mill to serve as a sort of unofficial assistant to Eddie Mays. There followed quite naturally a two-dog rental arrangement and an extension of the weekly lease to Monday mornings. Beginning in mid-March, each weekend thus saw a pair of humans with a pair of dogs making their way down and up the sloping street next to the Expressway, and through the other streets and parks of the neighborhood.

Since Julia's own injury had been to her left hind leg, when Jerry and Mildred would stroll with the dogs in tandem, the synchronized limping seemed to invite comments. Although most of these were interested or sympathetic, on occasion they could be droll, keen or even baldly hostile. In fact, it was one such unfriendly thrust which inspired Jerry to a notable *mot*.

On a Sunday morning when he and Mildred were with the dogs in a small pocket park on the fringe of the neighborhood, they came upon a young couple hurrying in the opposite direction.

Just as the couples drew abreast, the young man, who was tall and wore brown loafers without socks, remarked to Jerry out of the side of his mouth, "Whoa! TWO dogs! Say, fella, don't forget to scoop the poop!"

"Why?" was Kaplan's cool and slow reply, as he turned to fix the young man with a stare. "Don't you snoopy yuppies like our puppies' poopies?"

Another minor development concerned names. As long acquaintance ripened to fast friendship between the two rented pets, it seemed increasingly inappropriate to misdesignate the gender of the female, and so, at Kaplan's suggestion, she became known, after all, as "Julia."

Now it may be imagined that Rex and Julia would soon have produced an august brood of pups, but this, alas, was not to be. To put the matter bluntly, although the pair engaged in prodigious sniffing, they never progressed to the mounting stage. Since their compatibility was never in doubt, it occurred to people to wonder, "Is one or both of them too old?"

Once again it was Jerry Kaplan who took the lead, indelicately giving voice to this sensitive question on a Saturday afternoon in April at the guard dog store, where he, Mildred and Eddie were enjoying the ceremonial cup of coffee which now accompanied the weekly pick-up. But, if Eddie Mays knew the answer, he wasn't saying. He shrugged and smiled like the Sphinx, and neither did Mildred Schapp venture an opinion other than to shake her head and cast a sideways glance at the bumptious lumberman.

"Well," said Jerry, shaking off his slight embarrassment. "I guess I got to answer my own question, then." And, displaying what Mildred was coming to recognize as an unfortunate propensity for puns, he pronounced against the female: "Dogopause." The ritual groans of the other two ended this discussion, but the fact was, no pups.

As to human "pups," with the conventional preliminary of marriage, when Jerry raised this question after three glasses of wine at dinner that same night, Mildred's answer was decisive: "Oh, Jerome," she said, "how sweet of you! But why would we want to bother with all of that now?" And, as both dogs watched, she leaned across the table and gave Jerry a popping little kiss on the mouth.

Eight days later, on a Sunday evening, there assembled for the first time ever the complete circle of Rex. Present were: Jerry; Mildred; Eddie; Joe Bassano, the moving man; blind Charles Miller; Dr. Matt Brunn; and, naturally, Rex and his companion, Julia. It was just a simple get-together--coffee, danish, a few drinks-- in celebration of two sets of happy events. The first, of course, was Rex's recovery, and the other was Charles Miller's acquisition through the efforts of local politicians of a newsstand in an office building. This meant that the tall, thin, redheaded blind man and his mother could look forward to a higher standard of living, one which would include clothes bought new and even an occasional restaurant meal. And, as if that were not enough good fortune, a correspondence had just been started on Miller's behalf which might eventually put a permanent dog on the blind man's horizon.

So that Sunday at nine they all gathered in the "conference room" of the van line company, to which Bassano, as foreman of the yard, had access. This medium-sized, rectangular room was carpeted, newly paneled and dominated by a formica table. Into one of the long walls had been cut a sliding window which looked out on the reception area. Against the other long wall stood two glass-fronted cases that contained plaques and trophies commemorating bowling victories and sponsorship of organizations for children. Covering both end walls and all available space on the long walls were clusters of photographs signed by eminent politicians and show-business personalities. Bassano's prize showed a younger version of himself, wearing a bowling shirt, his hair thick and black and his face fuller and unlined. Standing with his arm around the moving man was a celebrity of about the same age and height as Bassano. This person wore a checked sport coat and a porkpie hat tilted so far back you could have knocked it off with a straw. Although his identity would have been apparent to most people from these clothes and from his distinctive, huge, pockmarked nose, anyone still in doubt --as no one tonight, other than Miller and the dogs, was-- need only have read the inscription:

TO JOEY--
    KEEP 'EM MOVIN', KID!
      AS EVER,
      JIMMY DURANTE

After the guests had admired the trophies, plaques and photographs, they gathered at a small bridge table set up in one corner to serve as the bar, and each helped themselves to their drink of preference. There were two sets of hosts tonight, for if Bassano was providing the hall, it was Mildred and Jerry who had proposed the event and paid for the refreshments.

Kaplan, in making the evening's first toast, also made clear his and Mildred's motive: "Here's to the dog of honor!" he cried, raising his plastic glass of rye. "To the wonderful dog who brought Millie and I together. Rex! Good health, boy!"

"Here, here," they all shouted, and, as they downed the evening's first drink, the object of the toast, hearing his name, looked up from the green carpeting on which he had stretched out.

Next to offer his own brief, but thoughtful, toast was Charles Miller: "To Julia," said the blind man warmly. "So her feelings aren't hurt." Although Julia was already asleep beneath the long formica table, her ears twitched.

Eddie Mays, in turn, raised a glass to Miller: "I just want to let you know, no hard feelings over the accident, Chuckie. And good luck with the new job."

Next with a brisk salutation was Dr. Matt Brunn. "Our hosts!" he called. "To you, Kaplan, and you, Miss Schapp!"

"Skol," "Cheers," "Here, here!" called Bassano, Miller and Mays, and now it was the moving man's turn to be mentioned. However, instead of being the object of a toast, he found himself the subject of a short speech.

"To our host, the capable Mr. Bassano," said Mildred Schapp. "Let me remind us all tonight that it was Mr. B. who, by teaching Jerry to call off an attacking dog, indirectly preserved the life of that unfortunate young drug addict last summer." Not surprisingly, most responses to this observation were weak and dubious. The single exception was the dog trainer's loud "Here, here!" accompanied by a vigorous nod.

Wanting to return Mildred's compliment, realizing also that Eddie Mays had not yet been honored, but forgetting the first two toasts, Joe Bassano now offered the most sweeping of the salutations. "To the lady," said the moving man with dignity, "to the dogs, and to my good friend, Mr. Ed Mays, Esquire."

After they had all cheered and once again sipped from their glasses, Doctor Brunn and "Doctor" Mays, in order to complete the round in style, toasted each other in time-honored fashion by locking right arms and simultaneously tossing off large, newly poured drinks. The onlookers applauded this feat with particular energy, and the first phase of the party thus concluded.

Next, the six friends settled around one end of the conference table. At Bassano's insistence, Eddie Mays was seated at the head, with the others ranged as follows: Mildred, then Jerry, on Eddie's right hand; Miller, Dr. Brunn and Bassano, on his left. As soon as the men were in their places, Mildred rose and circled the table twice, first to freshen the drinks and then to serve the coffee and danish, in order, as she put it, "to keep this happy occasion from turning into a drunken orgy."

When the guests had chatted, laughed, eaten and drunk for a few minutes, the proprietor of the guard dog store leaned forward in his chair, cleared his throat and prepared to speak.

"Order, order, please," he said, tapping his spoon against his coffee cup. "I wish to say a few words tonight. In honor of Rex here." The guests quieted down and, hearing his name again, the dog, who now lay behind and to the right of Mays's chair, once again looked up.

"Good, a speech," said Mildred. "Just the thing."

"That's right, boy," Mays continued, turning in his chair. "You won't be embarrassed, will you, fellow?" Then, as Eddie reached back to scratch the dog's ears, the chair began to tip.

"Whoa, careful there," said Dr. Brunn, and Mays righted himself just in time.

"Take it easy, Ed," suggested Jerry Kaplan. "We're all ears."

"Thanks, Jerr, I will, I will. I'll do just that. Okay, let's see." Eddie squared his shoulders, licked his lips and took a deep breath. Then he made as if to tap his cup again, but realizing this was unnecessary, he stopped the spoon in mid-air and put it down. "Okay," he repeated, "let's see."

"Get on with it, Eddie, will you!" said Dr. Brunn. "You look like a sailboat waiting for the wind to come up."

"Okay, okay," said Mays. Once again he breathed deeply and opened his mouth. But nothing came out, and Eddie began to blush. He turned in his seat again, as if seeking help from Rex, and then, silent and mortified, looked helplessly at the other guests, whose faces expressed various combinations of sympathy and amusement.

It was Mildred Schapp who came to the rescue of the tongue-tied speaker just as the doom-laden silence he had created was starting to descend on the entire company. "Gentlemen, may I?" she said. Relief was palpable, and Bassano, springing to his feet, needlessly circled the table with the coffee pot. "I, for one," she continued, "find Eddie's silence . . . touching, although, of course, I would be the last to deny its amusing aspect."

Those few words did the job. One by one, finding their voices, the other guests agreed with Mildred and began to make comments of their own, so that, before she could proceed, everyone was talking at once, Mays as enthusiastically as the rest.

"Tell us about the dog," someone cried, and among the other questions and requests were: "Let's hear your life story, Ed" "You Italian on both sides, Joe?" "How'd you lose your sight, Charles?" "Where you from originally?" "Is it true you had some college?" "How come so many kids nowadays want to be vets?" "Where'd you find Julia, Ed?" "What's that?" "Who's he?"

Now the festive group needed to be steered past impending chaos, and it was Charles Miller, this time, who set them back on course.

"Excuse me," piped the blind man in his loud, high voice. "I have a suggestion."

"Good, good," people said, "a suggestion." They quieted right down, and Miller continued.

"Since it was Eddie who started to speak first, and since we all seem to have so much on our minds, why not go around the table and let each person ask Ed a single question? About Rex, of course."

When the guests had universally applauded the neat logic of the blind man, they cheerfully acceded to his procedure, with only three provisos: questions, no speeches; no compound or follow-up questions; all inquiries must pertain to the guest of honor. Should disputes arise, they further agreed, such would be adjudicated (without appeal) by the Honorable Joe Bassano who, in Jerry Kaplan's estimation, "talks the most like a lawyer."

Who would be first? The privilege, someone said, should belong to Miller, since it was he who had invented the plan. No, it should be Mildred, who, besides being the only (human) female present, had broken the deadly silence.

"A foolish dispute," declared the judge, and he decreed that it would be Mildred, then Miller --"first, and almost first."

"In that case," said Mildred Schapp, looking thoughtful and pleased, "why not begin with first causes? Mr Mays, my question is, 'How did you get to know Rex initially?' I ask because something tells me that you two have a special relationship, that you must, as people say, 'go way back.' " This question, if predictable, was certainly legitimate, and Bassano directed Mays to reply, which he did with alacrity and thoroughness.

It turned out Rex had been "kennel-bred" in New Jersey by none other than Eddie himself and his own father, Buddy Mays. Furthermore, Eddie had not only trained Rex single-handedly, "up from a pup," but the very first dog in whose breeding Eddie had assisted, when he had himself been a teenager, was Rex's father, the show dog Mack. Swept away by memory, Eddie began to expostulate on Rex's unique qualities as a pup --his size, color, proportions, unusual hind-quarter strength, intelligence (he could bark arithmetically at six weeks) and so forth. This topic might well have swallowed the rest of the evening had not Judge Bassano invoked, at Dr. Brunn's whispered behest, "the gag rule".

"And that don't mean you tell gags now, neither, Ed. Next question: Robert Miller."

"Charles,'" said the blind man. "My question: How did Rex come to be trained as a guide dog?"

"Excellent question," commented Jerry Kaplan. "I was wondering about that one, myself. Way to go, Chuck!"

"Silence!" ordered Bassano. "Mr. Mays. Please."

Once again Eddie eagerly obliged. He began by repeating the fact that he, himself, had been in charge of Rex's earliest, general education --the "up-down stop-go sit-heel" phase. Then he told how, at the suggestion of Buddy Mays, they had brought the eager young dog to the Blind Dog Institute, which was only a few miles down the road from Mays Breeders. It was here, at the famed Institute, that Rex breezed through the three-month course in obedience and leadership.

"The last part was the hard part," Eddie concluded. "DISobedience training. See, they . . "

"DISobedience?' " interrupted the judge, forgetting himself. "You mean to tell me, first they . . ."

"Just shut up and let him explain, Joe," said Kaplan, and he received an angry look from Bassano, who did, however, shut up.

Eddie Mays then described that most demanding phase of a Seeing Eye Dog's education during which the animal is, in effect, taught to act against its own nature. For, if a vehicle or other menace should suddenly fly or fall toward the blind person, the dog must disobey the beloved master even to the extent, perhaps, of knocking him down.

"Interesting, Eddie, very good," said Dr. Brunn. "Who's next, Joe?"

"But I ain't . . ." Mays protested.

"Why don't you ask the next one yourself, Matt?" Bassano suggested, and the doctor obliged, surprising the other guests, however, by not asking a medical question.

"What's a young dog's most common failing?" asked Brunn, and from the readiness with which the question was put, it was clear that premeditation was involved.

Preparation was also suggested by the reply, for, when Mays began once again to speak, with a promptitude which answered that of the doctor, some among the guests began to suspect that Eddie must have spent years mentally rehearsing just such a performance as he was now giving. And their sense was accurate, for what Eddie Mays was in fact doing on this memorable evening was disburdening himself of the silent memories of decades. And, although not all the questions may have been exactly the ones he would have chosen to answer, Eddie was so eager that, not only did he find it easy to satisfy the questioners, but he spoke with a fluency which was, for him, uncanny. ("It must be the rye," Kaplan theorized, at one point.)

"Good question, Doc," Mays commented. "That one fault you ask of is friskiness --young dogs are all frisky. Dukey, too! Oh, whoops, uh oh!" He smiled. "Anyone catch that? I ain't told you that yet, did I? Rexie used to be named 'Duke.' But I better not go on about that now or Judge Joey here's going to cut me off again, right? So if you want to know about the name someone is going to have to ask it specifically.

"Friskiness. That was his only fault as a scholar. See, at our place he used to run along the fence in the grass, chasing the chickens from the farm across the road."

"Did he now?" asked Dr. Brunn, catching the judge napping with this interruption, a clear violation of the rule against follow-up questions. "Let me ask you, Ed, why did those chickens come across the road in the first place?" The vet winked across at Jerry and Mildred, who both smiled. Mays was momentarily puzzled.

"What do you mean, why did..." Then he understood. "For Christ's sake!" Before continuing, he raised an arm as if to strike the doctor. "Anyways, it's easy to get them to stop. When a dog starts chasing, you just throw a chain across his hind legs a couple times. That stops them right away."

"Hmm" pondered Mildred. "Some might find that cruel." As Bassano again failed to curtail the interruption, she continued. "But perhaps it isn't. After all, Eddie, you've already explained that these dogs are bred as workers. They must take great pleasure in doing things properly, mustn't they?"

"Exactly," Eddie replied. "You give a dog like Duke a job to do, feed him right, tell him 'Good Boy' when he does the job, and he's going to be one happy dog. A little pain don't bother a good dog."

"Hmm," said Miller, 'a little pain'."

"Who's next?" asked Bassano. "Jerry?"

As only two questioners remained, the others were disappointed when Kaplan, inert from food, drink and laziness, stuck to the subject of training.

"Do they train the blind people, too?" he asked.

Even Miller failed to look interested. Sensing their disappointment, Mays hurried over the obvious --the stages during which the blind man gets acquainted with his dog and learns to move with it, first alone, then in crowds and traffic. When Eddie did arrive at a detail he thought might interest the others, he lingered a moment.

"They even teach them to wear their clothes right and eat nice."

"Whoa, just a minute," objected Bassano, "you're jerking us off there, right, Ed? Whoops, excuse me, Mrs. Schapp. Sorry, Jerr."

"No, Joey, honest, I'm not," Mays replied. "See, no offense, Chuck, but lots of the blind been living alone for years, they get like animals. So when they first come to the school, the teachers show them how to eat nice. They set their plates up like clocks: vegetables at four, meat at eight, potatoes at midnight. And they sew different length threads on the inside of their clothes so's they'll wear the right colors together: no red with orange, for instance." Several of the listeners glanced down at their own clothes. "See, the Institute relies on public support, they got an image to keep up, so they don't want the graduates going around with their dogs and looking like --sorry, Miz Schapp-- like assholes."

To this, the second such apology, Mildred protested, explaining that she "had not been born yesterday," that she "knew all the naughty words." After a wave-like grin had rolled around the table, it was time for the final question, that of the judge and host, himself.

"Let's see." Bassano bit his lip, searching hard for the one question which would best satisfy what he perceived as a large, still unsatisfied hunger among the guests. "Ah ha," he finally said, and he asked his question with great care: "When Mrs. Schapp rented Rex from you, Ed, had he been with you all along? From when he was a pup, I mean."

"Excellent," said Charles Miller, expressing the pleasure of the group that biography would not, after all, be stinted in favor of education.

Mays smiled. "Thanks, Joe." Then he coyly looked at his watch and said, "But wait, look how late it is, almost ten-thirty already, people got to go to work tomorrow. Maybe we better can the rest of this until ..." Their faces ended the teasing right there. "Okay, okay," Eddie said, "but I will try to keep to just the main facts." He sipped his coffee, which was now tepid, the way he liked it. "In a word, Joe, 'No'. By no means. No. The truth is, there was a break of many years, many years. See, when my old man died --mom had already passed on when I was in my teens. Lung cancer, it was."

"Gee, I'm sorry to hear that, Ed," said Bassano.

"Shit, Joe, it was over twenty-five years ago." After this, no one interrupted again. "Anyways, when dad died, I sold the place. Business was slow, and it was too quiet a life for a young guy. So I went in the service, and after the war --Korea--I knocked around, did this and that, mostly with dogs, of course. I was even with the Police Canine Unit down in Philly when they started it.

"Then, after a while, I landed a real good job here with A A R F. My title was Chief Trainer and Caretaker. Business was great in those days --you guys can remember, can't you?-- all the factories and yards was open, most of them utilizing dogs. Yep, Doc here used to be on a fat retainer, didn't you, Doc? Of course, by then I had pretty much forgot about Duke, you know.

"It was years and years later before I found out what was happening to him during this same time period. By a big coincidence, a blind guy right here in the neighborhood had got him. Oh, I'm not sure if that happened straight from the Institute or if Duke done some other stuff first. So the guy keeps him a while, and then --what was the guy's name again, Doc?" Brunn shrugged. "Shit, it's gone. Anyways, after a while the guy passed away. Then Duke disappeared, or at least no one I spoke to later knew where he was, where he been. And then one day, just like that, some kids brung him in. Here. To A A R F. In a red wagon, no less. Kids!"

"It's always kids, ain't it?" said Kaplan.

"Yep. Now you got to understand, my friends, these kids couldn't of had no idea what Dukey meant to me. See, they was just giving it a try --they knew me for a kind-heart-- before they called the meat wagon, the S.P.C.A. Well, maybe you can guess my reaction. At first I didn't even recognize him. I mean it was years and years, and here was this poor mutt, filthy, full of vermin of many varieties, injured, a total mess. The poor dog must of had some kind of working over, he didn't even know where he was. So. What did I do? I called Matt, naturally. Remember, Matt? And he give him a shot just so's we could even begin to clean him up. And then when we started washing him, it hit me who he was. I can tell you, friends, I almost fainted right there and then. Remember, Matt? And soon I started crying, and I couldn't stop." Mays paused now to wipe his eyes. "You'll have to excuse me, folks, if I don't go into too much of the details of what happened after that. To be honest, it's too painful, still too painful, to recall certain details. Just remember one thing: this was Duke, my number one boy. Now try to picture him in the red wagon. Get it? Well, okay, enough of that.

"Anyway, the point is, this special dog had suffered a serious trauma, so I had to go right back to the drawing board, start him out again like he was just born. And, folks, you know what? I did it. I slowly retrained the boy.

"That was when he got his new name. 'Rex.' Hell, why not? A fresh start. He was still only seven, eight. I could see long rich years ahead, even though he looked old from his hardships: fur gone gray, a teensy bit withered in the quarters, nothing so terrible when you stop and think about it.

"Anyways, within a couple years, so help me if Rex don't seem good as new. Well, then, I was just starting to think, 'What next?' when you come in that day, Miz Schapp. So help me, I may not of showed it, but you was an angel from heaven to me. And now --I'm almost done-- I got to make a confession and an apology. It was a big risk I took, very unprofessional, too. Renting him, I mean. He could of attacked you, Miz Schapp. And another thing: I even lied about his age, he wasn't really all that old. It would have scared you, I thought, if I told you the real facts. I apologize, Miz Schapp, I really do." Eddie looked down.

"Really, Mr. Mays, no need at all," said Mildred handsomely. "In light of subsequent events, I must say I wish more people these days would take such risks."

"Here, here, Madam!" cried Dr. Brunn.

"Thanks," said Eddie. "Very kind of you, I'm touched. Of course the point of my taking the risk was obvious, wasn't it? I seen that you and the job you were offering was just the thing for Rex, a new life, the part-time aspect to ease him back into working, make the boy feel useful again. And it worked, Miz Schapp, one-hundred per cent."

Mays was finished now, and the group sat quietly for a moment, after which it was Charles Miller who spoke first. "Rex," he said simply, "has a beautiful spirit. And what a lovely story of friendship, Ed. After all those years."

"What impresses me," said Dr. Brunn, "is the dog's recuperative powers. Does everyone realize what he's been through in his lifetime?"

"It's his fighting heart, Doc," suggested Jerry. "Plus he ain't as old as we thought, right?"

"Jerry," said Bassano. "There I agree with you one-hundred per cent."

And with those words the party ended. Refusing all offers of assistance, and assuring everyone that he knew "where everything goes," Bassano showed his guests to the door, shook hands with each of them, and locked them out. Then Dr. Brunn suggested he might drive Charles Miller home, and after more "Good nights" the vet took the blind man by the elbow and guided him up the street to his car.

Since it was late and things would be rushed in the morning, and since they were right around the corner from the guard dog store, Mildred and Jerry decided to return Rex and Julia now, rather than keep them overnight. As the weather was clear and mild and they wanted to work off the effects of the party, they also offered to stroll back to the store with Eddie and the dogs.

Accordingly, a few minutes later Eddie Mays unlocked the plate glass door to his shop. Turning on the lights, he removed the leashes and left them behind the counter. They all proceeded to the edge of the kennel area, where Eddie suggested Mildred and Jerry turn back, so as not to waken those dogs which were already sleeping.

It was time. Mildred and Jerry quietly wished the dog trainer a good night. Kaplan solemnly offered his hand, and Mildred took Eddie by the shoulders and kissed his cheek. Finally, after giving Rex and Julia a few lingering pats, the couple watched as Eddie Mays and his limping dogs crossed the moonlit yard to the kennels.

EPILOGUE

Of course, the dogs did finally age and die. Rex went off on a March night and, like the survivor in many old human couples, a few days later, Julia hurried after. It was Jerry Kaplan who tearfully made the four-by-four double coffin of pre-treated two-inch yellow pine, and Joe Bassano who, in a small company van on a rainy Friday, drove the deceased and their survivors to a small cottage owned by Dr. Matt Brunn in the Catskill Mountains. There, in a grove behind the cottage, the animals were laid to rest in a grave which Dr. Brunn had called ahead to order dug by local workmen.

After a moment of silence, Eddie Mays took Charles Miller by the arm and guided him around to the far side of the grave. (Miller had judged it best to leave his own dog, Bob, home today.) Facing the grave, the blind man stood with the rain falling on his red hair and dark glasses, and listened to the footsteps of Mays as he rejoined the group. Then, clasping the lapel of his flannel suit coat with one hand and gesticulating with the other, Miller recited without preamble the eulogy he had composed in his room the previous night:

Let men be bold, let truth be told,
These two were a king and his queen
Of noble scions, their hearts like lions',
No bone in their bodies, mean.

To the lonely and the blind, ever were they kind,

These paragons of canine race.

They came, they saw, they overcame,

Leaving Earth a worthier place.

So let's raise a cup, drink it all up,

Here's afterlife to Rex and to Julia,

Let's hope where they are, whether near or far far,

There's food, water and sex, hallelujah

"Amen!" and "Here, here!" the people cry softly, then, and Mays walks back across to Miller. He takes him by the arm, returns him to the group, and, in a silent row, the six humans stand with bowed heads, as the rain thumps down on the dogs' new coffin.

Norman's Cousin

Brooklyn, 1981

It is difficult to explain how that confrontation came about, how it was that my cousin --short, plump, pale, freckled and sandy-haired-- and myself, very different, but presently his double, faced each other across the large, nearly empty room that Sunday morning and stared in silence for perhaps an entire minute.

"Who are you and what do you want?" he finally asked. The smoke from his interrupted cup of coffee drifted across his face as he spoke. I stood up straight and, aware that the other patrons were watching me, walked slowly over to him.

Leaning on the counter two feet to his left, I smiled into his face and said calmly, "Norman B ---."

A deep flush came up out of his shirt collar and climbed his face to the hairline, darkening the freckles as it went. It reminded me of a scarlet velvet theater curtain; the play was "Norman's Anger."

Cousin Norman, the son of my father's brother, had always represented living death for me. When I had last been in contact with him, Norman had been a middle-level civil servant responsible for the allocation of P ---'s municipal tax revenues. He had possessed a faculty for total recall of the daily newspaper, pretending to do so in the name of Informed Citizenry, but in fact relishing victory over anyone so foolhardy as to disagree with him about what an article had said. Even as a young man, Norman had aspired to the title of Family Patriarch.

Three years my junior, Norman had fathered two sons who must by now have reached high school. His wife I remembered as much taller and thinner than he. Even to think of Norman was to make me short of breath, but with a great effort of concentration I began to picture his fingers: stubby, with unbitten pink nails. Another detail I immediately remembered was that his breath was so sour you could taste it merely by licking your own lips.

These were the preliminary garnerings from memory, and now I was ready to begin work on the next stage, the creation of an approximate physical double. I do not keep photographs of people I detest, so I relied on my visual memory and a few quick viewings from crowds. Does it seem impossible that I could physically impersonate Norman? Even in the general resemblance that was my preliminary aim? Does the reader immediately think of height and frame as insurmountable barriers? A few commonplaces about appearance should dispel that misconception. "Oh, that color makes you look so fat!" "Don't wear those pants, they make your legs look so stubby!" Becoming short, fat Norman was not much of a challenge. Who was going to ask us to stand back to back? As to resources, by this stage of my career I was amply stocked with make-up, wigs, wardrobe and other props. Plus my single most remarkable talent, the capacity to mimic mannerism. With an hour's practice I would be able to do Norman's duck walk in my sleep.

In the event, it took less than a week for me to look enough like Norman that his wife, with a puzzled expression on her normally cool face, waved to me as I was disappearing into a crowd. But general appearance was only the start. I tested the impersonation just that one time before moving on to the next stage, research into details. I put the physical disguise away, so as not to "squander" it and so as to concentrate on the inward impersonation.

For this was to be my first three-dimensional performance. Even my most hitherto-demanding role, that of a subway blind man, had been little more than a stereotype, a cartoon. When I tried begging, a bit of self-abasement and a few droll touches were all it took to excite the compassion of my fellow travelers, the role's only object beyond the feeling of humiliation which was mine merely by virtue of donning the costume.

But this level of impersonation could no longer satisfy me, for at some point during my recent misery I had outgrown the flat two-dimensional impersonation. Perhaps I had lost a measure of my former playfulness. Or perhaps I realized even then that an effective way to eliminate someone is totally to become him. Whatever the reason, I could be satisfied only by a Norman that was subtle and deeply accurate.

So the next stage was to find out all I could about him. I began by looking through my files, but all I had were a few letters my father had sent me at college. They mentioned how Norman had been chosen President of This and Secretary of That, at N --- College of the P --- University. I was also annoyed to reread my father's many reminders about how P --- was a free university, an obvious criticism of my own choice of an expensive private university far from the city and, more important, from my unpleasant family. Even a careless reader will see in these letters what I had against Norman, but I leave such clues to the novelist or biographer. To tell the truth, I was glad there were no more written materials, for I did not want to postpone using my main method of research: spy craft.

Before I would be satisfied, I must know a great deal about my plump little cousin. I had specific questions in mind: exactly how did he now look; how did his stomach feel as he gulped down the last of his lunch and headed back to the office; and what was his smile like in response to the stink-eye his doorman gave him for the chintzy Christmas bonus?

Suddenly, the last year felt less futile. My obsessive multiple disguising now proved absolutely essential, for the variety of costumes I used in tracking Norman and his family almost bewildered me, myself. Both the capacity for quick changes and the generalized artistry I had perfected over those difficult months were now called upon to the utmost.

I began, not surprisingly, as the blind bum, this time embellishing the role with a false nose and artificial smell. In this guise, I failed to cadge money from Norman on the bus one morning. Of course, the money would only have represented a secondary gain, for I did succeed in observing his every facial expression as he read the editorial page of the P --- Bee, while I pretended to count my change and to transfer it from cup to pocket. Norman's lips looked dry as he read, and I noticed he had developed a minor eye tic, a fluttering of the left lid. Later that morning, I bought the edition of the Bee he had been reading, and when I saw that the main editorial was an impassioned plea for municipal budget cuts I wished I had checked Norman's trousers to see whether he had wet them.

Next, as a thin old lady in a red wig and trench coat, I watched him buying meat in a butcher shop on a Saturday morning. He examined a sirloin steak personally to make sure it was tender and properly marbled, and the way he fingered it gave me the embarrassing sensation of watching his foreplay with his wife. As he mauled the steak, I hoped he would turn it down, for the large, red-faced butcher seemed prepared to blacken his eye, and I would have liked to hear Norman rant about law suits. But he bought the meat, after all.

Watching Norman buy food was sufficiently informative and interesting that I risked a second "chance" encounter that morning, this one in a fruit store. Here he flashed a shark-like smile at me that almost seemed a murderous warning to the elderly to stay out of his way, and I was so discomfited that I fled the store without even making a purchase to cover my tracks.

In this stage of the preparations, I grew more and more thorough, for I had begun to sense that the actual moment of assuming the role was near. In fact, there were times when I ran from disguise to disguise rather too wantonly, risking exposure through excessive virtuosity. To give but a single example, I once found myself trailing Mrs. B. --- down Y --- Street in a prostitute's slit skirt, make-up and so on, but with the footwear from my previous disguise, that of a municipal garbage man pretending to be drunk on the job in order to see how far Norman would carry his "good citizen" act. He had settled for an unostentatious frown.

In all, I went through fifteen to eighteen of these disguises, and the number would have been much larger had I not used one disguise for spying on two, three, or even all four of the members of Norman's family. Naturally, my researches did not stop with the main subject. I spent a particularly informative Saturday afternoon on a roof across the street from their apartment, dressed as a bird watcher and using a pair of high-powered binoculars to watch Norman's pimply sixteen-year-old (whose straight black hair came from my own gene pool) frolicking on the rug with the family terrier, T ---. I had already heard a great deal about this T --- from Norman's cleaning lady, a garrulous Croat whom I once met in my own person at a coffee shop.

All these visual, historical and surveillant operations lasted a total of five weeks, during which I often missed work so as not to disrupt a delicate phase of the process. Now it was time to close in. The last stage before the impersonation proper must be confrontation. To get rolling, I needed mettle and momentum, and to achieve them I would use one last preliminary impersonation.

For weeks now, I had been conducting a mailbox lock-picking and letter-steaming operation, and I had discovered there was to be a large family party in honor of the golden wedding anniversary of the old family patriarch and his wife. Of course, I did not myself receive an invitation, having been struck from the family rolls after five years or more of ignored communications. From a penciled postscript on Norman's invitation, I learned he would be giving an "impromptu" speech. This meant he would probably be Windbag-in-Chief, and thereby vulnerable to public attack. The particular form of the attack, I would decide at the site. I relished the *poltergeist* role and reminded myself of another important reason for attending the party: last minute spying within the crucial milieu of the extended family. I anticipated that Norman would caricature traits I had already identified, providing a checklist for my findings to date.

To anticipate, my plan worked perfectly. By the time I left the party, my desire to impersonate Norman had been brought to the boiling point. In fact, I wound up leaving in the middle, for I could wait no longer.

Three days before the party, I put on one of my "Norman" outfits and left it on. In order not to have to keep changing back and forth, I simply skipped work altogether on those days. When the authorities called, I used his voice, pretending to be a personalized recorded message:

This is Mr. B ---'s cousin, Norman B ---, speaking. Mr. B --is ill and is unable at this time to come to the phone. I am staying home from my important position as Assistant City Comptroller in order to care for B ---, whose recovery is not expected to be protracted.

As the party approached, I had no doubt of my ability to slip unrecognized into the midst of my family. In the years since any of them had seen me in my own person, I had changed considerably. My hairline had receded, my eyes had sunk, my nose had grown sharp, and my ears, hairy and larger. My voice was now deep and raspy. Where once my lips might have been called sensitive, they now looked pained. Even my clothes hung differently, for I had shed the weight gained during the first difficult months, and many pounds more. Midway through my crisis, I had stopped eating, from a conviction that to eat in a starving world was obscene. I had also grown somewhat stoop-shouldered.

Of course, my invisibility was not completely dependent on these physical changes: my costume, make-up and wig would be impeccable. By now my talents for altering manner and personality were fully developed. After the last, intensive period of training, there was little to the art of impersonation that lay beyond my grasp. To name but a single facet, I had achieved outstanding physical dexterity. For instance, I had discovered one recent morning that I was able easily to brush my hair with one hand while simultaneously brushing my teeth with the other.

The night before the party, I slept little. I sat in an armchair in my bedroom dressed as Norman, imagining what he would say and how he would look during each of the several crises I would precipitate.

The only flaw in my costume the next day was that it was too warm. First, instead of showering or bathing, I took off my disguise as Norman, and did a little sponging up. Then, I put on make-up, including face-lifting materials, and a wavy, greasy black wig that fitted tightly to my scalp, already shaved for the wig I had worn as Norman. Then, the suit, a shabby sort of pseudo-formal garment, and I was ready to make my appearance at the party as a handsome menial of twenty-three or four whose origins might equally have been Arabian, Caribbean, Mediterranean, or perhaps even Oriental.

As I carried the food trays back and forth through the large living room in which the guests were assembled, I thrilled to the comments: my costume was a complete success. So handsome was my persona that female cousins and even a few hot-blooded old aunts lost the thread of their sentences.

"*Parla Italiano?*" asked a vaguely familiar blonde, leering at me through glasses with hideous frames, as I bent before her at the waist with a tray of little breaded hot dogs and toothpicks.

"No? Then, maybe, he *habla's espanol,*" suggested a hot old aunt whom I remembered as having pampered Norman and me equally when we were little. I remained momentarily silent, out of disgust, for she had spoken with her mouth full, having managed to ingest two hot dogs at once by means of a modified chop-sticking technique.

"Needuh, ladies." I employed a vague accent I knew they would fail to identify.

"Isn't he a doll!" someone else whispered. "excuse me, young man, but what lang ..."

"Tagalog!" I snapped venomously, and turned on my heel.

"That's a Filipino language, dear," explained a male voice I could not quite place. I hurried to the kitchen for more food.

"Everything okay, kid?" asked the avuncular bartender who served as crew chief. "Hey, you look overheated. Don' strain yourself so much, they're gettin' plenty."

"They pigs, eat too much, get sick." I grabbed a full tray, spun on my heel, and did my quick, short-stepped little walk back toward the living room.

Over two hours passed in this manner. An enormous amount of food and drink was consumed by the thirty-four guests, and by now quite a few toasts had been made, Norman's (unmemorable) included. Then, the moment for action arrived.

I suddenly found myself in the middle of the room holding a sandwich tray, feeling deeply sad and aimless.

"Why did I come?" I wondered. And the old feeling of contemptuous superiority to my family, alternating with self-loathing, began to roll over me. Hopelessly, I felt as if I were sliding backward into adolescence, and the prospect made me panic. The room turned into a loud blur of noise, smells and color. Everything was unbearably oppressive, especially the smells: liquor, perfume, flowers, smoke, sweat, meat. Lacking a plan of any sort and fearing that at any moment I might be unable to move, I rushed straight to the group of which Norman was center. Standing with my tray just outside the circle of their chairs, I studied them closely so as not to be caught off-guard by a sudden movement. They were five, in all, including the patriarch. Small, bald, crinkly-skinned and mottled, the old man sat facing me in an armchair. The rest, including Norman, whose back was directly in front of me, had drawn up a semi-circle of folding chairs around the patriarch.

As expected, Norman was holding forth, and I hesitated, pretending to be looking for a break through which to enter. The senile old man appeared oblivious to my presence as, still in a half-trance, I tried to catch the gist of Norman's droning speech: Baghdad, crying shame, living theater, Buddhist monks, television, Star Wars, circus fire eaters, incendiary devices, anti-fire suits, vehicles. Any fool would have recognized Norman's Platitude of the Day: how the media turn human tragedies to entertainment. The man's mind was so trivial, so predictable. I cleared my throat and began to edge the tray forward over Norman's shoulder. At that moment, the patriarch spotted me, apparently attracted by my movement. Turning red, he gruffly waved me away.

"Go away, boy, go away, don't want you now, can't you tell when a man is saying something important? That's Norman B --- speaking, boy, don't you recognize the man, that's our Deputy City Comptroller, boy! Hush, listen now! You'll learn something worth knowing."

"Very good, sir," I mumbled.

But the old man was overruled by several protesting voices. "No, no," they said. "Let him do his job, Uncle. Here, I'll take one. What are those?"

Edging into the circle, I lowered the tray so that they might see and take the sandwiches. But there were none: the tray was empty. For a second, except for a few exclamations of surprise, they were silent. Then one of them laughed, it caught fire, and in a moment they were all roaring.

I was not about to be bothered. The moment I felt a prickle of embarrassment, I caught myself, fought off the feeling, and became angry, instead. With a perfunctory, sneering "Sorry," I turned on my heel and took a few steps toward the kitchen. But then I heard something that stopped me dead. The laughter had hardly died down when someone who had evidently buttonholed Norman began to talk in a loud, confidential drunkard's voice. I stood stock still, my back to the group.

'How ya' doin' these days, Norm? Back at the old grind yet?"

'Yeah, just about." The affected nonchalance masked obvious fear, as well as obvious reluctance to have this topic broached. How had I missed such an important event in the history of my subject? The omission was flabbergasting. "Yeah, I'm back at work now, but the doc has me on mild exercise and no salt or arguments."

Pursing my lips, I hurried to the kitchen, as the other man laughed at Norman's quip. The revelation was not going to interfere with either my immediate or long-term plans.

I was allowed to serve only food because, I suppose, they were chary of letting new temporaries handle liquor. However, all the kitchen workers were busy as I hurried in, and no one stopped me when I pulled a large carafe of white wine from the refrigerator. I swept a white towel from a large pile and rushed from the kitchen once more, drying the dripping carafe as I went. I had not been in the kitchen more than ten seconds.

Still without hesitating, I crossed the living room rug toward Norman's wife, that tall blonde woman, attractive in what is called a "severe" way. She was sitting beside a similar woman in the corner opposite the circle of men, and the way they were leaning together suggested that they were engaged in intense gossip. I had previously noted that Mrs. B --- was wearing a frilly white shirtwaist, and I now observed with satisfaction that both women held empty wine glasses.

"Wine, madam?" I asked loudly. Before she could answer, I thrust the carafe at her, tilting it suddenly as if to pour. Her mouth opened, and she looked up into my eyes with alarm, for by then I had already made myself trip over the runner of a rocking chair. Desperately, she moved to catch in the little glass the wave of wine that descended on her, and I will say for her that she managed to half-fill the glass. The rest, however, made a direct hit, instantly soaking the white shirtwaist. Even in a bra, which I had been almost certain Mrs. B --- would be wearing, her interesting little breasts stared up at me like a pair of hungry baby birds. For a full two or three seconds, I stood absolutely still, staring back at the little birds. Then, I licked my lips and smiled a long, lazy, insolent smile. And, finally, far too late for her to suppose the spill had been accidental unless she were absolutely determined to believe this, I sprung into the expected actions, spluttering and extending the towel. Even then, I moved as if to dab her, myself, but she extended her hand and, when she realized the towel was soaked, flung it to the ground.

The events of the next few minutes were predictable. Blouse was plucked from undergarment and skin, and cries of "He did it on purpose" and "Don't be silly" rang round the room. Rushing in, the old bartender saw what I had done and, for the sake of the guests, called me a clumsy fool. Mrs. B --- was led by her confidante and another woman to one of the bathrooms, where they soon had her dried off, washed, and decked out in a reasonably suitable substitute garment. All this took four or five minutes. Then, back in the kitchen, my boss and the other workers gave vent to their delight at what had happened. Two or three approached me with congratulations, and one who had watched the whole act even remarked how pleasing the view had been before they got her dried off.

That had been my favorite moment, too, when I had stood there staring at Norman's wife's breasts while her failure to act assured me of her complicity. A close second was my reaction to the crew chief's mandatory rebuke.

"I am, I am, sorry, sir, ma'am," I had spluttered to no one in particular, in a marvelous impersonation of self-abasement. I even managed a blush, which I knew would look rather lovely through my light chocolate make-up.

Ten minutes after Mrs. B --- emerged with her entourage, I ducked into the bathroom, just in case there should be some secret message from her. I searched in vain, however. There were a few blonde hairs around the washbasin, but I was not so self-deluded as to suppose they had been left there intentionally.

My plan was to slip out of the party directly from the bathroom, which was off the foyer, but I once again impulsively changed my mind and got a fresh pot of coffee from the kitchen. Having noticed on a previous round that most of the men already had cups, I moved back to the patriarch's circle, which was growling desultorily about money markets and the food they had eaten. When they saw me, they made a few jokes --which I ignored-- about the wine spill and whether there was any coffee in the pot.

"Merr cuffee, gintlemin?" I asked, holding the pot in front of me, but not entering the circle.

Pivoting on his fleshy neck with effort, Norman fixed me with his eye. "I'll take some," he said, exaggerating the usual sour, insulting tone. He slowly extended his arm and held the cup out alongside his shoulder. The whole time I was pouring his coffee, Norman kept his eyes riveted to my face. He looked like a detective searching for signs of guilt, or maybe his stare was an admonition not to repeat with the coffee what I had done with the wine.

This was one of the most thrillingly dangerous moments of my entire career as an impersonator. I can say with pride that, as slowly as possible, I filled my cousin's cup to the brim, making *him* the apprehensive one. Stubbornly, he refused to tell me to stop.

When it was as full as it could be, I said with consummate obsequiousness and without a trace of a tremor in my voice, "I remembir you take it bleck, suh, correct, no?"

In response, Norman said not a word. Instead, he met my forced smile with the fat, sour nod I had noticed before, without emotion. Now that nod strengthened a thousand-fold my desire to impersonate him. I vowed to go straight home to practice the sour nod a thousand times before my mirror. It would be my trademark, the mannerism for which posterity remembered B ---, the impersonator, just as it remembers Houdini for his locks and shackles.

I made myself pour coffee for the two or three others in the circle who asked for it, bowed my way out of the circle, crossed the room and, setting the pot down on an expensive wooden table, left the party.

Concentrating on what must happen next, not looking at, or saying a word to, anyone on the street, I carried out my intention to forego the easy, but crowded bus, instead walking the two miles home. It had begun to drizzle, by then, but the air was still hot and sticky.

By the time I reached my apartment, little other than the costume remained of the Filipino busboy. Norman's nod was already built into my face. I deftly unlocked my door, flipped on the light, and crossed to the bedroom, tearing off the suit, the wig, and the rest as I went. In my underwear, I sat down at the dressing table.

It was time to say goodbye. I looked into the mirror at the busboy and, with a perfect nod, said slowly and dryly, "That was nice work with the wine, boy, she loved it." I waved him away.

"Thenk you, suh," he said with a smile at once grateful and sad, and then he disappeared forever.

There was no time to lose. I showered, put on Norman's deodorant and after-shave lotion, and dressed in the kind of clothes I knew he would wear the next morning, Sunday. By five o'clock I was once again seated at the mirror, ready to begin practice. I was on schedule.

Just before dawn, I awoke at the dressing table. I practiced a few last hours, then ate a doughnut and drank coffee to be certain my breath had the right degree of sourness. With a few deft touches, I freshened my make-up and put my wig to rights. Then, using the full-length mirror on the back of the closet door, I rearranged my pants, hidden suspenders and shirt, until I looked sufficiently stocky.

By eight-thirty, I was at the stop, waiting for the bus that would take me to the cafeteria where, for six consecutive Sundays, Norman had drunk three cups of coffee and read his newspaper from start to finish. In what seemed like seconds, the large green and white bus roared up, and I climbed on, careful not to mess my costume. I winked and walked past the driver toward the back.

"Hey, Mac," he called, obviously not knowing who I was, "what about the fare? You know, the seventy-five cents everyone pays to ride the bus?" Frowning severely I returned and, digging in my pocket, dropped all my coins on the tray beside him.

"Will that do? I'll expect an itemized receipt on my desk at nine sharp tomorrow morning. Got that, driver?"

"Sure, sure," he said, somewhat too familiarly. "Wait, here's your change, boss." I took it and moved toward the back, where I found a seat next to an old woman.

"Are you all right, young man?" she asked.

"Fine, thank you! And you? I do feel, Madam, that every consideration should be shown our elderly. The attitudes of the citizens of P --- toward the mature adult are shocking, no, pornographic. Count on me to speak out boldly on your behalf." She nodded, grateful to the point of speechlessness.

As the bus crossed town, I studied the situation while watching for landmarks. We were on the long shopping street that runs through this part of the city, and hordes of people crowded the sidewalks, even though it was still before nine o'clock. Up the side streets, knots of unemployed people were passing bottles around. Some children were already busy writing on walls and scrambling over parked cars and trucks. A few men were breaking into one car, and many people were flagrantly breaking the traffic rules by jaywalking and double-parking. Over everything hung the strong smell of oil. Distant sirens suggested fire.

A few blocks on, the streets began to be boarded up and smashed. Broken glass glittered. Letters, names everywhere, posters half-ripped from the crumbling walls. Between the buildings, empty lots like missing teeth. Everywhere, debris and garbage. Dogs chasing each other yipping across the holes. I spied a bum stretched out asleep in the middle of a vacant lot, a particularly large one. He was on an abandoned mattress. His face was bright red and his pants half down, exposing mealy buttocks and sagging belly. The mattress was coming apart in a way that made it appear that the grayish-white stuff was being excreted by the speaker, as he heavily breathed in and out.

A few minutes later, I glimpsed, somewhere to my left, the amusement park and boardwalk, but I carefully averted my eyes from the tracks, parachutes, towering cranes and other apparatus, for there must be no distractions or diversions now. Then, I saw the tall green letters on the white backing; it was time to get off. I pulled the cord, waited, climbed down the steps and crossed to the cafeteria. I was very calm, having pushed apprehension to the back of my mind. "One thing at a time," and "do it right before moving on" were my mottoes.

Taking a deep breath, I entered. He was not yet there. I crossed the room to the counter opposite the food line, leaned my forearms against this counter so that my face was partly hidden, and waited. Five minutes later, at nine thirty-one, Norman came in.

My first reaction was elation. I had guessed everything --except the shoes, that is, and this miscalculation was insignificant and one for which I could hardly be blamed. Norman was wearing the blue canvas deck shoes, whereas I had chosen the red joggers. I had been fooled by the changing of the seasons, not realizing how swiftly spring gives way to summer. But the rest was perfect. He wore the light blue sport shirt with the little green alligator, and the lightweight peach slacks, which I had pulled from the same pile in the same store as had Norman, whom I was trailing at the time. One other minor detail was off, I confess, but it did not matter: he was hatless. I had judged by the heat, and perhaps he felt it less than I did, or perhaps he had been influenced more by the overcast skies that day. Before he could notice me, I surreptitiously plucked the straw Panama from my head and flipped it into a large trash barrel beside the counter. A direct hit. I could decide later whether it was worth retrieving.

I studied. He had come in with the usual thick newspaper under his arm, grasping it at the bottom with a pudgy fist --with a hand, I mean. (One of these days I'll remember to stop insulting my own flesh and blood.) Any second now, he would look up and see me. I got my face ready: I was not going to cry. I haven't done anything wrong, Norman. But it was dangerous to assume he would realize my innocence. I knew how he would look at me, how hard he would make our reunion.

For the moment, as he walked through the line to the cash register, where they serve the beverages, his sour face was muted, a sort of Sunday-magazine sedation overlaying its tense, angry lines. Never putting the paper down, he ordered, waited, paid, then picked up the steaming white Styrofoam cup and walked halfway down the counter next to the cafeteria line, where he stopped. He carefully put down the paper and cup, first inspecting the counter to make sure it was dry. He stood with his back to the food line now, half-facing me. I was ready. I watched closely for the first reaction. Timing was crucial.

With a brusque movement, he yanked the first section of the paper off the rest. This time, he was not going to look around before he started reading. I breathed out deeply. With precise movements, he opened the first section to the last page, the editorial page, where he would find important source materials for this week's polemics and diatribes. His face an angry cloud, he took a quick sip of coffee and began to read.

By now, every movement was familiar. Each time wearing a different disguise, I had seen him do all this on six occasions. Each time, he had read and sipped for two to three minutes, intermittently blowing his nose between thumb and forefinger. Then, with a movement at once abrupt and careful, he had put the folded section of the paper on top of the rest, taken a last gulp of coffee, placed the cup on the counter next to the paper, and yawned and stretched for a full five seconds. Then, he had glanced around the room and, taking the cup, but leaving the paper, returned to the food line, this time through the wrong end (few people were ever on line) for a refill. Norman always brought back the original cup, not tolerating waste even as he took his pleasure.

This morning, he would never get to that second cup. Would he see me as soon as he started to stretch, or not until he scanned the room? I hoped it was the latter: I did not want to startle my poor cousin sooner than necessary. I watched and watched, waited and waited. Naturally, I was impatient.

But I did have to admit that the coffee tasted particularly good this morning, strong and fresh. And did I need it! I had slept poorly, due to the pressure of work. Oh, god, the paper was full of the usual crap about budget cuts. The suggestions seemed pungent, however. Maybe the old duffer had finally made good on his threat to retire and left the rag to that clever nephew I met at the party last month. Or maybe he had died. No, that would have been front page ... . Ah, Sundays! Have to get to those fucked-up reports again tonight. What a hash S --- has made of them. Half the statistical work down the drain, have to do it over, myself. Thousands pissed away! That blockhead S---, and not a goddamned thing I can do to get rid of him.

Finally, the minute has passed. The paper is on the counter, his arms are moving up, up, up. Now! There! His arms are frozen in the air, as if he were a robbery victim. The yawn has been cut off in its prime, as if he were a murder victim. He drops his arms, as if they were heavy sacks, his head goes back into his neck, then protrudes. He is staring at me. I stare back, the impulse to smile having been corralled by means of hours of patient practice. I, too, have developed the public manner, my dear cousin. For a minute, we stand there, frozen in the same sour, but puzzled frown.

"Who are you, and what do you want?" A few wisps of smoke from the nearly empty coffee cup drifted across his face. People watched as I walked across to him. Most looked very happy, as I had sensed they would.

I moved to a place two feet to his left, leaned on the counter, played with the edge of the paper, and smiled into his face, braced for the anger he would be feeling by now.

"Norman B ---," I said, in his voice. His face was very red, but so was mine.

"What the hell is this, some sort of sick joke? Who are you, and what do you want?"

Now I began to get angry, too. After all, why should I be spoken to like that?

"Who am I?' " I repeated indignantly. "'Who are you?' you mean. And what's the big idea? You some sort of prankster? Seen my picture in the paper or something, Bozo? Haven't you heard about appointments with secretaries, that kind of stuff?"

By now, the poor devil was staring at me with his mouth open. His face was scarlet and covered with sweat.

"Manager, manager, come over here, please!" From behind the cash register came a thin little fellow wearing a gray cafeteria jacket and pencil mustache. He hurried, but when he arrived, he seemed not to know what to say. I took charge of the situation myself.

"Look here, I'm Norman B---. I'm the Deputy City Comptroller. Here." I flashed my official-looking identification card.

"Yes, sir, Mr. B ---," said the manager. "But then who ... "

"Some sort of prankster, probably one of those pie-throwers." I was referring to a group that throws pies at important people in public. "Call the police, will you. Have your men hold him."

He motioned over a busboy and a short African-American man who had been sweeping. The whole time, Norman's mouth was working. He stopped being red, and began instead to grow pale. When the two employees were holding him by the arms and the manager had left to make the call, I suddenly clasped myself by the throat and made a series of grunts.

"Oh, uhh, uhh." I scanned the room in panic, saw the door marked "Men," and managed only to raise a finger before slumping to the floor. After that, everything was a blur of movement and sound until the sirens started. As soon as I heard them, I picked myself up, said I felt better and, on the pretense of going to the men's room, hurried from the cafeteria. (I want no publicity from this incident, for obvious reasons.) My cousin was still being held, silent now, having long since stopped trying to explain. When I slipped out the door, he was waiting for the police.

I have been busy, since then, but I have nevertheless taken the time to record these events scrupulously. Anticipating the question of why I have done so, let me call your attention to the similarity in spatial configuration between someone working at a dressing table and someone composing at the keyboard. To further explain why the art of writing begins to appeal to me, I have prepared the following statement for issue to the press.

November 18, 19--

Of all the ways in which we try to control our own destinies by controlling our world, two of the least objectionable are impersonation and writing. The impersonator controls the world by becoming it. The writer tries to capture it, as one might try to capture a mad bird in a net.

Simple

Brooklyn, NY, c.1993.

Mr. Johnny Jukes did not think it normal to spend ten minutes warming up a one year-old car on a sunny May morning. Just like *them* to need an alibi to sit still and have a little fun. This one's silly secret sin was (*ooh*) R&B. And maybe he didn't want to have to fight the Saturday morning traffic aggravation while he was trying to enjoy himself. Typical: guy had his music up nice and loud, but his car windows all shut and the AC off, as not to offend nor man nor nature. (Yeah, but what about those emissions, Jack?) He looked like a little cooking turkey in there, little red-faced guy with reddish almost real-people hair, sweating and swaying to --beat that, of all things-- *Trick Bag*. Word! The wonderful, the one-and-only ... *Trick Bag*.

Life was rich. Johnny smiled and gave the passenger-side window of the man's car a tiny little tap. But, whoops and damn, the man jumped, anyhow.

Now Johnny Jukes always counted on people not to be alarmed. He hoped his attire and his demeanor might suggest one of those harmless Jehovah's Witnesses, those strange folks who warn you about the end of the world, then tell you to go on and have a nice day, regardless. When people had had a moment to take in the neat haircut and blue suit, then they could notice the big gray canvas bag slung across the shoulders of the suit, and then Johnny would gesticulate with the little white slips of paper, pantomiming whether they would let him stick one under the driver's side windshield wiper. And he wouldn't say a word yet, neither, since he knew they had to be pre-prepared for the experience of his sonorous tones.

The little turkey man in last year's Nippon puddle-jumper glanced across at Johnny. Then, he turned off the radio and the engine, leaned over and rolled the window down a few inches. He used a lot of wrist, cool trying to be cooler, which was good.

"Heey," said Johnny softly. "Bee-eau-ti-ful day." He gestured toward the silent radio. "Say now, that was *Trick Bag*, wasn't it? WRFR?" The man nodded, waited. Should Johnny tell him? He chuckled (let the man think it was some private joke), opened his mouth, changed his mind again, closed it, then just for one more second, hesitated. Damn! Angry for making it so obvious he was covering his tracks, sure he had undercut the effect of the patter before it was even started, Johnny pushed on, nonetheless.

"Say now. Mind if I just put one of these on your window, friend? 'Kinky telephone sex at ninety cents a minute'? Nope. 'Bargain basement oil change'? Nah, not that, neither. Nope, just some plastic slipcovers. May I?"

Because the guy wore an expression generic to this neighborhood, Johnny could read his mind like it was "Dick and Jane": *At a time when a single subway token costs a dollar-and-a-quarter, why is this neatly-dressed African-American gentleman, no longer in his first blush, passing out advertising circulars for maybe a penny apiece?* The mind reader sighed, tired by the sameness.

"Sure, go ahead," was the reply, expected, but Johnny was agreeably surprised by the deep, loud voice, by the set of heavy pipes the Lord or someone had placed inside this man's skinny little neck. "No, wait," the man added. (And what was this? He was rolling his window all the way down?) "Here, give me a bunch of them."

While the leafleteer groped in the bottom of his bag, the Samaritan was rewarded with some extra patter, half-way sung: "Thanks, friend, and I know that when you've read the literature you'll want to hurry to your nearest telephone in order to order a set --or two-- of these fine prophylactic coverings, sure to make your furniture last and endure, and sure to make your love life smooth and pure." The last nine words were a standardized test, and Johnny watched the man's wheels turn --fast.

"Sure," he said. "Whatever that means." Passable --not bad, in fact. "And don't worry, I'll keep the slips a while before I throw them away." Which meant he had correctly guessed there were spies out there, prowling the sidewalks and peering into the garbage cans, checking for bunches of slips to make sure the peons --distributors-- earned their pennies. The man held out his hand, palm up, and waited.

"Hey!" said Johnny. "Fee fie fo fum, I sense the presence of a gentleman." And, groping in the bag, "Well, well, what do you know, you're my last customer. Freedom!" He scraped the last twenty or so slips from the bottom of the bag, shuffled them into a neat pile and handed them over with a flourish.

A salute, a smile, a wink, and Johnny Jukes was striding across the street to a mid-sized American car, dark green, not too old, which he unlocked and entered. He rolled down his window, raced the engine and roared up the block.

The little redheaded man watched the larger, Black man disappear. Then, he stacked the slips beneath a flat rock on his dashboard, closed the passenger-side window and cracked his own a couple of inches. Re-starting his engine, which ticked and purred, he immediately moved forward, following in the wake of the bigger car. The moment he turned the corner, he flicked the radio back on. The second hour of the WRFR Saturday Morning R&B Extravaganza had just begun. Like a reward for the small good deed with the slips, the first song was the excellent *Can't Be With the One I love, So I Love the One I'm With*. Off to the cleaners!

-2-

It was a windy day, and as soon as the redheaded Mr. Oliver Nelson pulled into the supermarket parking lot (hurrying, conscious of his wife waiting for the things she needed in order to start dinner), the plastic around his suits started flapping and he noticed that the tarmac was practically carpeted with circulars. Hundreds of them, swirling everywhere, each one red, green and blue on a yellow background. This considerable mess reminded the alert and retentive Mr. Nelson not only of the slipcover slips, but of a peculiar announcement he and his wife had heard on the radio the previous fall.

It was the Sanitation Commissioner, come on the air to request public assistance in sweeping and bagging leaves, which was fair enough. But, for some reason (inebriation, perhaps), the political man had waxed lyrical.

"This is the fall season of the year," he announced, "when the streets of our fair city are covered with millions of leaves, leaves of every hue and color: red, yellow, orange, green, blue and brown."

This blunder brought mirth to Oliver and his wife, and Oliver remarked, "Blue, eh? I suppose it isn't all that surprising these days -- what with pollution, narcotics, synthetics, cloning and all-- that there's a lot of confusion about the natural world."

"What we clearly need," Mrs. Nelson replied, "is a World Naturalness Court. Hey, what harm would it do to add one more to all the pleasant-sounding, ineffectual world bodies?"

And then, as he remembered it, he had suggested that the W.N.C. be headquartered in Zurich or The Hague, after which they had stopped pounding the idea.

Oliver parked, turned off the engine with the radio still on (commercials), locked up, then tramped through the circulars (supermarket "specials") and through the automatic IN-door to meet ... the slipcover man.

Except now he was the grocery bagger. The same guy. He had shed his suit coat and put a red apron over his nice (white) shirt, (red) tie and (blue) pants. As Oliver Nelson came in, the other man happened to look up, and, obviously recognizing Nelson, he spoke without breaking rhythm in his bagging.

"My man!" he said. "Slipcovers? What's happening?"

"Shopping time." Oliver stepped alongside the bagger, then moved a little closer in order to get out of the stream of shoppers that had followed him into the store. Curious about this man and his two jobs, Nelson tried to think of a tactful way to pry.

"Rush hour," the man said, sounding apologetic because he could not pause to chat properly. He lifted out a double roll of paper towels to make room at the bottom of a bag for a half-gallon of orange juice, then laid the towels back in flat, on top of the other items. A smiling Black child now looked up from the top of the bag. "Little soul brother," the man remarked with a smile and a gesture, as he started right in on another bag. "It's always busy in here around noon on Saturdays." So he had been there previous weeks when Nelson had shopped.

"Right, I know. Uh, did you finish ... uh ...?" Nelson saw the man reading his mind.

"Hewers of wood and drawers of water,'" he began, then went on non-stop. (Was he drunk with fatigue or just talking to relieve the tedium of his task?) "I know what you want to know, friend, and I'll give you the answer, free of charge. Why not, you obliged me before, right? Still got those slips out in your car, right?" Without waiting for an answer, he winked and went on gabbing, even as, with quick, precise movements, he went on bagging. As he divulged information, he kept glancing at Nelson, as if to see how he was taking it, and Nelson, aware, nodded every time the man met his eye.

"Four jobs altogether. Weekdays, eight-thirty to four-forty-five, I'm a midtown mail room menial. Second, I'm the custodial superintendent --janitor-- of my residence. Three and four, you already know. Today and tomorrow here, probably twelve hours total, which would be seventy-three-fifty, net, if you're wondering. And this morning, thirty bucks, three-thousand leaflets, which two of my kids are still out unloading the last of those. Why? Now ask me, 'Why?'"

Resisting an urge to say, "Because you need the money," Nelson said, "Why?"

"My wife don't work but one job --secretary-- because we don't want our two kids who are still at home with us to become no latchkey kids. Oh, no, not in this day and age." He came up for air. "Yes, it's hard. Yes, we get by. Yes, I should of stayed in school all those years ago. 'The things I used to do,'" he sang softly, then muttered, "And shouldn't of." Then sang, "And didn't used to do." And muttered, "And should of." And concluded, "Any questions?" He smiled and started on another bag.

At this point Nelson noticed that the man was perspiring in the air-conditioned store, that his forehead shone. He had some gray and a widow's peak, and Nelson silently guessed (afraid to do it out loud, for what if the man was actually thirty or sixty?) that he was in his mid-forties. Which gave him a good fifteen years on Nelson.

"You know, I do have a question, but ... "And as he heard himself starting to ask, for some reason Nelson reminded himself of the Langston Hughes character, that *faux naif* observer of Harlem life, Jesse B. Simple.

"Go on, friend, speak up, no question too stupid or embarrassing. Don't worry, if you overstep, I'll shuck and jive, I'll circumvent."

"Okay. Thanks. Just one, then, please. Why did you laugh? On the street before? When you recognized that song on the radio."

"Recognized that song'?" Nelson felt himself the object of another appraising glance, a serious one. "*Trick Bag*? 'Why did I laugh?' You ready?" Nelson nodded. "Well, you may not believe me, Mister ... uh, I didn't catch your name, did I?"

"Nelson. Oliver Nelson."

"Pleasure," said the man, then muttered, "Huh! Play a little tenor, do you?" An allusion Nelson had heard before. "Jukes. John Jukes." And then there was a moment's hesitancy, and then a quick touching of palms initiated by Mr. John Jukes. "Mr. Oliver Nelson, sir, you may not believe me, friend, but I laughed because I ... well, yes, I *wrote* that song. That was *my* song. Fact of the matter. Yes, sir, I *wrote Trick Bag*."

"No kid ... "

"Gospel. In fact, that particular tune, *Trick Bag*, was one of the three or four biggest hits my brother and me ever had, way back when. You ever hear of us, friend? 'Ladies and gentlemen, Jarvis and Johnny Jukes, the Jukes Brothers.' We were big time in the Sixties, yes, the Sixties was our time. Once, 1962, I believe it was, we had two songs on the Top Hundred R&B charts at once: Trick Bag, and another one you probably never heard of --wasn't as good-- called *Lady Dee-Dee-Lilah*. Yes, sir, the Jukes Brothers."

"Well, it does ..." Nelson started to lie, trying to be polite.

"Sound familiar,'" Johnny Jukes continued for him. "Thanks, anyhow. That's okay."

Sensing that the monologue had run down, Nelson was thinking of something else polite to say when he looked up just in time to see that he had drifted out into the aisle and was in danger of being steamrollered by a young woman with spiked green hair, pink jogging suit, and elaborate sunglasses. She had shoved her change into a pants pocket and scooped up two bags just packed by Mr. Jukes, and now she came ploughing silently through the narrow aisle. Hopping aside,

Nelson accidentally brushed shoulders with Johnny Jukes, who was bagging away again and jumped at the contact, without comment.

"Excuse me," Nelson said. "Sorry, but..." He returned to the aisle, calculating intensely. "The Jukes Brothers," he thought. The name really did seem vaguely familiar, but the ages and dates were wrong. For, if this man was now in his forties, he would have been a child in the early Sixties. Besides, the song, *Trick Bag*, sounded like it came from the Fifties, or even earlier. Well, maybe the song was ... ageless. Or the man was.

Johnny Jukes laughed. "Say now," he said, "you look like you trying to count without using your fingers." Nelson smiled sheepishly, and then the bagger at the next counter, at whom he had not yet looked directly, also laughed. This was a fat man, also black, also not young, also with a shiny forehead, but with a little mustache, as well. Now he laughed a phlegmy laugh for several seconds while, like Mr. Johnny Jukes, he never broke stride in his bagging. That he had listened to the whole conversation was obvious.

"Yessir," said the fat man. "It's every word of it true. Pinch yourself, friend, you talking to Mr. Johnny Jukes, himself, ain't no dream. Now, as for all those songs him and Brother Jarvis wrote, the damned shame is, the damn shame is ... he lost them. Yep, he lost them. Every last one of them. You see, this man here was so hard up, didn't have a nickel to squeeze the Indian over on to the buffalo, so ... so he had to sell away all those good songs. Sold away the rights to every last one of them, didn't you, Johnny? Every last one of them. For a song, too!" The fat man bent over with laughter.

Johnny Jukes, bagging as ever, frowned, and Nelson sensed that he was now speaking --half-singing, actually-- to himself rather than to Nelson or to his co-worker. "That's true, yes, it's true. I may have been wrong, but I sold the rights to those songs. Sold them for a song! A sad song, not a sweet song, no, sirree!" Then he was no longer singing. "However, I did save my own two legs from being broken. Or worse. Fact. And another fact: since --when was it?-- June Something, Nineteen-Hundred-and-Seventy-Four, I have never again placed no single wager on those four-legged creatures piss your money right down on to the ground. No, sir. Never again, neither. Huh!"

Nelson was embarrassed by the man's obvious pain. As for the next-aisle man, he had been bent over laughing during most of Johnny's lament, bagging from a crouch.

"For a fact," he now said, then added, laughing, "and while you're at it, friend, check out the grapefruit, two for eighty-nine. They're good, I had one for my own breakfast this morning. Sweet as sugar. Right, Johnny? Sweet as ..."

"Sugar. Fact of the matter."

Johnny still seemed lost in sad reminiscence, and then Oliver, not knowing what else to say, impetuously and most unfortunately, played the fool.

"Say," he ventured with a sly wink, "this isn't your brother here, is it? This isn't Jarvis, by any chance, is it?"

The baggers looked at each other with an unmistakable "Who's your friend?" expression, and Nelson, sharply embarrassed, experienced a sudden, palpable change in the weather, against which he had no protection.

"Shoo! You kidding?" Johnny said, and after that words seemed to stream out. "Look here, Mr. Oliver, you go along and shop now, you hear. Thanks for your time, but then again I don't mean to be wasting your whole day with the story of my life and hard troubles. But, hey, thanks again. Need some slipcovers, my man? Nice talking to you now, Oliver. 'Nelson' is your other name, right?"

"Right, that's right. Okay, then, so long, Mr. Jukes. Talk to you again, I hope. Goodbye to you, too, friend."

"My man," said the other bagger, seeming conciliatory. "See you on your way out, then, right? Goood, goood."

And, as Nelson headed toward the row of carts to the left of the registers, he heard Johnny Jukes say, "Nice fella! 'Jarvis'? You? Shit! No way! You about as much like my brother, Jarvis, as Mr. Oliver over there is."

"No way' is right," the other man agreed, as Nelson pushed his cart past the registers. "And thank God for small favors! Ladies and Gentlemen, the man himself, Mr. Johnny Jukes."

"And now we're going to play a little *Trick Bag* for you all," and Johnny hummed a few bars. And then they kept on laughing, talking and working while Nelson shopped, hurrying now.

Soon he was back, and he chose Johnny's friend's register, where the line was shortest.

"Yours is shortest, if you don't mind."

"How's he going to mind?" Now Johnny Jukes felt like teasing his uneasy new acquaintance. "It's his *job*, Nelson. Go on, unload that cart, man."

So the two baggers worked on, and Nelson watched in silence. When the money had been paid and the change and receipt tendered, Nelson wished both men a nice day. The fat man nodded.

"You have one, too, now, Nelson," said Johnny Jukes, feeling a bit contrite as he watched the little red-haired man push his cart out through the electric door. "You take care now, you hear?"

And then he thought again of what Nelson had said about George, here, being his brother, Jarvis, which must have been intended as some kind of little joke, but which stung because of the "look-alike" connotation and because it made Johnny wonder if, in fact, Nelson had disbelieved his whole story --told so many times that by now it sounded thin even to his own ears-- of the songs he had written and the money he had lost, way back when. And then he wondered why he even cared whether the man believed him or not. A foolish habit, he decided. We're in the habit of wanting them to believe us.

On each of the next few Saturdays, Oliver Nelson met Johnny Jukes and his "partner" at the market. They made small talk, including a few running slipcover jokes. Oliver did not see Johnny leafletting again, but he did not think it his business to ask, and Johnny, who had been working another part of the neighborhood, never thought to offer the information. Then, one Saturday, Oliver, a computer consultant, was on an emergency call, so his wife shopped. The following week, on his way in, Oliver saw Johnny's friend, but not Johnny.

"Left town," the friend replied, sounding sad and thoughtful, to Oliver's question. "Personal business,' I guess you might call it. Probably gone for good."

"Oh? I'm sorry. I hope ... well, give him my best if you're in touch." Later, Oliver was checked out by the young woman (African-American) at Johnny's register. As she was bagging his groceries, Oliver turned to Johnny's friend and said, "You know, a lot of people seem to be disappearing these days."

The man looked at him and said, "You're right. Fact of the matter."

And, sure enough, Johnny Jukes never did reappear at the market. And, in times to come, when he would recount the events of these days, Johnny would always begin by saying, "And then there was that time I got *boosted*."

-3-

"*Oyez, oyez,*" cried the Bailiff. "Superior Criminal Court, Princess County, is now in session. The People versus James R. Johnson. Judge Victor R. --Moth? North?--" (inaudible: was that *N* as in *Nelson*, or *M* as in *Morris the Cat*?) presiding. Everyone must rise and remove your hats, other than those worn for reasons of religious persuasion."

Oliver Nelson and forty other perspective jurors rose. "Moth" (Nelson maliciously assumed) came in. He was a big, jowly, red-faced bird with half-glasses and a white tonsure. He sat. He cleared his throat. They waited.

They also serve .... By the time he had been called to this courtroom, Citizen Nelson, in his third day of jury duty, had stopped worrying about the urgent pleas for help left on his answering machine by clients whose systems had crashed, had given up trying to read the newspaper or anything else, and was busy drooling and staring at the peeling, swimming-pool-green walls of the hot, crowded jurors' holding pen. The announcement of his name on the P.A. system had jump-started his heart, and up to the eighth floor with forty-odd others he had gone. Yes, sir, yes, sir, two elevators full.

When his throat was completely cleared, Judge Moth laid out some facts (in a high-pitched voice): the charge was Grand Larceny; the alleged felony, shoplifting a diamond engagement ring of "some considerable value." The trial should take no more than a day or two (for those worried about missing more than the total of two weeks which people on jury duty were required to miss of work, vacation or unemployment). The Judge then made a little speech, familiar to Nelson (and everyone else, presumably) from TV drama, about the presumption of innocence, etc.

Next, he asked if anyone could not serve fairly on this case, and, of the ten or so who tried to get off, two, a fat man wearing a yarmulke and a bee-hived young woman who looked like an aerobics instructor, were sent back down to the jury pen with cards initialed by the Judge.

At this point, Nelson's right-hand neighbor whispered to him. The man was tall, thin, nervous, and about Nelson's age.

"These people are either lazy, stupid or too honest," he observed.

"Oh?"

"I think the case will be fascinating." Nelson glanced at the man and saw pale blue eyes sparkling with excitement as they darted around within the confines of wire-rimmed glasses. "I mean, how could someone shoplift a diamond ring? The security…"

"Quiet!" barked Judge Moth, not even looking up. He was scribbling in a little book, penciling in, as Nelson imagined, a golf or tennis date he had just remembered.

Then, at a secret signal, the Bailiff, a tall, fat, redheaded gent in white shirt, dark tie and doorman's pants, slipped out a side door to the judge's left and returned almost immediately with two men, whom he parked just inside the door, where shadows made it impossible for Nelson to see their faces. He was, however, able to form general impressions, of a stout man wearing a yarmulke (a man very similar to the one who had just been excused), and a Black man wearing a dark suit and white shirt, but without tie or handcuffs. Nelson assumed that these were, respectively, lawyer and defendant.

Once again, Judge Moth cleared his throat, and Nelson sensed that the serious business would now begin.

"The Assistant D.A. assigned to prosecute this case and Counsel for the Defense are in conference and should be joining us briefly. Meanwhile, in the interests of saving time" (Nelson mentally overruled his indignant objection) "if anyone on the panel is acquainted with either the presenting witness or the defendant --and there are only one of each, in this case, plus the arresting officer-- you should speak up now so I can dismiss you. Bailiff!"

The Judge had made himself very clear. In fact, he might just have well have said (if such things were said), "Get it, folks? Pretty much a judgment-call here, the Reb versus the Colored Gent."

An absurd tableau was formed when the Bailiff motioned the two men into position on either side of him for the crowd to inspect, while he stood between them with his freckled arms folded like a referee right before a boxing match.

"Now before we begin the lengthy process of jury selection, I must ask you once again if ..." Because the Judge was going through the motions so hastily, the interruption that now occurred caused something like a verbal head-on collision.

"Excuse me, Judge Moth --I mean, Your Honor-- I do."

Nelson was both embarrassed and tickled to hear his own voice booming across the crowded courtroom. As he spoke, he stood up, threaded his way to the nearest aisle, and approached the Bench. All eyes upon him, Nelson felt what it must be like to be a daytime TV star.

Of course, this disruption was not merely capricious, since the defendant was Johnny Jukes, the man who, not six weeks before, had given him slipcover ads, bagged his groceries, and told him significant episodes from what Nelson had come to believe was more or less the man's real life story. Yes, Johnny Jukes. ("But what was this "James R. Johnson" business?)

Nelson watched Johnny's eyes doing what the computer man thought of as scrolling: rolling through data at a rapid clip. There seemed to be an enormous amount of data in Jukes' memory banks, and, for a few seconds, he seemed to go through it at multi-gigabyte speed. Then, he had the file he needed.

"Slipcovers!" He pointed at Nelson.

"*Trick Bag*!" Nelson grinned, adding a little bow.

It was as if they had performed the Boy Scout handshake.

"Excuse me?" said the Judge, sounding faintly jealous. "Er, would you gentlemen mind ..." and he beckoned them closer.

When Nelson had briefly explained, the Judge briefly deliberated. Then, he leaned down and looked him in the eye.

"All right, sir," he said, "can you be fair, or do you want me to dismiss you?"

Nelson glanced at Johnny Jukes. He saw that his momentary excitement had faded into an impassiveness that presumably betokened a tedious time already in the hands of the law. Standing At-Ease, eyes down, Johnny wore that unmistakable *che sera, sera* look. Nelson experienced a rush of sympathy.

"No, Your Honor," he said, in profoundly dispassionate tones. "I don't see why such a ... slight acquaintance would pre..."

"All right, Mr. Nelson," the Judge interrupted. "Thank you, I get the point. Of course, we should really stop now and wait for the D.A. and the ... but, while we're waiting, Mr. Johnson, suppose *you* try to decide, as well ... of course, you are not obliged to render a formal response, other than in the presence of Counsel, but you might just want to ... think about it ... now ... to save time ... later. So. Do you have any..."

As he said all this, the Judge seemed distracted, and he kept glancing toward the side door.

Johnny Jukes shrugged and said softly, eyes lowered, "Why not? Good as any."

Not sure exactly what that meant, Nelson waited for Jukes to say more, but, instead, there was a sudden disruption. For, through the side door burst a young, sweaty little man followed by still another (the third) heavy-set man wearing a yarmulke and in need of a shave. It was the latter, taken by Nelson to be the Assistant D.A., who spoke.

"Excuse us, Your Honor," he said in the clipped tones of a public speaker. "As you know, the D.A. and I have been trying all morning to resolve this matter before it goes any further. (And, off the record, we just spoke to the insurance, and they concur with our ... agreement.) At any rate ... if you would be so kind, your Honor ..." And he gestured toward the side door.

"One moment, ladies and gentlemen," said the Judge, his face visibly brighter. Descending from the Bench, he rushed stage left, gesturing for the defense counsel, D.A., witness, defendant and Bailiff to follow.

The courtroom was abuzz. Then, suddenly, impulsively -- goodness knows why-- Nelson rushed after the others. It took him only a few steps, of course, to collect himself and stop.

As he applied the brakes, a few people laughed, and his erstwhile neighbor cried out, "Go on, don't stop now, go get 'em, pal!" which stoked more laughter.

Impulsively playing the clown, getting a few last laughs, Nelson faced the jury panel and shrugged. But, before anything more could happen, back came the Judge and the five others. The rest was anticlimactic.

"You won't have to search your soul, after all," the Judge said to Nelson, gesturing him back to his seat. As he retreated, Nelson saw Johnny Jukes looking down at his feet, in visible gloom. The Judge then concluded the proceedings with a homily, at each stage of which Nelson saw members of the congregation mentally signing off.

They were the rock on which the system rested. Each and every member of the panel should know how much he appreciated their patience. No time or money had been wasted, since, in point of fact, it had probably been the presence of the panel and the onset of the selection process which had awakened the defendant to the reality of his situation, prompting his --better late than never-- plea. And thus, concluded the ponderous Judge, did the wheels of justice turn.

As no cross-examination was permitted, Moth's little peroration stood as uttered, but Nelson bet that few of his compeers had been convinced of anything beyond the fact that the old Judge could wield a mean platitude and hoist a heavy load of specious crap in the service of hearing his own voice.

Sheep-and-goat like, they were then divided into first-weekers ("Return to Central Jury") and second ("Room 101: see Mrs. Winston-Smith"). Slowly, then, the would-be jurors filed out, while the principal players left via the well-used side door.

But ... but ... but how very annoying! Instead of the speech, why hadn't the Judge given the people some idea --a glimmer, at least-- of what had happened at the jeweler's that day?

In this frame of mind, Maverick Nelson turned right, instead of left toward the elevators, muttering to anyone who might have been listening that he needed a rest room. He found one, made a token deposit, freshened up, exited and, still stalling, roamed the corridors in the direction away from the elevators, wondering how far he would get before a guard stopped him. He knew there must be muggers here, too, but doubted that any would be in action.

Then, as he rounded a corner, his heart jumped, for he came face to face with Number Three, the defense lawyer. And, behind the lawyer, just being led into a grimy service elevator by the redheaded Bailiff, was, yes, the man himself, Mr. Johnny Jukes.

"Johnny!" Nelson cried. "Where are they...?"

"Call me, Nelson, I'm in the book: James R. Johnson, One-Two-Five Sterling. I'll make bail, be home tomorrow." The doors closed.

"So you know my client," remarked the lawyer, who was looking back and forth from his watch to his appointment book.

Nelson seized the opening. "Some case," he said. "And some speech: 'the wheels of justice.' Tires are shot and she needs an alignment." The lawyer smiled, and, before he could duck back into his book, Nelson had begun to plead.

"Look, I've been on jury duty eight days now, haven't been on a case yet, I'm bored out of my skull. And now...At least tell me what this case is about. Please. One moment of your time. One. And don't worry, I don't really know the defendant. I mean, he once checked me out at a supermarket. And I swear I won't tell a soul. Oh, my name is Nelson, by the way, Oliver Nelson."

Noticing momentary uncertainty on the lawyer's part and guessing that the man was unsure of whether to introduce himself, Nelson seized his hand, shook it, and looked him in the eye.

"How do you do," Nelson said. "Please. You can trust me."

The lawyer chuckled. "You know, Mr. Nelson, you look like my wife's cousin. You sure your name isn't Horowitz? Mine is Bash, by the way, Ira Bash." He put his finger to his lips. "Not a word. Shh." Then, he laughed, and Nelson relaxed, happily aware that he was in the presence of a raconteur. "Sure. But what do I care, the case is over, anyway." Still, Lawyer Bash looked up and down the corridor and lowered his voice. "In a nutshell, then. See, my client, Mr. Johnson, was in a jewelry store, one of those places with all the separate little booths on R&B, we call it --Rocks and Baubles-- Way. (That's A Hundred and Forty-Seventh Street, in case you don't know. We got funny names for everything, nowadays.)

"Anyway, he told me his son, who is just graduating High School, God bless him, was about to get engaged. The boy had asked his father to come with him to look at rings because, when he --the son-- tried it alone, he wasn't treated with respect. You know what I'm talking about, right?" Nelson nodded, and Bash pressed on.

"Anyway, Mr. Johnson --according to Mr. Johnson-- was on his lunch hour strolling around, when he remembered the boy's request. So, on impulse, he goes into a big store and finds his way to the booth of the man you saw in the courtroom just now --the witness. You got that much, Mr. Oliver?" Again, Nelson nodded.

"Good. Then, something highly unusual happened. Listen carefully, Horowitz --uh, Nelson. When Johnson inquired about 'inexpensive diamond engagement rings,' the dealer, who was polite, but also seemed nervous, took a whole tray of rings out of the locked display case. 'Cheap crap,' he called them, garbage, with settings, but no stones, or with chips, zircons. Poor quality, semi-precious stuff. You see, he told my client he was just showing him these 'by way of contrast.' Johnson figured the guy was being a salesman, coaxing him into the higher echelons.

"So they looked at a couple, and then the jeweler put that tray back and took from the same display case two or three individual rings that he called 'the real thing': rings with one-to-two carat diamonds on fourteen- or eighteen- carat gold bands, stuff worth two, three grand and up. Got that? You'll note, too, that the guy hasn't even inquired yet of Mr. Johnson as to the actual sum he wants to spend. Then --get this!-- he hands Johnson ..."

Lawyer Bash came up for air and glanced at his watch.

"Oh, God! Shit! No!" he said. "I got another case to present in front of that bastard North in half an hour, and I haven't even looked at the brief yet. He'll have my balls in soup! I'm sorry, Nelson, I really am, but I really have to go."

"But ... but ... please ...what...?"

"Oh, shit!" He sighed. "Okay, what the hell, in a nutshell: when Johnson leaves the store, the guy runs out after him and gets a cop, and they grab him. He accuses him of boosting one of the rings, one of the good ones. See, they claim they find this zircon on him, and the merchant says he must have passed the diamond on to a confederate or something. Though why the hell he would take the ... well, it was complicated.

"Anyway, Johnson is a two-time loser, a 'discretionary persistent,' they call it. This is Grand Larceny, a 'D' felony, so, believe it or not, he could have been looking at fifteen to life." He noticed Nelson's expression.

"I shit you not. So, when he saw the jury about to be formed, he got scared, copped a plea. No other witnesses, but there were prints --

naturally-- on the zircon. So he copped, Attempted G.L., an 'E" Felony, eighteen months to three years. And, as it turns out, he may actually have to serve some of that time. Medieval, right? Well, Victor North is a tough old bastard. Which reminds me. "Again, Bash looked at his watch. Then he grabbed Nelson's hand, pumped it and started to move away.

"Wait! But why ... what do *you*..." Bash, anguished, looked back.

"What do *I* think?' They always ask that. Fishy, the whole thing is fishy. One witness --a presenting, no less-- purely zirconstantial evidence --sorry-- the guy leaves Johnson holding a ring worth supposedly forty-five hundred dollars? The zircon in his breast pocket? Give me a break, the whole thing is a set-up if I ever saw one. It would strike a fucking imbecile dead and buried two hundred years as a fucking set-up. A fucking, fishy set-up."

"Also --I know, I'm confusing you, I have no time-- also, my client is a family man, claims he works four jobs, the ring's insured, of course, so the D.A. accepts the plea. So does the insurance guy, and Johnson's going to have to pay a little something to society --to the company, that is-- maybe on the order of six months."

Again, Bash looked at his watch. His face was desperate. "Look, Mr. Nelson, seriously, now I got ... "

"But what do you think really...?"

Bash sighed heavily. "Didn't I just answer that? 'What do I think?' The guy's innocent. But they're all guilty, anyhow --of something. Haven't you heard? You must read the papers, Oliver, you must know how stuffed up the criminal justice cistern is, what with all that penny-ante drug crap. Okay. What do I *really* think? Okay. I think the *gonev* store owner is in some kind of deep shit financially —I bet he plays the ponies or something-- and he's trying to grab forty-five-hundred lousy bucks from the insurance company so his legs don't get broken. Something like that, that's what I really think."

Bash sighed, but Nelson could not tell whether it was over the injustice or his own increasingly desperate situation.

"And lots of luck to the bastard! I hope the insurance company sends out a tough cookie that'll squeeze his nuts good and hard for him."

A quick pump of the hand, and the eloquent Counselor Bash was once again on his way --but not without a parting word.

"Call Mr. Johnson for yourself, Oliver. He'll tell you the rest. You heard him, he's in the book. Peace!"

"Thanks. I will. Peace!"

"Call Mr. Johnson." Which was exactly what Nelson had been thinking the whole time Lawyer Bash was racing through the story.

-4-

It had been the tenth of June, the year 19--, when the trial of the alleged notorious jewel thief, James R. "Johnny Jukes" Johnson, nearly took place. On an unseasonably hot evening precisely four calendar days later, Appellate Justice Oliver "Oyez" Nelson, with Mrs. Associate Justice May Walker-Nelson standing at the ready in order to note possible corroborative evidence, sought and secured the telephone number of said Mr. J.R.J.J. Johnson.

After encountering two busy signals over a period of some thirty minutes, Justice Nelson was finally successful in making contact with Mr. Johnson. Their conversation proceeded as follows:

ON: Mr. Jukes, please.

JJ: Who wants him?

ON: This is an acquaintance of his. My name is Oliver Nelson. I met Mr....

JJ: Nelson! My man! This is Jukes speaking. (That's my stage name, by the way, real name's "Johnson.") What's shaking, my man?

ON: Oh, not much. Yourself?

JJ: Oh, well, can't complain, can't complain. What can I do for you?

ON: Well, nothing, really. I just called to ask ... you said...

JJ: Oh, that. Right, right. Well, I got three months. Suspended, thank the Lord --and thank the Judge, who much as said the guy was full of shit. Which he was, which he was. In fact, my man Ira Bash and me been talking about a counter suit. That'd fix the son of a gun. (*laughter*)

ON: Oh, good, that's good news. But, say, what really...

JJ: ... happened? I was waiting for you to ask. You got a couple minutes, Nelson? And be honest now, you sure you want to hear another Johnny Jukes real-life story episode?

ON: To tell the truth, that's why I called. Oh, where have you been, by the way? I haven't seen you at the market, on the street, anywhere.

JJ: Oh, well, let's ... it don't matter. Let's just say, things change.

ON: I'm sorry, I didn't mean to...

JJ: That's all right, that's all right. Where was I now? Oh, yes. This is what happened. See, the whole thing was a frame-up. Man says I boosted his ring, but, in actual fact, it was *me* that got *boosted*, if you get my drift. Yes, sir! See, the guy handed me a goddamn ring with a big rock in it, then just walked away. Talking some nonsense about getting me this other prize diamond of his "just to look at" from the safe in the back. Whole thing was just weird. I'm standing there with the thing in my hand, wondering *what* is going on. And I'm afraid to put it down because, heck, someone might steal the thing! At one point --can't remember when, exactly-- I even looked up and seen this close-circuit TV they got, but all I can see on it --get this-- is a cat! A cat! Washing herself just inside what must be the back door of the place, a door with bars, just like a you-know-what ... jail. That's the security they got in a jewelry store? That's it? Hey, piss on my head, but don't tell me it's raining. If you get my drift.

ON: I get it, all right. What a fishy business!

JJ: Could say. Guy comes back, I hand the thing over like it's a hot potato, and I'm out of there! Minute later, out on the street, and the guy jumps me. Him and a cop, that is! 'Course they don't find no diamond on me, just some "zircon" he showed me in the store and then planted on me --with my prints on it, naturally. But the guy starts shouting about some "confederate," how I must of already passed the diamond to some "confederate." Can you beat that for shit!

ON: No, I don't think I could beat that for shit, Mr. Jukes. But why didn't you let the matter...

JJ: ... come to trial? Almost did. But, the more I considered, looking at all you people, the jury panel, I mean, they might not of picked a jury full of people all fair as yourself, Nelson, you dig? And, well, I mean, there was a whole lot at stake. So I took the plea -- swallowed my pride, you might say-- just let the thieving bastard have his way.

(*pause*)

ON: What a world!

JJ: Could say.

(*Small talk ensued. A tentative plan was formed to get together for lunch, after which the conversation was terminated.*)

Immediately thereafter, Mr. Justice and Mrs. Justice Nelson took it upon themselves to try said case in Dinner Court. Based on the testimony of Counselor Bash and of the Defendant, Mr. Johnson, the Justices were unanimous in reaching the following determinations:

1. Mr. James R. Johnson, a.k.a. "Johnny Jukes," is fully and finally acquitted.

2. Furthermore, the Court issues a Directive that the Grand Jury is to convene for the purpose of considering whether there is evidence sufficient to indict the merchant (name unknown) for insurance fraud, which is (the Justices assume) a "D" Felony.

-5-

Oliver Nelson never did see Johnny Jukes again. Their paths did not happen to cross, and Nelson kept putting off the lunch plan, primarily because he suspected it would only have caused mutual embarrassment. A deeper and darker reason, which he also admitted to himself and to his good wife, was that he feared becoming entangled with Mr. Jukes, who, though clearly more wronged than wrongdoer, did seem to lead a life which, if interesting, was marked by conflict and by what Mr. Nelson euphemistically characterized as "controversy." While Nelson would always tell himself that he believed Mr. Jukes about both the ring and the history of *Trick Bag,* a shadow of a doubt nonetheless remained.

Without subsequent renewal or enrichment, Nelson's slight acquaintance with Johnny Jukes has gradually resolved itself into two stereotypical fantasies.

In the first, Johnny Jukes is wearing black-leather pants and a poppy-colored silk shirt, sweating, standing alone in a spotlight. Darkness, lights, music. Johnny is playing electric guitar for thousands of dancing, screaming kids.

In the second, James R. Johnson is out on a hot dusty road, squinting at the camera and wearing a khaki jumpsuit, a battered hat, and the ball and chain.

As for Johnny Jukes, he never really considered calling Oliver Nelson. Although he would have been polite about accepting a luncheon invitation, he experienced no surprise or regret when none came. For a while, he retained a vaguely positive image of the feisty little redheaded white man, and then, gradually, he pretty much forgot him.

Meanwhile, life moved on. Partly in response to the sequence of events during the 1960's in which he had lost the rights to some two-dozen rhythm-and blues songs, partly in response to his experience in the 1990's of pleading guilty to a felony he had not committed, and partly in response to many other life experiences of a nature kindred to the loss of songs and the false plea, James R. Johnson chose to become, in the late 1990's, a member of the organization popularly known as The Jehovah's Witnesses.

Now, if Oliver Nelson ever again happens to be in the right place at the right time, he will certainly encounter a somewhat changed Johnny Jukes. In fact, he may very well see the man in the dark suit and tie walking along a tree-lined street, chatting with other neatly dressed men and women, while their well-behaved children follow quietly behind. For all these good people are out there every Saturday morning in the service of the Lord.

ANOTHER NEW NEIGHBORHOOD

1995-the present

In 1995, my wife and I bought an apartment in Greenwich Village. My sense of this neighborhood had been formed in the early 1960's, when I shared a cheap apartment in the East Village with a friend from college. To me, and many others of my generation, Greenwich Village was Bohemia, the land of jazz and marijuana.

But by 1995, this had changed, and in the subsequent twenty-eight years, the changes have accelerated. Everything has become expensive, and the Bohemian elements have retreated to various corners that now seem like museum displays. Two universities have engrossed much of the real estate. Commercial realtors, hand-in-glove with politicians, have ruined the shopping, driving out thrift shops, shoemakers, and luncheonettes in favor of boutiques, high-end restaurants, and banks and chain stores.

The cast of characters with whom I have interacted is also changed. As the old people in my co-op building have relocated or died, rich young people have moved in, taking on mountains of debt to buy their domiciles, and bringing in new values that are as alien to old-timers as was the street life of South Park Slope to my younger self, in 1975.

In place of Jim Fahey and Bobby Langford, many of my local interactions have been with shills for city agencies and two universities. Not that my main adversaries, both men, are completely uninteresting. One, a construction manager, is also an escaped Jew from Albania; the other is an ombudsman for the city bureaucracy who doubles as an ecological activist. The ever-increasing litigiousness of our times keeps me from so much as naming these men. Besides, the reader would find any detailed account of our contentious, repetitious interactions, tedious.

The main themes of these interactions have been noise and dirt, which head the updated list of my anxieties. Construction projects and malfunctioning machines are the culprits. There has been one further change of note: instead of cars and the subway, my transit options have become buses and subways. After the first decade, or so, keeping a car in Manhattan became untenable. We could neither afford the hours circling the streets nor the money for a garage space.

Of course, the move from Brooklyn has also had its advantages: better access to cultural and other facilities (at least until Covid-19 struck), and better options for walking (enhanced since Covid-19 reduced street traffic). But, in terms of anxieties, I seem to have carried the old ones from Brooklyn along with me and added new ones, both specific to Manhattan and incidental to age.

Voir, Dear

Manhattan and Chicago, 2000's

Actors/Characters (with doubling):

1. The father/husband/J.D. #2: a seventy-something widower, retired from his job with the Transit Authority, also a long-time writer of fiction, lives in New York; old Russian-Jewish immigrant, retired cab driver.

2. The daughter/wife's voice: an only child, thirty-something, a free-lance economic journalist, between partners, lives in Chicago; her mother (as a voice).

3. Judge Solomon/ J.D. #2: the fair-minded judge; old man, Russian-Jewish immigrant, retired cab driver.

4. J.D.#1: twenty-something go-fer for C.S.I.

Settings:

1. Split stage: the father's kitchenette, daughter's living room. A weekday evening, after both have eaten supper. Through the windows, rain in New York; snow in Chicago.

2. Empty, spotlighted, darkened stage representing a courtroom and the Central Jury room.

Scene 1

Daughter: So . . . what else? . . . Weren't you supposed to start your juvenile delinquency today?

Father: Yesterday. Jury duty, I'm already finished. Ding, dong, the wash is done.

Daughter: Witch is dead.

Father: Time off for general . . . uh . . . bullshit.

Daughter: Good behavior. Go on, please. Time Out?

Father: Granted. Funny you should have played that one, because I met two J.D.'s today, one of whom really was sort of a juvenile delinquent.

Daughter: Hmm, good. Tell me more.

Father: I got called to a panel this morning, a veritable dog.

Daughter: Voir dire. Dad! Remember? Time out?

Father: Oops, sorry.

Daughter: That's okay, go on.

Father: So, anyway, my dear. You've never been called, have you?

Daughter: Actually, I was, here in Chi-Town, during the summer. But I postponed it because I was busy with the GMI annual report.
Father: Oh, yes. How did that one turn out?

Daughter: Well, you know, it's what I do. Rent, food, a life (mutters) sort of.

Father: What? Oh, understood. Where was I? They need 14 people, 12 regulars, 2 subs.

Daughter: 'Alternates.' I know —everyone knows that—from TV. Assume intermediate knowledge.

Father: Thank you, I'll take that as a narrative alert. Isn't it odd how, even during time outs, we still sound like we're playing our game?

Daughter: True, it must be . . .

Father: So they called a crowd of people down from Central Jury—eighty—and herded us all into a courtroom. Try to guess the judge's name. It's easy, the watchword for wisdom.

Daughter: Judge Solomon.

Father: Yep. Looked like a nice guy, too. Eloquent, minimum of jargon.

Daughter: In short, a pargon—sorry, paragon.

Father: And he looked like he had only one wife—there was a wedding band—and no porcupines.

Daughter (a bit sourly): Ha ha, that one again!

Father: Sorry. Anyway, so the two cretin lawyers—I don't know where they get these guys . . .

Daughter: 'Cretin lawyers'?

Father: A hard-body Italian prosecutor who asked the prospective jurors such obviously inappropriate, insinuating questions that the judge kept admonishing him.

Daughter: Got it. And, let's see, a fat one, balding, with dandruff all over the shoulders of his cheap black suit.

Father: Blue.

Daughter: Most TV defense lawyers—I'm assuming he was Legal Aid—look like that. Go on.

Father: Okay. The case—I can tell you now, since obviously I wasn't picked—was about a mugging. The defendant was this pathetic-looking kid, also wearing a cheap suit—black, er, the suit; him, too, for that matter—and a tie his mother must have knitted.

Daughter: Maybe she helped him tie it, too.

Father: Time in?

Daughter: Not yet. Let me get this straight. You didn't want to be on the jury? you did?

Father: According to the loose-lipped prosecutor, even though no one was shot, a gun had allegedly been flashed. So, even though it wasn't clear by whom, it sounded as if jail time was a real possibility. Since I didn't believe incarceration could do anything but hurt such a young man and, by implication, everyone else in society, and since, before I'd heard the evidence, I wasn't so arrogant as to assume I could persuade a jury to vote for acquittal . . .

Daughter: Here, here! Author! Author! You didn't want to be chosen. Did you get questioned, or did they fill the jury before you had your chance?

Father: I had my chance. But first let me tell you about the other two J.D.'s.

Daughter: Narrative suspense.

Father: Okay, let's see, then, where to . . .

Daughter: The juvenile delinquent.

Father: Right, I first noticed him when he was called to the jury box for his, er . . .

Daughter (interrupts): Don't say "venereal disease" or anything, Dad. Time is still out.

Father: His voir dire. As he was walking up with the others—they do eighteen at a time—I thought he had either dressed to be rejected or was just completely inappropriate. I could hardly believe this guy!

Daughter: This is good!

Father: Guess what he looked like.

Daughter: You tell it, it's your story.

Father: Thank you, my dear. Well, then, can you picture a hip-hop Humpty Dumpty?

Daughter (laughs): Let's see: those voluminous short pants, buzz cut, Metallica tee shirt, gold chain, and a big tattoo on one leg.

Father (laughs): Very good. A dragon. I saw it when he swaggered past on his way to the box.

Daughter: And . . .

Scene 2

JD #1 (reading from questionnaire on laminated card): Let's see, Numero Trey: "Are you a native New Yorker?" Yes sir! Born and bred in Brooklyn. That's New York, isn't it? Right here in the good old U.S. of A.

Judge: And do you now reside in Manhattan, sir?

JD#1: I most certainly do, sir, in the downtown area.

Judge: Your occupation?

JD#1: I'm a go-fer for C.S.I.

Judge: Well! That must mean you know police officers and possibly even, er, other people involved in the criminal justice system.

JD#1: I'll say! I do, indeed, know such persons. Yep, a whole bunch of cops. And I meet numerous criminals, too, bad guys, in my work. Numerous. Plus several of my own friends, even close friends, have done serious time.

Judge: But not you, yourself, sir.

JD#1: Yep, I mean, nope. Never been inside, myself—except to visit, or when we were shooting—ha ha, the show, that is.

Scene 3

Daughter: You're not going to tell me J.D. Number One was actually . . .

Father: He was. I couldn't believe it, either. I mean, he was among numbers nine to eleven of the jurors chosen, and there were still more than forty of us waiting to be examined, so it wasn't as if . . .

Daughter: Hmm. Strange machinations of the so-called system of justice. We can infer, perhaps, that the guy satisfied some obscure idea of balance: race, age, whatever. But go on.

Father: Oops! Can I call you back? Nature . . .

Daughter: Me, too, let's take five.

(They hang up. Fade, then two toilets simultaneously gurgle as he speed dials. She picks up on the first ring.)

Daughter: So. When were you questioned?

Father: In the next batch, right after lunch. By that point, my chances of being selected were five out of eighteen—assuming they would finish filling the jury from our group. Anyway, when it was my turn … heh heh.

(short silence)

Daughter: Dad? Hello? Are you there? Did you do something you, er, shouldn't have?

Father: Yep. I did.
Daughter: Oh, no! You acted crazy or told some ridiculous lie. I hope it wasn't construed as contempt of court.

Father: Well, yes and no. The judge didn't admonish me or anything, but . . . well, contempt may have been involved. You decide.

Daughter: What did you do, Dad!

Father: Well . . . did I ever show you that short story I wrote about the shoplifting incident? I must have written it more than fifteen years ago, before I retired from my day job with the T.A.

Daughter: I do seem to remember that story. I think you wrote it ... the summer we rented the wonderful farmhouse in Maine.

Father: You have some memory!

Daughter: It was called . . . something with . . . 'groove' . . . 'bag'? Oh, no, don't tell me you . . .

Father: Wow! That's right, "Trick Bag."

(At that moment, the daughter's call waiting signals.)

Daughter: Darn! Sorry, dad, I have a call. I'll put you on hold, okay?

Father: Okay.

(She talks for a short time, laughing, looking animated, while he sits in an exaggerated attitude of patience. She comes back on the line.)

Daughter: Sorry. It was a friend. I said I'd call him back, but that it might be late.

Father: "A friend?"

Daughter: Dad! Play by the rules.

Father: Sorry. Where was I? Oh, yes, the story.

Daughter: Which of the jury selection questions were you ostensibly answering?

Father: The one about knowing someone who's been in trouble with the law.

Daughter: Oh, no! And you pretended . . . they let you tell that whole long story?

Father: Well, no, part of it. You see, I used a trick from my own bag. My initial answer was, "Well, actually, I do. Quite a close friend."

Daughter: So they had to ask. Which of them bit? the judge or one of the lawyers?

Father: Heh, heh. Wise Justice Solomon, himself.

Daughter: He asked you to elaborate?

Father: Yep. (mimicking judge) "Briefly, please, sir."

Daughter: But that didn't stop you!

Father: Nope. I got up to the part where Johnny—remember, that was his name?—is accosted by the security guard. Then, at last, Solomon did stop me.

Daughter: Why'd you do that, Dad?

Father: Well, as my friend, the shrink, might say, "The act was probably over-determined."

Daughter: Ha!

Father: If I understand my own motives, I think that, A, I knew—or hoped, since after Hip-Hop Humpty anything seemed possible—they would disqualify me for having befriended a convicted felon –like the guy in the story did. And B . . .

Daughter: Yes, 'B.' Obviously. Even assuming 'A' is true, let's get to 'B.'

Father: Of course, I'm not really sure, but . . .

Daughter: Never mind, there's already been a lot of guesswork in this conversation.

Father: True, true. Okay, I told the story because . . . well . . . I wanted to see if it was ... credible.

Daughter: Ah, yes, that story never got published, right? Was it . . . credible?

Father: If you'll allow me to introduce J.D. #2 now, I can circle back to my own role in these events. All the parts are related, you see.

Daughter: So are we.

Father: The point of the story will be more forceful if I tell it this way.

Daughter: I'm sure it will, but . . . look, I don't mean to hurt your feelings, Dad, but this conversation has become annoyingly circumlocutious.

Father: That's blunt! But true. Okay, okay, I was just . . . I don't know what . . . trying to . . . shape the narrative.

Daughter: So . . . again, was your story credible?

Father: Okay, okay. First tell me, would you have found it credible?

Daughter: Hmm, depends. Honestly? Well, I can't remember having been unable to suspend disbelief when I read it. But I was only twelve or thirteen, and if you had pretended . . . hmm, I'm not sure.

Father: Well, the judge let me get up to the part where the narrator posts bail for Johnny. Then. . . .guess.

Daughter: He politely suggested you'd said enough, he got your drift, thank you, and you should—briefly—answer the remaining questions *(sotto voce)* and go directly to jail.

Father: Ha! I heard that! Not exactly. He called the lawyers to the bench, the three of them whispered behind their hands like they do, and, then, he dismissed me.

Daughter: Do you think he realized you were pulling his . . . ? Or was he just moving things along?

Father: Well, I wouldn't swear to it, but normally he wore a sort of sympathetic, inquisitive expression, and by the time he stopped me he looked like he had smelled a rat.

Daughter: Like he had snorkeled a reef? smoked a reefer? snookered a Roman? Damn! Sorry!

Father: "Sorry"?

Daughter: You know, for violating "time out."

Father: That's okay, time in. Where were we? Yes, he made me stop. But so what? That was the point —one of the points. Remember? I didn't want to be on the case.

Daughter: Sorghum gumbo!

Father: Sour grapes? No, no.

Daughter: Whatever. Let's move on.

Father: To J.D. Number Two.

Daughter: Right! To John Denver. John Deever. John Dean—no, that's "Howard." Wait, there was a "John Dean," too, wasn't there? Jeffrey Daumer. Johnny Damon.

Father: Wow! You must have been storing those up.

Daughter (modestly): Well . . . not really.

Father: Jew. Displaced.

Daughter: Oh.

Father: He was in the same group as Humpty, right before lunch. I'll describe his virtual divination.

Daughter: I scorn the point. We should have a no-repeat rule.

Father: Generous, my dear. True. Q. and A. okay here?

Daughter: Q. and A-okay.

Father: May I refer to them as 'J.S.' and 'J.D'?

Daughter: Proceed, sir, without fucking asking!

Father: Wha . . . ? Further ado. I'll recommence in mobster style, then.

Daughter: Marinara sauce. No, in *medias res.*

Father: Wow! Good for you, that was a hard one!

J.S.: "So you were not born in this country?"

JD#2: "No, your chonor. Rahsha."

Daughter: And the witness—you—will now be permitted a boondoggle of the J.D.

Father: Brief description. Ashkenazi, seventy to seventy-five. Careworn, grizzled, respectable dark suit, white shirt with top button buttoned, no tie, black-rimmed glasses with a small American flag decal on the right earpiece, the one on my side—on the other side, too, I later ascertained.

Daughter: Excellent, father! Water dog.

Father: Well done. Tin yams, my dear, if I may throw you a Serbian babushka.

Daughter: Thank you. Softball. And thank you, too, Pater. Proceed.

Scene 4

JD#2: But now I am U.S. citizen, your honor.

Judge (very fast): Good. What's your occupation, marital status, and do you currently reside in New York County—in Manhattan, that is?

JD#2: My occ . . . I retire, drive cab fourteen year. Yes, reside . . . I reside, my wife, she dead ten year.

Judge: I'm sorry to hear that. One moment, please. Will the prosecutor and . . .

Scene 5

Daughter: So they dismissed him?

Father: Then and there. We'd been told several times that fluency in English was a so quit nagging.

Daughter: *Sine qua non.* Time out again, please?

Father: Time out. But the judge neglected to have the man excused altogether. He sent him back to Central Jury.

Daughter: Wow! Interesting. Was that a mistake?

Father: I don't think so. Solomon was too sharp to make that kind of a mistake. No, I think he saw how much J.D. 2 wanted to serve, so…

Daughter: Oh, no! He left him in the pool? Why do you think he wanted to serve so much?

Father: Who knows? loneliness? needed the money? improve his English?

Daughter: What about "the wheels of justice"?

Father: I hate to say it, but I don't think it would have mattered—not much, anyhow. Assuming a case with him as juror ever reached the deliberation stage, he would have probably just sat there and nodded, made the right noises, gone along with the majority.

Daughter: I'm not sure I buy that. Suppose someone asked him to justify his vote. What if the jury was divided?

Father: He would probably have touched the side of his nose, or something, made the "intuition" sign. You know how those Russians are!

Daughter: I'm still not convinced. In fact, I don't think you have any idea why Judge Solomon did what he did. Look, it's getting late, and I should probably call that guy back, if only to be polite.

Father: Okay. Shall we say good night, then, my dear?

Daughter: Well, almost. One more question: did you see J.D. again? Number Two? I like him.

Father: Me, too. Yes, I did. It was during the interminable lunch break. I got back to Central Jury early and saw him looking out of a big picture window over the rooftops of Chinatown toward the Manhattan Bridge. He looked melancholy—not depressed. It crossed my mind that he might have been a professor or something in the old country.

Daughter: Did you speak to him?

Father: I did.

Scene 6

Father: Some view!

JD#2: Yes, beautiful. I love New York.

Father: You drove a cab, correct?

JD#2: Correct. But why . . . ?

Father: I bet you could name all the streets down there. We're looking north, aren't we?'

JD#2: Actually, excuse me, sir, but east: Mulberry, Mott, Elizabeth, Bowery, Chrystie, Forsyth, Eldridge, Allen, Ludlow, Suffolk, Clinton, Pitt—no, sorry, Ridge, then Pitt—Columbia, Baruch Drive, Baruch Place, the F.D.R. Drive, and, finally, at last, we come to the East river. That is not a street, of course, however. (He puts his hand on the father's arm, smiles gently, and looks into his eyes.) You watch out for me, please, Mister? Sir? You stay close, and when I not understanding. . .

Father: Well, sure. Yes, I can do that.

Scene 7

Daughter: And ?

Father: But, then, I was dismissed, so . . .

Daughter: Don't worry. He'll get somebody else.

Father: Yes, I'm sure he will. Even so . . . When I was dismissed, I had to return to Central Jury, and I spotted him there, reading the paper, or something, in a corner.

Daughter: So you weren't just sent back to the jury pool?

Father: No, dismissed. I got my ticket, no delay, and I left. To my shame, I didn't even say goodbye. It felt like I was running away from him.

Daughter: Don't beat yourself up, Dad. I think you showed good . . . judgment... Well, it's getting late. I suppose I really should say good night. We'll talk again? Soon?

Father: Always a pleasure, my love. Soon. Good night, dear.

Daughter: Good night, Dad. (She hangs up, then punches "redial." One ring.) John? Hi, Annie. Sorry, honey, I was talking to my dad in New York.
(She laughs happily, fade out her half of stage.)

(Father sits with his hand on the phone.)

Wife's Voice: So there you are again, Paul, with your oiled marmalade frangible hibiscus on the bleak rebus. Did you enjoy it, dear? How is she?

Father: With my old man's freckled hand on the black receiver. Yes, I did, Ellen. Very much, thanks. She's fine.
Wife's Voice: Good, good, dear, I could tell you haven't lost a step. Go get ready for bed now. And don't forget to brush your teeth. Use the eclectic tortoise.

Father: Electric toothbrush.

Wife's Voice: I'll be waiting.

(Exit father. Fade out his half of stage.)

Carla, the Copy-Shop Girl: A Tale of Canal Street

Manhattan, 1851 & 2003

NOTES

1.Both the "Bartleby" scenes and the modern scenes use text from the Melville story. Generally, it is unaltered, except for a spliced sentence or omitted/added word or phrase, here and there. The exceptions are added scenes, such as Act 1, #4 (Ginger Nut meets Lulu), where Melville's text is augmented and woven into new material.

2. The "Bartleby" sections turn out to be in metrical prose. They could almost all be formatted as verse, which is what I do when it seems to suit a scene's rhythm. Sometimes, however, these are left as prose.

3. Time of day can be indicated by big clocks in both offices.

SINGERS

BASS: Ed/Turkey/Grub Man

BARITONE: Narrator/Dave

TENOR: Nippers/Ginger Nut

CONTRALTO: Carla/Bartleby

MEZZO-SOPRANO: Sally

SOPRANO: Lulu

ACT ONE

1. Prelude

FRAGMENTS OF A LOST GNOSTIC POEM OF THE 12TH CENTURY

by Herman Melville

[This to be sung during the opening photomontage, possibly by the bass who plays Turkey. The song serves to introduce indirectly the motif of ancient ruins and dead walls.]

tableau, video:

Wall Street/1850'sCanal Street/2000's

blank wallstawdry, colorful, teeming street

B'way: horses, teeming crowdshordes of shoppers, traffic, monitors

Sunday bustle, Trinity Church, Pearl Paint, inside and outside, the P.O. (same), fade to Trinity graveyard

Found a family, build a state,

The pledged event is still the same:

Matter in end will never abate

His ancient brutal claim.

Indolence is heaven's ally here,

And energy the child of hell:

The Good Man, pouring from his pitcher clear
But brims the poisoned well.

2. Trinity Church, the graveyard: Fall, 2003:
Carla sitting on a tombstone, reading as she eats & drinks
She reads, opening duet . . .:
narrator introduces self: Carla introduces self:
"I am a rather elderly man ""Just a poor working girl"

Narrator:

I am a rather elderly man. For thirty years, my avocation has brought
me into contact with a singular set of men about whom nothing that
I know of has ever been written. I mean the law copyists --or
scriveners.

Carla:

I'm just a poor working girl, I take life as I find it. Actually, no, I'm
an artist--a painter, primarily conceptual-- but, to pay the rent and buy
the groceries, not to mention art supplies, I work at a copy shop,
unnamed, ten blocks south of Canal Street. (No free advertisements
for the running dogs of capitalism!)

Duet:

An elderly man a poor working girl

thirty years, my avocation a painter, conceptual

a singular set of men pay the rent, buy the groceries

I mean the law copyists no free advertisements

or scriveners for running dogs.

[She eats, drinks, reads on].

Narrator:

I waive the biography of all other scriveners for a few passages in the life of Bartleby, the strangest I ever saw, or heard of.

But first I must mention myself, my employees, my chambers, and general surroundings, for such is indispensable to an adequate understanding of the character about to be presented. *Imprimis* ...

Carla:

A near-minimum-wage slave, I make ten bucks an hour, eight-hours a day, five days a week. Plus two ten-minute coffee breaks, and forty-five minutes for lunch. And, oh, yes, there's overtime --abundant, but totally random.

I live in a one-room rat hole above an army-navy store smack in the heart of Canal Street. This serves as my "studio." I wake up with paint on by doze.

My diet, though scanty, is healthy and balanced, tofu, bean sprouts, carrots, and --as they used to say-- curds and small whey. --which reminds me ...

Duet [*like the first*]:
I waive the biography near-minimum-wage slave
of other scriveners ten bucks an hour
Bartleby, the strangest forty-five minutes for lunch
But first I must mention totally random

my employees, my chambers a one-room rat hole, Canal

an adequate understanding   as they used to say

Imprimis ...which reminds me ...

[she looks at watch closes book, finishes lunch, stretches, heads back to work]

3. More on the narrator

Turkey, Nippers, Ginger Nut introduced

[a few minutes later]

back at the office, the daily round *intro of Ed, Dave, Sally, Lulu*

Narrator:

As I was saying:

In the cool tranquility of a snug retreat, I do a snug business among rich men's bonds. All who know me, consider me an eminently safe man.

The late John Jacob Astor, a personage little given to poetic enthusiasm,

had no hesitation in pronouncing my first grand point to be prudence.

I do not speak it in vanity, but simply record the fact.

John Jacob Astor, a name which, I admit, I love to repeat. For it hath
a rounded and orbicular sound to it, and rings like unto bullion.

John Jacob Astor,

John Jacob Astor,

rounded and orbicular,

rings like unto bullion.

[the copy shop, workers at their stations ...]

Sally:

Is everyone back from lunch? Right, then!?

Hear ye, hear ye, lunch hour is officially over.

So stand and deliver --that is, reply.

In order to plan the rest of the day,

remind me, me, me of which job you're on

and when you expect to be done.

Ready, then? Ed? Edward? Ed?

Ed:

Aye, aye, Ma'am. At your service, as usual.

Current job: digital poster lamination.

Instrument: the Harbin/Price Five-Thousand.

Number of copies to be completed: ten.

Time of completion: let's say, two-forty.

Sally:

Good. Since you're already at the H-P,

I'll send you another small batch.

Matte stock or glossy, just read the job orders.

Dave? David? Dave? Stand and deliver!

Dave:

Here I stand, Milady --that is, sit--

at my trusty word-processor.

[aside:

and it's "David," not "Dave," by the way.]

I'm formatting a resume

for some art-student dingbat.

Though long, it's poorly organized,

so I'll have to do a lot of c & p.

Two more resumes after this.

I expect to be finished by three.

Sally:

Very good, Dave. Since that one's so demanding,

we'll switch you over to color copying

for the rest of the afternoon. Okay?

Dave:

You're the boss, Sal. That sounds just dandy.

[aside:

although my brain may turn to candy]

Sally:

Very good, then, Dave. And last, but not least,

we come to you, Carla. Carla? Carla? O, Carla mia?

Carla:

Sorry, Boss, I was busy wool-gathering,

just let me finish this skein.

[aside:

rounded and orbicular

 rings like unto bullion.]

No, seriously,

I'm doing b & w copies,

multitudinous copies, vast as the sea,

five-thousand of the suckers --let me see,

about fifteen hundred to go ... which means

--let me get out my slide rule-- at eighty per,

I'll be finished by, say, two forty-eight.

Sally:

Good. So I'll put you on b & w, too,

but difficult originals, faint or smudged,

twelve cents a copy, I have a few hundred,

which should keep you busy till five.

Carla:

When pains need to be taken, count on me.

Sally:

I do, dear, I do. Questions, then? No?

Good, we're all set. Work on, my beauties!

[Lulu comes in from back, drying her hands, seems about to ask what she should do, but Sally has already started checking out chits at the cash register, so Lulu just shrugs and goes back to the cafe. Fade.]

Narrator:

As a point of information:

of my two copyists, Turkey and Nippers,

the irritability and consequent nervousness

of Nippers were mainly observable

in the morning (... indigestion).

So that, Turkey's paroxysms,

only coming on about twelve o'clock,

I never had to do with their ...

... eccentricities at one time.]

[shrugs, points to clock to indicate that it is now early afternoon]

[Turkey and Nippers return from lunch, the former drunk, the latter subdued. They take their hats off, go to their desks and begin copying, Nippers quietly and Turkey making an enormous fuss, cursing, grinding his teeth, moving his chair back and forth noisily, blotting and ripping up documents, spilling his sand-box, breaking his pens. The narrator comes around the corner from his cubicle.]

Narrator:

Turkey, Turkey? My friend, my good friend.

Might I have a word with you ... in private?

[He beckons him to the cubicle, then continues]

Turkey ... friend, I don't know how to say this,

valuing your services as I do

[aside:

the morning ones, that is],

Now that you're growing ... older, might it not

be a good idea to... abridge your labors ...

[Turkey seems about to protest]

on Saturdays, at least, just Saturdays

[aside:

when you always seem at your worst].

After twelve o'clock, dinner being over,

it might be best for you to go home

to your lodgings and rest yourself till tea time

[aside:

after which, you may do as you please.]

Turkey *[holding a long ruler]:*

Please, sir, allow me to assure you that,

if my morning services are useful,

how indispensable, then, in the afternoon?

[aside:

not to mention the money. How will I live?]

With submission, sir, I consider myself

your ... right-hand man. In the morning,

I but deploy my columns. Afternoons,

I put myself at their head and charge the foe

[gesticulates with ruler]   --thus!.

Narrator:

But the blots, Turkey, what about the blots?.

Turkey:

True, but, with submission, sir, behold these hairs!

I am getting old. Surely, sir, a blot or two

of a warm afternoon is not to be

severely urged against gray hairs. Old age

--even if it blot the page-- is honorable.

With submission, sir, we both are getting old.

With submission, sir, we both are getting old.

*[The narrator starts to reply, but instead throws up his hands, nods in
reluctant agreement, then resignedly gestures Turkey back to his own
desk, where Turkey mops his brow, then resumes his furious activity. The
whole while, Nippers is shaking his head in disapproval as he quietly
copies away.*

*Fade. Then, Ginger Nut brings an envelope into the narrator's cubicle, is
given another, runs out of the office.]*

4.Duo: Ginger Nut, Lulu

This sets up Lulu as another fan of C's, and sets up GN & L as witnesses to the crime in Act Two

[a few minutes later]

WE, WHO ALSO SERVE, ALSO HAVE FEELINGS

Lulu:

My name is Lucy, but call me Lulu.

Carla gave me the handle

my first day on the job.

It stuck, I think she's great.

By profession, I'm the coffee girl

for the copy shop: I run the cafe

--"Java Bytes"-- isn't that tacky?

A minimum wage slave, alas,

I do score the occasional tip.

"Big tits, tiny tips," said bastard Dave.

Nobody laughed, but him.

The half-wit thinks he's smart.

Ed says not to mind him: "Lulu, be cool."

But that's easier said than done.

No, I find Boy Dave highly annoying.

In fact, some day, I hope to hurt him.

And just you wait and see, I will!

Yes, I will. Oh, well, where was I? Oh, yes.

My job may be low, even peripheral,
but there are worse jobs in the world.
Lots worse. How about so-called modeling
for magazines with names like "Bend Over"?
(Yes, I did that. I'm not proud of it.)
Here, I try to be pleasant and useful
by doing all sorts of small things.
"Like what?" you ask. Huh! "Like what"?
Like collecting waste paper, recycling,
(save a tree!) and cleaning all the lenses
on the costly machines --that's what!
I also watch the copy clerks copying,
I'm waiting for my chance to move up.
Okay, I know that being the operator
of a black-and-white copy machine
for eight or ten bucks an hour
is not life's highest calling, but, hey,
I'm just trying to make my way.

Besides, furthermore, and in addition,
I'm trying to "find myself," as they say.
To do so, I hang in the East Village,
in Tomkins Square Park and adjacent streets,
tormenting the yupping-class residents
with god-awful noises at ungodly hours.

I also boost smokes and hot magazines,
and I attend all the moshes and raves,
endorsing my paycheck over to CBGB's.
And, oh, yes, I think I may be gay.
Like Carla, I wear a nipple ring --no big thing.

Where do I live? Really! Please!
In a roach-and-rat hole, one-room
paint-peeler, shared with three pauperous others.
Communal bog and bath, unspeakable,
at the end of a stygian hall.
Our place -- this palace-- is on Third and C.
My roommates do hard drugs --not me!

Want to know more about Lucy?
Two parents, Catholics, alas,
with nine --count them--children.
(How did you guess? I'm the eldest.)
They live ninety miles north of the city.
My dad's a nice guy, very hard-drinking,
works in a garage, he can fix anything.
Mom, of course, is a housewife, plus she
does some telemarketing from the home.
They're real. I love them. What else?
I did three semesters at SUNY, New Paltz,
majoring in Fine Arts, I love to silk-screen.
Will I go back? Who can say? Okay, that's it.

Oh, yes, just one more thing: I hate babies.
Really. I do. I can't stand them. [imitates one screaming]
Eeeeeeeeeeeee. [exits, working]

Ginger Nut:
What is this place? The address must be wrong.
[checks address on envelope from law office]
Hmm. Oh, well, I'll just rest for a moment.
[sits at cofee bar, playing with a spoon]
"Ginger Nut." Does that sound like a real name?
I was nicknamed by my colleagues,
Turkey and Nippers. "Turkey"? "Nippers"?
Names for fowl and implements, not for men.
The single exception is Bartleby.

That, I believe, is his real name,
which is odd, considering that he is
--odd, I mean, a ghost with a genuine name.
But never mind, what difference does it make?
The fact is, they named me for a cake,
a flat, round spicy cake which they all love
and which, along with apples, Spitzenbergs,
I'm always sent to purchase. Copying
legal documents, as my employer says,
is "a dry, husky sort of business."

My dad, a carter, sent me here to lift
the family fortunes. My employer
(full of witticisms) quipped that my pa
"preferred the bench to the cart for his son."
Not that I mind it here. I think of myself
as more than a ...messenger: I'm also
a sweeper, a cleaner, student of law.
I have a small desk of my own,
the draws of which are full of nutshells.
My employer once joked --another bit of wit--
that, for me, "the noble science of the law
 is bounded in a nutshell." So he thinks,
but how can he know what I think?
I'm sure the law is difficult, dense and, er ...
abstruse. Perhaps, even stygian.
*[He spies Lulu and crosses to the copy shop. They circle and sniff for a few
moments.]*

Lulu:
Hi? Hello? I'm Lulu. I like your suit.
Very retro, very cool. What's your name?

GN:
Call me "Ginger Nut." "Lulu"? A nickname, too?
You seem ... outlandish. What work do you do?

Lulu:

I'm the coffee girl, I run the cafe

here at the copy shop. What about you?

GN:

"Copy shop"? You could call the office

where I work a "copy shop," too.

But I'm not a copyist, myself,

not one of the scriveners. No,

though I aspire to that station,

for now I'm just a messenger.

Lulu:

And I'm just a poor coffee girl.

We're not so different, then, are we?

GN:

True, both, in a sense, servants of servants.

Lulu:

Yet we, who also serve, also have feelings.

GN:

That's very well said:

"We, who also serve, also have feelings."

GN and Lulu:
Yes, we, who also serve, also have feelings.

GN:
In fact, my own, at times, are quite complex.
As I weave my way through the crowds
on lower Broadway, the sunlight gleaming
off bright and varied buildings,
hurrying to the Court or Custom House
to buy apples and cakes for my colleagues,
I often feel ... well ... calm and happy,
at one, you might say, with the world.

Lulu:
How sweet! I've had that feeling, too
[aside:
 sometimes pharmaceutically induced]
When Carla takes me out to lunch,
or Sally says what a sweet girl I am
and how I'm meant for bigger things
 ...yes, that gives me a significant buzz.

Lulu and GN:
Yes, we, who also serve, also have feelings.

GN:
A "buzz," is it? "Furthermore, and moreover"

(as my employer is wont to say),
I'm particularly amused --buzzed, that is--
by the new man in our office, Bartleby.
He won't do nothing but copy.
No errands, no proofreading, no nothing.
Frankly, I think he's a bit loony!

Lulu:
These days, the world is full of "Bartlebys,"
and most of our tunes are loony.
But, if someone in our shop did that
--preferred not to help out, whatever--
Sally --the boss- would just kick his ass
right out the door. Believe me. But why don't ...

GN:
Yes, indeed. In point of fact, why don't ...

Lulu:
. ... I don't see why we don't ...

Narrator *[from wings]:*
 Ginger Nut, Ginger Nut. Oh, dear,
where is he when we need him?

GN:
Oh! I have to go, alas, they're calling,

but I'll try to come back soon, Miss ... Lulu.

Lulu:
That's cool, Mister Nut. Glad to have met you,
and have a good day. Hope to see you soon.

Lulu and GN:
Yes, we, who also serve, also have feelings.

5. I Prefer Not To/ ... Work Overtime.
 This scene further defines the dynamic of the two offices.
[both in the afternoon, later the same Fall]

[Early on in Bartleby's tenure at the law office, the narrator at his desk, finishes looking over a document of which there are two copies]

I PREFER NOT T0 (1)
Narrator:
Bartleby!
[holds one copy out back over his shoulder]
Come help me examine a small paper.

Bartleby:
[from alongside, behind the screen which separates his desk from the narrator's, B. goes on copying as he answers in a "mild, firm voice"]
I would prefer not to.

Narrator *[stunned]:*
What?! Bartleby? Did you not hear me?
[as clearly as possible]
Come help me examine a small paper.

Bartleby:
[still behind the screen, same voice]
I would prefer not to.

Narrator:
"Prefer not to"?
What do you mean? Are you moonstruck?
I want you to help me compare this sheet here
-- just take it!
[he leans around the screen, thrusting the paper. Bartleby comes to the corner, does not take sheet]

Bartleby:
I would prefer not to.
[goes back]

Narrator *[aside]:*
Did you see that? His face was composed,
his gray eye dimly calm.
Not a wrinkle of agitation.
Had there been the least impertinence,
doubtless I should have dismissed him.

[looks hastily at watch, then looks around corner, where B. is copying away. Turns back, shrugs]

Narrator:
Nippers! Nip ...
[N. appears almost before the narrator calls him]

Nippers *[calmly, with a little bow]:*
Sir! At your service! Sir!

[Narrator thrusts copy at him and Nippers instantly begins reading, while Narrator checks]
Nippers:
Twentieth September, *anno* eighteen fifty-one.
J.M. Bailey, Esquire, Two Exchange Place.
Before the Court of Chancery. *Imprimis*:

[fade to the copy shop]

THE "I PREFER NOT TO WORK OVERTIME" SONG

[Everyone at work at machines except Lulu, who is in the back drying cups and saucers]

Sally:
Oh, Carla, *mia*, some overtime tonight?

Carla [absently]:

Thanks, boss, but I would ... prefer not to.

[The other workers all laugh, knowing why she says that.]

Sally:

Ha ha! What a funny way to put it!

Are you being sarcastic, dear?

Well, then, okay, in that case, ha, ha,

I'd "prefer not to" pay you this week.

I'm a bit short. Are you okay with that?

Carla:

Whatever, ha, ha. I'd prefer to be paid.

Ed:

I'd also ha ha ha prefer

not to do any more copying,

at least not in this ha incarnation,

but thanks ha for not asking, anyhow.

Sally:

You, too, Ed? Watch out, or I'll "prefer"

to kick your ass ha ha right out the door!

What's going on here? Some kind of joke? on me?

Dave:

I have no preferences, ha ha, myself.

[aside:
Oh, just one: I'd prefer --no, I'd like to--
sleep with Carla. In point of ha ha fact,
I'd love to jump her bones. Heh heh. I would!]

Lulu:

No coffee, anyone? Hee hee, I won't bring it.

Ed:

Thanks, ho ho, Lu. I'm sure that we're all ...

Dave:

       ... underwhelmed by your har har non-offer.

All *[including Sally now]*:
    {We would prefer
    {We would all prefer
    {We would all certainly prefer
     {not to!

Carla *[aside, going into washroom]*:
    But "not to" ... what?
[closes door, then opens it, looks back]
    We'd prefer not to say. Ha ha.
[closes door again, fade]

6. [back in the copy shop, as they work, they talk]
[a few days later]

FIRST CONCEPTUAL ART SONG
Ed:
Paul Kos, Joseph Beuys, Donald Judd,
Dan Flavin, Hanna Darboven,
and Sol Lewitt. Lewitt, Carla?
Isn't he the one who said,
"Perception is subjective"?
It may just be me,
but that seems significantly stupid,
a kind of lame tautology.

Carla:
Yeah, right, Ed, well, everyone says
something stupid now and then
(hopefully not too often).
But that doesn't negate
the value of ... blah blah.
Speaking of conceptualism,
some of it is significantly witty.
Have you ever heard, for instance,
of the Big Tailed Elephant Group,
that hot new gang in the P.R.C.
--People's Republic of China?

Ed:
In point of fact, indeed, I have.
The handle evokes the days of the queue.

Dave:
Actually, it does sound familiar.

Carla:
Yeah, right, Dave! "Actually,"
everything sounds "familiar" to you,
even when you don't have a clue.
But, since you've heard of the movement,
I'm sure you've also heard of Qiu Zhijie's
gang-buster piece, "Repetitious Copies"?

Dave:
Actually, I can't say ...

Ed:
... that you have.
Obviously some reference to our own sad vocation.
Isn't he the one who made that costume,
"half white collar, half peasant"?
I saw it on the Internet
("Heard it on the grapevine.")
A socialist yang-ying joke, I opine.

Carla:

No, Ed, wrong guy, that was Luo Zidan.

I know, all those Chinese names sound alike,

but, nevertheless, I'm impressed, I really am.

Dave:

As for us, what are we?

What costume would suit us,

the white-collar educated

with no-collar jobs?

We're the all-American,

fifty-fifty,

cotton-polyester,

tee-shirt workers.

Ed:

I'm not even sure I'd call us "workers," bro.

"Minimally-employed slacker" is my own m.o.

Carla:

My favorite Big-Tailed Elephant piece

is by Chengying: "Kite with a Severed String."

He picks this random street, where he puts down

a throne and some scissors. Then, he flies a kite

that he calls "the Kite of Past Emperors."

Ed:

... after which, of course, he cuts the string ...

Dave:

... symbolizing severed ties to the past.

You might say he's kissing Communist ass.

Carla:

There's more to it than that, though.

As the kite drifts slowly

to the ground in the distance,

Liu, himself, assumes the throne ...

Ed:

... thus making another statement.

I mean, what's that pompous line from Shelley

"... poets are the unacknowledged legislators"?

Carla:

Of course, someone else could come along

with a kite called "the Kite of Past Artists."

Snip snip. But I'm certain Chengying thought of that.

Dave:

So did I, it's completely obvious.

But why are we talking of China?

Is there a reason for that?

Is it somehow more "conceptual"
because it is happening there?

Ed:
Well, it does seem especially outrageous
to think of all those japes and gags
going on under the noses
of the Commie gerontocracy,
which, I take it, is a main point
of the conceptual movement:
outrageousness, a kind of dada,
a dada based on ideas, not objects,
or, you could say, if you meant to be cruel,
a desperate straining after the new.

Carla:
That's harsh, Ed! It really is.
And I thought you were a friend.
But what did you just say, Dave:
"Is there a reason for that?"
Well, then, before we return
our limited powers of concentration,
alas, to work, and I have a huge
lamination to finish by five
--that's "lamination," not "lamentation,"
I always have plenty of those —

but let me round off this discussion
with two more sentences from Chairman Sol,
after which, "to be continued":
"Rational judgments repeat rational judgments,"
and "Irrational judgments lead to new experience."

[Dave, with a "whatever" gesture, moves off to do some work]

Ed:
Pardon me once again, Carla.
I don't intend to be perverse,
but that kite piece seems very rational
What could be more rational than satire?
And, secondly, take you, yourself:
you're the most rational person I know.
"Rational"? has it occurred to you
to think of Bartleby, himself
(whom I know is a favorite of yours),
 as a proto-conceptual artist?
 Beginning with nihilistic denial
of the value of human endeavor
--indeed, of civilization --
his path is absolute and logical.
Or, to out Le-witt you, if I may try:
"Irrational thoughts should be
followed absolutely and logically."
That may be why you love the story so.

Carla:

Yes, perhaps it is, hmm, perhaps, it is.

I mean, "conceptual"? "rational?" ...

they share a porous boundary.

Ed:

And speaking of that copy piece in China,

how is your ...

Carla:

Thanks for asking, Ed. I think you mean

my big "blow-down, blow-up" project.

Well, it's ... ... going on... proceeding ...

moving forward, as usual.

But let's leave that for another time.

Meanwhile --lamentably-- back to lamination.

[they separate, both go off to work]

7. [morning, sometime before Christmas, in the law office]

"I Prefer Not to" (2): the melee

Bartleby:

At present, I would prefer not to be a little reasonable.

[Nippers comes in, suffering from indigestion and a bad night's sleep]

194

Nippers:
"Prefer not," eh? I'd prefer him,
if I were you, sir. I'd prefer him,
I'd give him preferences, the stubborn mule!

Narrator:
Mr. Nippers, I'd prefer that
you would withdraw for the present.

[Nippers sourly withdraws. Turkey, deferential, enters.]

Turkey:
With submission, sir, yesterday
I was thinking about Bartleby here.
I think that if he would but prefer
to take a quart of good ale every day
it would do much towards mending him.

Narrator:
So you have got the word, too.

Turkey:
With submission, what word, sir? What word, sir?

*In making his bow, Turkey crowds the narrator, causing him to jostle the
screen into Bartleby, who is hunched at his desk]*

Bartleby:

I would prefer to be left alone here.

8. Finale: *[right before/around Christmas, same year (2003): the Christmas party: new machine introduced, C & Ed get together, cell-phone duo, Dave's rage]*
THE BOSAKI PATTER SONG

Sally:

Men and ...er ...

 [Lulu runs in]

--good!-- women,

your attention, please!

I have some announcements to make.

[they pound the tables, etc.-- drum rolls]

Thanks to all of you, thanks to your efforts

(not to mention my superb management),

we're back! out of the red! all the way back!

Returned to profitability, yes,

without a single penny from FEMA.

For the first time in two long years,

although not huge, bonuses shall be paid.

{they cheer and applaud]

And also ... and also ... more drum rolls, please

[more drum rolls]

I hereby present the Bosaki X4593,

the new, the very new Bosaki.

It can do anything.

Carla:
Anything, boss?

Ed, Dave, Lulu:
Anything?

Sally:
Well, almost anything.
to wit (heh heh):
[and she demonstrates]:
Arguably,
the world's speediest machine,
the Bosaki X4593
gives you
one hundred copies per minute,
 standard size,
color or black and white,
enlarging or shrinking
to the 128th power,
that's --get out your slide rules, boys and girls--
600 p.p. per hour.
And with the simple blue-button operation,
even you can work it, Lulu, dear.

Lulu:
Merci beaucoup, Boss.

May I press the button?

Sally:
No! Not yet! Don't touch it!
Er, er, then, where was I?
Yes, the heavy-duty offset stacker
will collate, staple, hole punch
--that goes without saying--
upside down, backwards and forwards,
while the digitalized multiflex camera
turn slides to transparencies,
or vice --da da-- versa. Or when we wish ...

Ed, Dave, Carla, Lulu:
Or when we wish ...

Sally:
--and we will, yes, we will--
Mr. B. will do eighty per,
eleven by seventeen
--that's A-three images, of course.
Admit it, folks, Mr B. is quite a horse!

[for a minute, as they banter, she plays the machine like a virtuoso]

Dave:
Yes, yes, Boss, it's terrific, of course,

they always are.
And, when they break down
--which they always do--
the repairman is never far.

Carla:
Don't be so cynical, Dave,
you negative wanker!
Can't you see she loves it?
And don't you appreciate your bonus?
So I say, Oh, brave new world ...

Ed:
... that hath such gizmos in't.

Sally:
Please, folks, please, I need your attention.

Lulu:
[aside:
I feel like I'm back in (God forbid!) school.]
Is this still the Christmas party?

Sally:
It is, Lulu, dear,
and this is my ... present,
so shut up --please.

Where was I? Oh, yes,

If speed is not your priority,

we can have six --six-- pick points per,

plus cover insertions

[they start to fool around, wander off a bit.]

[Sally goes faster and faster]:

Wait, wait, please don't applaud yet,

just a few

[aside: dozen] more features:

there's your magazine-type finishing,

to wit: fold, saddle-stitch and trim, or ...

C, D, E, and L:

or if we prefer ...

Sally:

Yes! the Optional Document Binder

--hereafter referred to as ODB--

which --yes!-- offers perfect binding.

And

[aside: almost]

   finally,

multi-lingual pagination,

annotation, plus our new holy "TERROR"

--i.e. "Translator of Electronic Registers"--

which insures reliability

with stock ranging from ...

Carla:
Paper, oh, paper, how I love paper!
I even love the word: "PA-PER."

Sally:
And last, but ...

C, E, D and L:
... not least, and finally ...

Sally:
to minimize possible down time...

Dave:
But there won't be any down time, Boss,
these new machines are always perfect.
There's never any down time till there ... is.
Plus, I hope you all remember
everything the Boss has just said.
for, yes, there will certainly be a quiz.

Sally:
How many times have I told you, Dave,
not to call me "Boss"? I hate it!
I'm an enlightened modern employer,

and you kids are my pretend-family.
[drinks, throws away cup]
Now, as I was about to say,
in other words, i.e.,
the Bosaki X4593 can easily
copy the phone books
of all five boroughs
in a single lunch hour.

Carla:
Really?
In forty-five minutes, Boss ... er, Sally?
(Our lunch "hour," that is.)
And yellow pages, white or both?
That makes a big difference, too.

C, E, D and L: Yes, what, exactly, do you mean? An hour?
Forty-five minutes? Yellow, white or both?

Sally
That's what I like about you all,
you're so ... alert
[aside and impertinent]
Well, er, white, of course,
and ... er... actually ... Manhattan
[aside:
surprisingly few residential listings]

Plus, I was speaking in round numbers,
referring to the ...er... proverbial "lunch hour."
I was speaking hyperbolically.
Haven't you heard of hyperbole?
"Proverbial hyperbole"?
After all, this is only a ... speech.

Carla:
"Proverbial hyperbole," indeed.
But a real lunch hour is sixty minutes,
and that's what we really need.
Consider our digestion, Sally, dear.

E, D and L: Yes, consider our digestion
A real lunch hour is what we need.

Sally: Well, not to make any rash promises,
but we can put the matter under discussion
[aside:
since I've already decided to do it]
and I'm sure we can find a way
--tied, of course, to increased productivity.

Carla: Well, that sounds very good.
"Productivity"?
No problemo.
If Bosaki works faster, so can we.

E, D and L: So can we.
Sally: Agreed, then! So.
Let's all drink to Bosaki X4593.

C, E, D andL: Here, here, here,
yes, here's to Bosaki X4593.

Dave
[aside:
I wish I could smash a bottle right over its … prow.
Luckily, though, I'm ruled by reason]

Sally:
What's that, Dave? Never mind!
 And while we're at it,
in the spirit of the season,
let's not neglect our older machines:
the printers and scanners,
the black and white copier
that earned our first dime
--or was it a nickel?--
 the fax, the phone, the laminator,
even that relic, the Selectric.
Faithful servants all,
stalwarts at their stations,
let's drink to them, too.

Ed:

Ah, yes, the dear Selectric.

[aside:

For those of our customers who,

for reasons of temperament or age,

are crazy-glued to the past,

we offer an IBM Selectric.

We wheel it out upon request,

right up to your electric wheelchair.]

C, E, D and L:

Here, here, here,

the older machines,

here's to them, too!

Carla:

Just like us, Boss, your faithful employees.

Lulu:

Speak for yourself, you "older machine."

Carla:

Don't get your knickers in a twist, dear,

you're not even a copyist, let alone a machine.

[Ed and Dave egg them on, and they start to mock-box. Then, Ed gallantly steps between them, and Carla and Ed shrug and wink at each other]

Sally:

Food, everyone, the coffee bar is now open!

C, D and E:

Ugh! two-day old Danish? We can hardly wait.

Sally:

Right. Help yourselves. It's all on me.

[She whips out shopping bags from Katz's, 3 Chinese restaurants, and Russ & Dghtr]

Surprise! Surprise! I ordered in!

[She gestures to the coffee bar in back, where a big table is revealed, covered with food. They cheer and rush back there. Lulu cranks up the music and they all dance, C. w/Ed, Sally and Dave (jealous) and Lulu in a trio. After a bit, Sally breaks away. Lulu pulls a face at being left alone with Dave, who is dancing badly and obliviously. Sally comes back around giving everyone their little red bonus envelopes. They are all pleased.]

Lulu:

 Wow! it's a fifty! I live for big tips!

[After they dance some more, Carla and Ed whisper, separate, and, then, from opposite sides of the room, sing on their cell phones, including the speech tags:]

Carla:

"You're cute, Ed. Are you gay?" she inquired.

Ed:

"Not really," he replied with a shy smile.

"Where do you live?" he asked, moving things along.

Carla:

"My place is too small," she bluntly informed him.

"Any significant others?" she asked, trying to sound casual.

Ed:

"Nothing serious, dear, how about you?"

Carla:

"Oh, several, you honey, but no long-term contracts.

But that's enough talk!

Shall we go ring the doorbells of ecstasy?"

[C & Ed re-converge, and, hands on each others' bottoms, move toward the cafe, where a couch can be seen in the back corner of the stage.]

Dave:

That fucking asshole, Ed!

Hey, maybe Carla's one, too.

Oh, God, Merry Christmas!

ACT TWO

9. Prologue: *[the gnostic poem again, a duet this time between Sally and Lulu, accompanied by images of empty interiors, law office/copy shop]*

Found a family, build a state,

The pledged event is still the same:

Matter in end will never abate

His ancient brutal claim.

Indolence is heaven's ally here,

And energy the child of hell:

The Good Man, pouring from his pitcher clear,

But brims the poisoned well.

10. *[C & E at lunch in Trinity graveyard again, reading together: the deficient views, blank walls, nature: Maine, Hamptons] [the following Spring, 2004]:*

THE DEAD WALLS/NATURE DUO

Carla:

Listen to this, Ed. I love this part: *[reads]*

Narrator:

"My chambers were upstairs,

at Number (blank) Wall Street.

At one end, they looked upon

the white wall of an interior

of a spacious sky light shaft,

penetrating the building

from top to bottom.

This view might have been considered

rather tame than otherwise ..."

Narrator, Ed and Carla:

 ... deficient in what landscape painters call 'life.'

Ed:

"Deficient," indeed!

"call life," ha ha!

Here, let me read the next part

--though I practically know it by heart... *takes book]*

Narrator:

"But, if so, the view from the other end

of my chambers offered, at least,

a contrast, if nothing more.

In that direction,

my windows commanded

an unobstructed view

of a lofty brick wall,

black by age and everlasting shade,

which wall required no spy glass

to bring out its lurking beauties,

but for the benefit of all

near-sighted spectators,

was pushed up to within

ten feet of my window panes.

Owing to the great height

of the surrounding buildings,

and my chambers

being on the second floor,

the interval between this wall and mine ...”

Narrator, Ed and Carla:

“... not a little resembled a huge square cistern.”

Carla:

"A huge square cistern!"

I love that "cistern."

The word, the image, oh, my!

Have you also considered "deserted as Petra"?

Ed:

(... a city known, by the way,

 for excessive litigation)

or "my bust of Cicero"?

Carla:

which 'you' "would

as soon have thought of turning

out of doors" as Bartleby.

And what of "the last column"

Narrator, Ed and Carla:

"of some ruined temple"

Ed:

or "Marius brooding"

Narrator, Ed and Carla:

"among the ruins of Carthage"

Ed:

"... not a little resembled a huge square cistern." *[narrator leaves]*

Why are we so taken with those words, dear?

Sort of obvious, isn't it?

"Not a little resembled"

that gaping hole two blocks from here

Carla:

... over which we've brooded for more than two years.

Ed:

Indeed! And "not a little resembled"

our own denatured lives, as well

--or yours, at least, Carla.

Look how pale you are.

Not to sound like your mother,

but I worry about you. I do.

Oh, don't start that again, Ed!

Nature, like life, is overrated.

I don't do "country." I just won't go there. *[Ed starts to protest]*

I know, don't even say it:

your parents have a place

in Maine that looks out over miles

of scenic mountains and pristine forests.

You love to watch the clouds drift by

and to swim in the pristine lake

which the locals call a "pond."

Seventeen hours in a car, just to look

at five pretty mountains? No, thanks!

Besides, summer is two months away.

Are we sure that we'll still be alive?

No, when I feel the need to see bovines,

I'll subway up to the Met and feast my eyes

on Claude Lorraines and Constables.

A single day in Maine would be, for me,

a month of tedious misery.

Ed:

Okay. So don't come to Maine.

Swelter all summer here in the city,

with this graveyard, your only oasis.

Yes, think your sad summer thoughts,

secretly hoping some rich college friend

will invite you to her time-share

in the Hamptons for the weekend.

Half a day to get there, half to get home,

and, in-between, more noise and crowds

just like the ones here --plus a free sunburn.

Carla:

No, Ed, I hate the Hamptons, too

Actually, I prefer Canal Street.

Canal Street. Ah, Canal Street!

To me that's real nature,

better than the chichi beaches,

better than that postcard landscape

you're always waxing over.

Hamptons! Maine! both are *nature mort*!

No, dear, I prefer the anthill,

the sidewalks full of vendors,

where we can get our shoes repaired

or partake of a tasty snack

for prices even paupers can afford.

No, Ed, I really do prefer Canal Street.

The cheap food, free smells,

 the garbage, the noise,

and all those truck drivers

stuck in cement-like traffic,

admiring my equipment

with their "hubba hubba's,"

while their huge tattooed arms

droop from the windows

of their belching monsters.

Ed:

Oh, dear! Are my arms too thin, Carla?

Should I get some tattoos?

Learn to drive a sixteen-wheeler?

I'll do anything you say, dear.

Carla:

You're sweet, Ed, one of the best,

but you also remind me why

I have multiple love interests.

Keep nagging, you can be replaced!

Besides, it hardly matters if ten

or twelve of you sicken and die.

Ed:

Whoa! Thanks a lot! Oh, well, I guess.

that's one way to look at love,

but, sadly, I'm a serial monogamist.

So I worry about your health, C.

That's all. I can't help it.

I'll stop loving you when I can.

Carla:

Yes, that's all. You're the best, Ed.

A sweet and funny man.

[She kisses him, they pack up and leave.]

11. the 'I prefer not to' sequence (3)

[over time, at the law office]

Bartleby *[in a singularly mild, firm voice]*:

I would prefer not to.

Narrator:

"Prefer not to"? Eh? What's that?

[aside:

Still, I should have as soon thought

 of turning my pale plaster-of-paris

 bust of Cicero out of doors]

[time passes]

Bartleby. Come here, please.

Bartleby *[in a flutelike tone]*:

What is wanted?

Narrator

[aside:

But his decision was non-negotiable.]

[more time passes, the narrator comes into the office unexpectedly on a Sunday, finds B. in dishabille.]

Narrator

[aside:

I questioned him about his life.

 Twice, there was no reply. But then ...]

Bartleby *[looking above the narrator's head at the bust of Cicero]:*

I would prefer not to. I would prefer not to.

[more time passes]

Narrator:

Bartleby, come here, please.

[no answer]

Bartleby!

Bartleby:

At present I would prefer to give no answer.

Narrator:

But be a little reasonable.

Bartleby:

At present I would prefer not to be a little reasonable.

[more time passes, the narrator brings B, who is staring at his window in his dead-wall reverie, a document]

Bartleby:

I have decided to do no more writing.

Narrator

Why? How now? What next? Do no more writing?

Bartleby:

No more.

Narrator:

And what is the reason?

Bartleby *[indifferently]:*

Do you not see the reason for yourself?

Narrator

[aside:

I looked steadfastly at him,

and perceived that his eyes

looked dull and glazed.

Instantly, it occurred to me

that his unexampled diligence

might have temporarily

impaired his vision.

I was touched.

Days went by.

Whether his eyes improved or not,

I could not say. To all appearances,

I thought they did.]

Bartleby:

I have given up copying.

Narrator:

What! Suppose your eyes

should get entirely well

- -better than ever before--

would you not copy, then?

Bartleby:

I have given up copying.

12.

[a few days later]

SECOND CONCEPTUAL ART SONG

[Everyone is busy copying. Dave finishes a pile, carries it to the counter, where he signs off on it, looks with furtive interest at the sign-off sheet, then stretches, takes out his cigarettes, puts one in his mouth, heads for the door, looks at his watch, then reluctantly turns back, puts the cigarette behind his ear and returns to the counter, where, after furtively scrutinizing the sheet again ...]

Dave *[solus]*:

Copy, copy, copy, that's all we ever do.

And to what end? To make life easier

for a bunch of bankers and shysters,

developers and architects,

not to mention the colleges, all busy

turning out people like us --our copies.

How I hate this job! I hate it so!

Our miserable status, the measly pay,

the monotony, the illegality,

it's all illegal. Call me Cassandra,

a Cassandra of copyright,

but I bet we'll all wind up in jail.

[Enter Carla, Ed and Lulu]

[aside:

Time to suck up, to hide my real feelings.]

Hi, guys! What was that again, Carla,

that conceptual piece you mentioned

the other day? "Blow-down, blow-up?"

Why not tell us more about it?

Carla:

Well, thanks for asking, Dave. As you must know,

for quite a while now, I've been making art

from political statements. Here's how I do it,

the down-and-dirty details --shhh:

[pretends to look around for spies]

I take a sound byte, verbatim,

and copy it over and over,

each time smaller and smaller,

until it's unreadable,

at which time, you could say,

the physical words mirror

the magnitude --or mini-tude--

of their content or meaning.

Dave:

And that, of course, is the "blow down."

Clever, clever!

[aside:

In actual fact, it sounds like a crock]

Carla:

Are you being sarcastic, Dave?

It's often hard to tell with you.

Dave:

No, no, I really meant ...

Lulu:

Don't mind him, Carla.

Everyone knows Dave's an asshole.

Dave:

You watch what ... bitch!

Sally *[joining them]:*

Hey! hey! No fighting in the copy shop!

Carla:

Anyway, as I was saying,

the second stage is deconstruction,

the "blow-up." Taking the same sound byte,

I find all the give-away words,

the ones that show what the evil empire

has in mind, what they're really up to.

These I enlarge, over and over,

bigger and bigger, until,

ultimately, they become posters,

thirty-six by forty-eight

in digitalized color.

Sally

[aside:

Which I hope you've been paying for!]

Carla

[to Sally, as if she has heard her]:

Which, of course, I always pay for.

Ed:

And, finally ...

Carla:

... the presentation, the "show,"

which, every morning, snow, sleet or so on,

my public eagerly awaits:

the blow-ups, the blow-downs,

the latter in descending sizes,

each copy on a separate sheet,

and the former, as mentioned,

on large, full-color posters.

Yes, every morning, they appear,

as if by magic or heavenly decree,

in multiple public places,

actually posted there, in the semi-darkness

of the New York night, by my corps

of trained assistants --that is, by me.

Dave:

Give us an example

[aside:

of this lame crap.]

Carla:

Thanks, Dave, I thought you'd never ask.

Ever since the big invasion,

I've been focussing on --what else?-- Iraq.

Take the official reaction

of the Coven of the Wicked

--er, Coalition of the Willing--

to the murder of that Shiite cleric,

Muhammad Bakr al-Hakim.

(Stale news, I know --only an example.)

According to their spokesman

(and I quote): "The Iraqi police

have our full cooperation

in this important investigation.

I pledge that the Coalition

will do everything possible

to see that the perpetrators

are brought to justice."

I used those words for a blow-down.

See the way I tiny-fied them?

[she produces the sheets, which are projected]

Ed:

That does have the true ring of falsehood.

But let me guess the "blow-up." Something like:

"The coalition are perpetrators.

Do everything to see them brought to justice."

Carla:

Very good, Ed. Exactly.

[shows them the poster, which is also projected]

Lulu:

Hey, this is like a parlor game. It's fun.

Dave:

You're such a lame brain, Lulu.

[she flips him the bird]

Sally:

No fighting in the copy shop!

But you're right, Dave! "Lame" is the word.

What's worse, this "game" is stupid.

Sophomoric! No, worse, unpatriotic!

Have you forgotten what they did to us?

Does thirty months seem so long to you?

I guess I'm too old for this kind of thing.

[stalks off]

Ed *[calling after her]*:

 A matter of opinion, surely, Boss?

 Many still dispute the connection

 between September Eleventh

and the ... oh, well, she isn't listening.

Dave:

Still, she has a point ... sort of ...

Carla:

... but she's wrong.

The connection remains unproven.

Dave:

Whatever. Hey, I'm a-political!

And I do get what you're doing.

But I have a different question

--actually, an aesthetic qualm.

According to Le Witty Chairman Sol,

 "the process is carried out blindly."

[aside:

 I read that last night to snow you]

But your "blow-ups" can hardly be said

to be "carried out blindly."

Ed:

Whoa, Dave, good point! Excellent!

If the execution were truly blind,

wouldn't the blow-up --"The Coalition

are perpetrators," et cetera--

read something more like, "Our the up to do-do"?

Or would that be too much like "da-da"?

Carla:

Hmm, there's a thought. It even has a ring.

"Our the up to do-do." It's like the I-Ching.

You guys could be conceptualists, too.

Ed:

Oh, no, not me, you know I don't do art.

Lunch, I do, with pleasure. But art? Never!

Dave:

Here, here! I don't do art, either.

Does the city really need more artists?

[aside:

In fact, I'm a second-year film student,

struggling to pay tuition and fees.

But there's no need to tell them that just yet.

A boy should keep his secrets.].

Carla:

Well, guys, it's been a real pleasure.

But enough palaver! Let's do some work.

To be continued at a later date.

Ed:

Remind me to call in sick that day.

 I'll stay in bed, reading.

Dave:

Bad dog, Ed! You're the one who's sarcastic.

[goes over to another machine to work]

Ed *[to Carla]*:

Just kidding, darling. My breath is bated.

Carla:

Yeah, thanks. But remember, Ed:

you can be replaced. Easily.

[a quick, furtive little hug. after which they exit and Dave comes back.]

Dave

[aside:

Whatever. That should do the trick.

Hi there, hello, I'm David, the prick.

Yes, I go along with them --for now!

Why, you ask? You'll find out... quick.]

13. *[at the law office, Turkey, who has been eating ginger nuts as he copies, finishes a document with a flourish]*

[afternoon again]

Turkey:

At last! Ta ra ta ra ta ra.

[The narrator peers around the corner in time to see Turkey —again with a flourish- fold the document, moisten and slap a ginger nut down on it, then grind it in as if to seal the document, before realizing his mistake and looking abashed]

Narrator:

But but but ...

Turkey:

With submission, sir, it was generous

of me to find you in stationery

on my own account.

[Flabbergasted, the narrator retreats to his cubicle. Turkey regards the ginger nut seal with wonder, while Nippers shakes his head and quietly goes on copying.]

14. *[At the copy shop, Ed is working. Carla, working nearby, listens with amusement]*

[a few days later]

THE COPYCAT SONG

[an odd sort of love duet]

Ed:

Do you know, Carla, dear, I've been thinking ...

Carla:

Oh?

Ed *[performing for her, an aria]:*

Yes, on this matter of copying,

copying, yes, copying, copying:

consider the implications.

Imitation, as Lord Byron said,

is the sincerest form of flattery.

Copying, by that name, smells sweet:

"Copy"? yes, yes, "plagiarize?" no, no,

and never never never "cheat."

Hey, writers, scholars, too,

have robbed the quick and dead.

Did Plutarch or Suetonious threaten to sue?

No, in art, as it is in life,

the point is to get ahead.

Fair is fair, it's open season

in commerce as it is in art.

Carla:

Yes, it's true, we copy without question,

with total lack of discrimination,

everything from dry legal briefs

to seriously salacious selections.

Ed and Carla:

Yes, we copy everything

Ed:

from single sheets

Carla:

to novels of profundity and weight.

Ed:

And, what's more

Carla:

--what's much more--

Ed:

whether the copy is new or old

Carla:

the author, quick or cold

Ed:

we never hesitate

Carla:

we never stop to worry

Ed:

about the so-called "laws

Carla:

 of intellectual property."

Ed:

For, frankly, my dear, who gives a damn!

Carla:

We're much too busy for such legal spam.

[They now sing to the audience, pleading their case]

Ed and Carla:

Why, it's a practical matter, you see.

Carla:

For suppose we were more fastidious?

Ed:

The customers would go someplace else,

Carla:

and within two or three months

Ed:

this desirable commercial space,

Carla:

eleven-thousand square feet,

Ed:

suitable for retail or wholesale,

Carla:

would be ... available

Ed:

for lease

Carla:

with option to sell.

Ed:

As for us? the boss, plus four employees?

Ed and Carla:

Like garbage, we're out on the street.

Ed:

Yes, here in the copy shop,

Carla:

the laws of intellectual property

Ed:

are certainly moot

Ed and Carla:

--though (of course) meet.

And, finally (to wax operatic):

Carla:

Cosi fan tutte,

Ed:

"the way of the world."

Carla:

where everyone

Ed and Carla:

every boy and girl

Carla:

parrots ideas

Ed:

and opinions

Carla:

and shops around for beauty.

Ed and Carla:

So copy copy copy, never stop:

that's the law of the copy shop.

[They hug, then wander off, still laughing and talking]

15. *[narrator moves, hears B evicted, then how B. finally arrested]*

[over some time]

Narrator:

Eventually, the conclusion became inevitable: I asked him to leave: "Will you or will you not quit me?" He, of course, preferred not to quit me. Inevitable: since he will not quit me, I must quit him. But that was not the end of it.

In my new quarters, I thought all was going well, until, one day, a perturbed-looking stranger appeared. "Are you the person who recently occupied quarters at Number (blank) Wall Street?" He proved to be a lawyer: "You are responsible for the man you left there. He refuses to leave." "I shall settle him, then --good morning, sir."

Postponing the inevitable, I received a note from the new landlord, informing me that the writer had sent to the police and had Bartleby removed to the Tombs as a vagrant. At first I was indignant; but, at last almost ... approved.

16. *[Dave, apparently alone in the shop late at night, reading from two books, Carla's copy of "Bartleby" and Jonathan Edwards' "A Careful and Strict Inquiry into Prevailing Notions of the Freedom of the Will."]*

[very late at night]

Dave:

Carla must have left this.

[sniffs Melville volume]

Mmm. Oh. Oh.

[sighs, pulls himself together, reads from Melville]

"Some days now passed, during which at leisure intervals I looked a little into 'Edwards on the Will' and 'Priestly on Necessity'"

[from Edwards]

... Let's see: Edwards: "A Careful and Strict Inquiry into Prevailing Notions of the Freedom of the Will." What a mouthful!

"An act of the will is the same as an act of choosing, or choice."

No kidding!

"It is the glory and greatness of the Divine Sovereign, that his Will is determined by his own infinite, all-sufficient wisdom."

Ah ha, I get it: since we're made in God's image, so must our wills be created in the image of his. Huh! where's the "freedom" there?! Totally bogus.

[drops Edwards, picks up Melville]

Back to Melville:

"Gradually I slipped into the feeling that these troubles of mine, touching the scrivener, had been all predestinated from eternity, and Bartleby was billeted upon me for some mysterious purpose of an all-wise Providence, which was not for a mere mortal like me to fathom."

[slams the book shut]

Yeah, right! People find solace where they can.

But that's not how I see it. And neither,

I bet, does Carla or her hero, Bartleby.

 [as he runs around, vandalizing the machines, Lulu and GN appear from the back and look on, astonished]

No, I'm the one who's doing this.

Sparked by anger, greed, desire for revenge,

by my character, personality

--whatever-- I'm still the agent, the one

who's doing this. My act belongs to me.

[breaking several bottles over the Bosaki]

And here's to Bosaki X4593!

Lulu *[aside, to GN]:*

Holy tamales! He's flipped his lid.

GN *[to Lulu]:*

Flipped his ...? I'd say he's gone loony.

Dave:

I -- yes, I, not my id, not my anger--

have wanted to do this for months.

Unlike, say, Lulu, a creature of impulse,

[Lulu flinches, hides for a moment]

whose "choices" resemble compulsions

I consider. I decide. And I act.

Ha ha! Whee! Yes! Ah! Yes! This feels so good!

Lulu:

Maybe we should try to stop him.

GN:

I don't think so. He seems dangerous.

Anyway, it's too late, he's broke everything.

Dave:

[scooping the cash from the register]:

And here's a little something for tuition.

My conscience is now in remission.

"Hey, writers, scholars, too,

have robbed the quick and dead."

Well said, Mister Lover-Boy, Mister Ed!

And so the copy shop does its bit

for the arts and higher education,

supporting poor film-makers --like me!

Let's see...

[quickly counts the money]

a whole half-credit at NYU.

[calming down]

Some day, investigators of the mind

will pinpoint the site where our impulses

are sorted, weighed, and acted upon.

The site will, itself, remain autonomous.

Yes, I'm the one who has done this.

My mind to me a magic kingdom is.

[He turns out the lights and, laughing, leaves. GN and Lulu peep out from rear.]

ACT THREE

17. [**Third Prologue**, *this time showing dead walls, ruins --Petra,
Carthage, Rome, Ground Zero-- a trio sung by Carla, Ed and Nippers]*

Found a family, build a state,

The pledged event is still the same:

Matter in end will never abate

His ancient brutal claim.

Indolence is heaven's ally here,

And energy the child of hell:

The Good Man, pouring from his pitcher clear

 But brims the poisoned well.

18.*Act Two [the copy shop where Ed and Carla arrive at work to find
Sally and Dave already looking over the chaos. Lulu watches furtively
from the back]*

[still Spring, 2004, morning after vandalism scene]

Sally:

We're finished, ruined, history.

Sixteen-hundred dollars missing,

plus the damage to the machines

--my machines, my lovely machines--

in amounts still-to-be calculated,

probably hundreds-of-thousands,

which will cause our insurance rates

to soar again --not to mention down time.

My machines! My poor, beautiful machines!

We're finished, ruined, history.

Ed:

Have you called the police yet, Boss? How awful!

Sally:

The police never solve these "victimless" crimes.

We'll keep it in the family, if we can.

Ed:

"Victimless?" I'd say we're all the victims.

Carla:

But who did this? Did someone break in?

Dave:

No signs of forced entry, an inside job.

Lulu

[aside:

Right! Inside your demented brain]

Dave:

Why don't we search all the lockers?

Let's get to the bottom of this!

Lulu

[aside:

Liar! At the "bottom of this" is you!]

Sally:

Let's start with the facts. Who closed up last night?

[looks at Carla]

It was you, Carla, wasn't it?

Carla:

Well, yes, but when I left at eleven ...

Dave:

Anyhow, we all have the keys.

Hey, I'm the one who opened this morning.

Lulu *[running in]:*

I can't take any more of this bullshit.

[points to Dave]

He did it! I saw him! You hypocrite!

Dave:

Be careful, Lulu, dear! I'll sue your ass!

Lulu:

Sue away, dick head. I saw you.

Besides, I have wit ... a witness.

Sally, Ed, Dave, Carla:

A witness?!

Lulu:

Well, yes, except he isn't ... here right now.

Sally:

Who is he?

And what was he doing here last night?

Lulu:

Well, actually ...

Dave:

... he doesn't exist.

Everyone knows she has it in for me.

[Lulu and Dave have to be kept apart.]

Sally:

Whoa. Simmer down. Let's do this calmly.

Let's start at the beginning. Now, Lulu ...

[fade, exit all, then enter Ginger Nut]

Ginger Nut:

A "witness" from the eighteen-fifties ...

Talk about unreliable!

"Inadmissible evidence!"

"Objection sustained!"

But never mind! Lulu will find a way.

[GN exits]

19. *[shortly after the narrator has learned that B is in The Tombs]*

[lights up on an empty walled space, jail yard. The narrator creeps up to a slumped Bartleby, facing a high wall from which he never turns]

Narrator:

Bartleby!

Bartleby:

I know you.

And I have nothing to say to you.

Narrator:

It was not I that brought you here,

and, to you, it should not be so vile a place.

Look, there is the sky, and here is the grass.

Bartleby:

I know where I am.

[lights down on Bartleby, up on the Grub Man]

Grub Man:

Is that your friend?

Narrator:

Yes.

Grub Man:

Does he want to starve? If he does,

let him live on the prison fare, that's all.

Narrator:

Who are you?

Grub Man:

I am the grub man.

Such gentlemen as have friends here

hire me to provide them

with something good to eat.

Narrator *[slipping him some money]:*

Is that so? Then, I want you to give

particular attention to my friend there.

Let him have the best dinner you can get,

and be as polite to him as possible.

Grub Man:

Introduce me, then, will you?

[lights up on Bartleby. Grub Man bows.]

Your sarvant, sir, your sarvant.

Narrator:

Bartleby, this is a friend.

You will find him very useful.

Grub Man:

Hope you find it pleasant here, friend.

Nice grounds, cool apartments.

What will you have for dinner today?

Bartleby:

I prefer not to dine today.

It would disagree with me:

I am unused to dinners.

Grub Man *[astonished]:*

How's this? He's odd, ain't he?

Narrator:

I think he's a little deranged.

[lights down on Bartleby and the Grub Man]

20. *[a few minutes after last copy shop sequence.]*

Sally *(alone)*:

Sixteen-hundred bucks. I thought I knew her.

But there was all that political crap

and all those expensive posters,

for which, of course, she says she paid.

No, I shouldn't have looked the other way.

And to smash all my beautiful machines …

[Enter Carla.]

Carla:

I'm really sorry, boss, that ... this has happened.

We're all the victims of this "victimless" crime.

It's terrible for everyone. I'm sorry.

Sally:

You should be sorry, dear, very sorry,

because the evidence points to you.

Carla:

What! No way! What are you talking about?

Sally:

Well, you did the register last night,

and you also counted the clicks.

Sixteen-hundred dollars missing.

As for the machines, I can't imagine

what you were thinking. The rage! All that rage!

Carla:

Come on, boss, I'm not an angry person.

What's happened to your common sense?

The clicks? the cash? They matched when I checked them.

Someone must have taken the money af ...

[Sally holds up a handful of cash]

Sally:

That's enough! Let's cut the crap!

Sorry, but I found this in your locker.

Four hundred-dollars. Where's the rest?

Carla:

You searched my locker. What a load of shit!

I was saving that money for ... never mind!

What a load of shit! She searched my locker.

I can't get over it, I can't believe it.

Sally:

Not just ...er... yours, we searched everyone's,

but this is all we found. Can you account ...

Carla:

What! Can I "account" for my own money?

Fuck you, Sally! I won't "account" for it.

I won't "account" for anything.

I can't believe …

Sally:

Well, then, you leave me no choice.

I won't call the police, but you'll have to…

Carla:

Whatever. I don't care. Do what you please!

[she storms out, leaving Sally, sad]

Sally:

What a sad day! I thought I knew her.

[fade]

21. *[The Narrator returns to The Tombs. Joined by the Grub Man, he realizes B is dead.]*

[a few days later]

Narrator:

Some few days passed, and I returned. The yard was entirely quiet. The surrounding walls, of amazing thickness, kept off all sounds. The Egyptian character of the masonry weighed upon me with its

gloom. But a soft imprisoned turf grew underfoot. The heart of the
eternal pyramids, it seemed, wherein, by some strange magic,
through the clefts, grass-seed, dropped by birds, had sprung.

[lights up on the jail yard, Bartleby's corpse, as it is about to be described]

Strangely huddled at the base of the wall,

his knees drawn up, and lying on his side,

his head touching the cold stones,

I saw the wasted Bartleby.

But nothing stirred.

I paused;

then went close up to him;

stooped over,

and saw that his eyes were open.

Otherwise he seemed profoundly sleeping.

*[he reaches down and touches Barleby's hand, shivers, lights up on the
Grub Man]*

Grub Man:

Eh, he's asleep, ain't he?

Narrator:

With kings and counselors.

22. *[Sally has fired Carla, Lulu repeats that she has a witness, but when GN appears, Sally repeats what he feared: an unreliable witness. Lulu and GN tell Ed what happened. He is less skeptical.]*

[a few days after last copy shop scene]

Sally:

To get the insurance money,

I filed a police report, after all.

Oh, they went through the motions

--the case is open, but, of course, unsolved.

Meanwhile, I know the truth. So I've fired her,

but called it a "lay-off" --I know, I'm soft.

My final, sad act as Manager.

Five long years, building this business,

including the last, horrid thirty months,

the aftermath of disaster.

Why, I kept those three kids employed

when business had slowed to nothing,

even hired Lulu, created a job

--the coffee bar, ha! just what we needed!

Yes, for almost a thousand days now,

I've kept this place going. At first,

just hanging on, we printed leaflets

for the families of the missing,

and designed inspirational posters

like that one that won the prize:

a fireman's hat, his ax, the dog, the gloves

--everything, but the man, himself.

That was the winner. Whose idea was it?

Carla's, of course! With Ed and Dave's graphics.

And I thought, yes, I thought that I knew her.

[enter Lulu, leading an uneasy GN]

Sally

Oh, no, not him again, the boyfriend,

the unreliable witness!

Lulu:

Come on, Sally. Won't you even listen?

Sally:

Actually, I have an appointment, dear.

If you need anything, talk to Ed.

As of today, he's Acting Manager.

[aside:

And, as for me, I'll be starting a new

--and a much better-- job.] Exits.

[Enter Ed, hurrying past]

Lulu:

Ed, please, won't *you* listen to us?

Ed:

I've heard it second-hand, but go ahead.

Is this the witness? How do you do?

Make it quick, please. I have a lot of work.

Ginger Nut:

How d'you do, sir? I was here that night,

visiting Miss Lucy, my friend.

We saw everything, we heard it, too..

Ed [becoming interested]:

Oh? Well, then, begin at the beginning.

Lulu:

Thanks, Ed, you won't be sorry.

See, we were hanging out in back,

it must have been after midnight.

Then, we heard this crazy laughter

and the sound of breaking glass.

It sounded like Halloween, or something.

We peeped out. It was Dave! He was insane!

And then …

[fade]

23. *[Ed is reading an e-mail, which we simultaneously see Dave gleefully composing]*

[a few days later]

Ed & Dave:

"Dear Ed: So, regretfully, I must resign.

A slot has opened in a famous class

with a famous director, a chance

too good to resist, especially

since, by coincidence, a small bequest

from an old aunt will just about cover the cost.

So give my best to everyone,

especially, of course, Carla and Lulu,

not to mention Sally, the boss.

Oh, and best to you, too, Ed. Of course. Ta. Dave.”

Ed:

“A small bequest from the cash register,”

he means. The dirty bastard! Good riddance!

[enter Carla, wearing nice Spring clothes, in a hurry]

Carla:

Congrats, Edward, couldn’t happen to a ...

I hear she made you Manager.

Ed:

“Acting” --which is exactly what I am,

a make-believe, virtual manager.

But here --she also left something for you.

[he gives her an envelope, in which she finds four bills]

Carla:

Oh, wow! It's my four-hundred bucks!

She gave them back, after all! But what did ...

Ed [*not meeting her eyes, because he is lying*]:

She didn't say anything, just left it.

[*aside:*

Call it a parting love token:

This way I know you won't refuse]

Carla:

Well, this is really terrific.

And don't be so self-effacing!

I know you'll grow into the job.

[*an awkward little pause*]

So. Ed. Anything else? Not that this is ...

Ed:

[*jumps up, takes her hands*]

Don't even say it! Please! Don't say that word!

You're rehired, darling, the authority's mine.

Don't leave! I want to be with you all the time.

Carla:

Oh, Ed, you're so sweet. We'll get together,

don't worry. But I've given it some thought.

Sally agreed to say she laid me off,

which means I can collect Unemployment.

Right now, that's the better option. See,

I got some good news today, a phone call

from an East Village gallery:

a two-person show in the middle of June.

Ed:

[releases her hands]

That's wonderful, C.! Congratulations!

Wow! We're both headed for riches and fame!

[grabs her hands again]

But why not stay on here, too? Keep working

to pay for the groceries, rent and paint.

I'll let you do those blow-ups … at cost!

I swear! I'll be a benign employer.

Carla:

Of course you will, Ed, I know that.

But to coin a phrase, my sweetheart ...

Ed and Carla:

I prefer not to.

Ed:

How did I know that was coming?

But ...

Carla:

... goodbye for the moment, Ed.

I'll call, we'll have coffee, we'll read together.

[kisses him, runs out, enter Lulu from back]

Lulu:

Hey, Boss --can I call you that now?

We need to go over those orders.

But wasn't that Carla? Is she ...

Ed:

She isn't.

She just got a show, she's not coming back,

she wants to be a full-time artist.

Lulu:

Well, I certainly wish her the best.

But how sad, Ed --for you, for us. Won't she ...

Ed:

I hope she doesn't hate this place.

She says she'll come visit ...

[gathers himself]

but life goes on!

I have some new ideas --involving you.

How would you like to be a copyist?

And, if so, do you think your friend, Ginger,

could double up with his messenger job?

No offense, Lulu, but I've realized

we could save quite a bit of money

by cutting the coffee-bar hours.

Lulu:

Yes, and yes, to everything! you're right!

Oh, Ed, I'm so thrilled! You won't be sorry.

This shows you're management material.

As for Ginger, he'll be the coffee boy

--man-- I'm sure he can jing --juggle his hours

[aside:

not to mention his centuries]

Ed:

Great, then, that's settled. Slap hands on the deal.

[they spit on their hands and slap five]

Lulu:

I'll get the order forms, boss, just a sec.

[Ed rests his head on his hands on the Bosaki, looking sad. Fade]

24. Postlogue: *[C's room, which is plastered with her posters. C. is having the show soon, and is preparing a piece for it, the faux resume. Narrator comes to C's room. They sing "Ah B, Ah, Humanity" duet. She*

leaves for the Job Center, and he sits on her bed in silence w/ his (beaver)
top hat in his hands]

[early June, 2004]

Carla *[at work on a poster]:*

Ah! finally! the faux resume! done!

the piece de resistance for my show!

When people move on, it's good to take stock.

My real vita, of course, is very sad:

dog walker (multiple),

camp counselor (day),

 and --sigh!-- copy-shop factotum,

my last and best "position" --pitiful!

[works away].

Let's see, how shall I present this? Ah, yes!

A torn page from an artist's resume,

found on the floor of a ... copy shop.

Yes, a torn page. Page Two,

 items forty-seven to sixty-four.

[as the items are read, they can be added to a large projected poster,
perhaps scrolled down]

"Forty-seven: A.D.A. Aid to Dependent Artists.

Grant (restricted). New York City

Department of Social Services." Hmm.

That reminds me ...

[looks at watch, then works on for a while, music playing]

fifty-two: "Drawing accepted to group show.

Owner deceased. Trianon Gallery."

[aside:

Get it? "try anon." A pun.]

[works on]

fifty-seven., the chicken joke:

"Anticipated one-person show: Chicken Space

(a co-op)"

[aside:

ha ha, a chicken "co-oop."

"Gallery Disbanded."

{aside: or should I say, "Artist Plucked."]

This next one is esoteric,

"Seven paintings accepted,

Three-person show,

Fischer-Laufer Gallery,

 Lease not renewed."

[aside:

"Fischer-Laufer!" Catch that, folks?

"seven paintings"?

"loaves and fishes"?

" three-person show"?

May their lease be resurrected! Amen.

[works on]

Sixty-one: "Guten-Luks Gallery: work lost."

Sixty-Two: "Constance Cropper: incorrectly hung."

Sixty-three: "Hooper-Greenbach:

Work confiscated by I.R.S."

[works on]

And, finally, the last one.

How sad, how ... forlorn.

"telephone call contemplated

to the Ars Longha Gallery."

Ah, me! the joys of self-pity!

But!... all is forgiven, I have a show!

Meanwhile, I also have an appointment

[looks at watch again]

... in forty-seven minutes

at the (quote) "Downtown Job Center"

--they've banned the word "Unemployment."

[She stretches, sighs, drinks from a mug, runs behind a curtain,
returns dressed to go out --a summery outfit-- looks at her watch
again, sits down carefully on the bed, begins to read]

...one little item of rumor, which came to my ear a few months after
the scrivener's decease --how true it is I cannot tell-- that Bartleby
had been a subordinate clerk in the Dead Letter office at
Washington, from which he had suddenly been removed by a change
in the administration. Dead letters! Does it not sound like dead men?
Continually handling these dead letters and assorting them for the
flames?

[enter Narrator, wearing light frock coat and beaver top hat]

Narrator:

Sometimes he takes a ring from out the flames

--the finger it was meant for, perhaps,

molders in the grave;

Carla:

.. a bank-note sent in swiftest charity

Narrator:

--he whom it would relieve

nor eats nor hungers any more

Carla:

...pardon for those who died despairing

Narrator:

... hope for those who died unhoping

Carla:

... good tidings for those who died

Narrator:

stifled by unrelieved calamities

Carla:

On errands of life

Narrator:

these letters speed to death.

Carla and Narrator:

Ah, Bartleby! Ah, humanity!

[They look at each other. Carla touches up in front of the mirror,
then leaves. Narrator sits down on the bed in silence w/ hat in his
hands.]

Author's Note:

Carla… remains a draft-libretto in search of a composer. In its
present form, it is a kitchen-sink draft, the assumption being that
librettist and composer will pick-and-choose as they shape the opera.

Selling a Car: Eleanor's Story

Manhattan, Brooklyn & Queens, 2003

-1-

Not that my husband, Bob, is a bad guy, or anything. Actually, if you've read "Buying a Car," his New York picaresque set in the dog days of the Beame administration, I'm sure you'll agree that, in a silly sort of way, he's a sweetheart. This time, instead of buying a car, Bob and I have just finished selling one. Twenty-eight years later, his quirks —the guilty little jokes, and so on-- have not gone away. In fact, he's so upset about how we sold the car that he can't allow himself the pleasure of writing this story.

"Why don't you write the damn thing, yourself?"

I must admit that this outburst was triggered by my teasing. I shrugged my shoulders, saying nothing. Surprise, Bob!

The Camry, as you may know, is the world's most popular used car. Our family now owned two of them, and we decided we could manage with one. Bob made some noises about cutting needless expenses and harmful emissions, but the real reason was that we wanted to give Lisa, our daughter (age 23), a present, a big chunk of cash --which she needed, and we couldn't afford to give her. Her dad thought that selling the car and giving her the money would be a tactful way to avoid insulting Lise's independence. As I said, Bob is sweet. And he likes to think of himself as subtle. (BTW, Lise was born in 1980, or as Bob still jokes, "TC. 3" --that is, the third year in which we owned the Toyota Corolla.)

The car in question: a 1993 Toyota Camry DX four-door sedan; white, with blue seats; "loaded" (air, cassette, four new tires, anti-lock brakes, power everything); mileage, below 44K; asking price, 6K; book value (from dealer, with warranty), $6,225. Our other Camry is also a 1993, but it has higher mileage and, hence, lower book value.

If Bob was so sensitive about Lisa's feelings of independence, why didn't he just let her sell the car, herself? Well, the main reason was that he wanted to play the car game again. Also, partly a reason and partly a justification, was that he had more experience, more "savvy," than she did. (Of course I didn't say this, but I think our little girl is probably ten times as street-wise as her dad.)

Bob also had the time. The car-selling process transpired in June, when Lisa was very busy (as an assistant teacher in a nursery school), whereas Bob was already on summer vacation from *his* teaching job -- the same one as in 1975: still teaching English at Brooklyn Community College, Ebbets Field campus. But he was no longer with SMILE, that program having been scrapped during the 1980's, along with a host of other desperation measures from the '70's. Bob had been mainstreamed into the regular English Department, and he had since risen through the ranks to Associate Professor, with tenure (and a tonsure).

Like Lise, I was also very busy, just then, but I had my own reasons for participating in the process. The first was curiosity, left over from our adventures as a young car-buying couple twenty-eight years before. A second reason was protective: my man wasn't getting any younger (few people do), and I wasn't sure he could still cut it out there on the streets.

Bob offered one final sweet, and possibly even valid, reason for taking the initiative. "Lisa has a sentimental attachment to her car. She wouldn't be objective about selling it." Yeah, right!

The car was one of two means of transportation --the other being an old bicycle-- given to her by Bob 's mom in 1997, when diminished vision and balance precluded further driving or pedaling. (She died in early 1998.) As it happened, Lise wound up parting with her two sentimental modes of transportation almost simultaneously, for around the time we finally sold the car, someone stole the bike. She had been parking it for about a week --chained, of course-- in an areaway in front of her building in a so-so Brooklyn neighborhood. This may not have been wise, but there was little choice, because she had just moved to a place where there was no storage space for bikes.

All three events --the move, the sale, and the theft-- took place in June, almost two months ago. I'm writing this account —or starting to-- to help fill my quiet two-week vacation at our summerhouse in the Catskills. Stoic Bob is stuck in the sweltering city, holed up at the public library working on a major article that he hopes will remove the "Associate" from his title.

For about seven years, he --we-- had been inactive in the used car-buying field. It had been that long since we bought our other Camry, a sand-colored four-door sedan, from a Mrs. Lillian Borowitz, a recently widowed seventy-something who lived in one of those famous, but ordinary, houses built in Levittown, Long Island right after World War II. I had heard about this car from a colleague (now dead) who knew Mrs. B. from I-forget-where. Bob had jumped at the chance to buy this car, even though it had cheated him of the chance to go off on some wild goose chases before allowing himself the triumph of buying another good used car.

I'm skipping over three or four cars here, and over twenty years. If Bob were writing the story, you'd probably hear in detail about each of these cars, but, believe me, they were acquired through commonplace, uninteresting processes. Like many men, my husband is into self-dramatization.

Mrs. Borowitz's Camry had been a supremely easy buy of a supremely good car: mileage, in the low sixties, price, somewhere in the high three thousands. (We have more money now, so who's counting?) The transaction, consummated over cookies and seltzer at the widow's kitchen table, had a strong family feeling. I liked Mrs. Borowitz, although she was nothing like my mother (R.I.P.) —or Bob's, for that matter (R.I.P., too).

As it happened, from Mrs. B's kitchen window, one could look out across a sunny field to the jail where Amy Fisher, the infamous teen-age mistress of that car mechanic whose name sounds like "Butt Fuck," was incarcerated for trying to kill Mrs. B.F. Don't ask me why I include this detail. It's very Bob-like, isn't it?

-2-

The opening of "Selling a Car" will be narrated from the point of view of an interested by-stander --me. I stood by as Bob made his first moves to sell Lise's Camry. By now, his car-dealing skills were almost rusted through. His first false move was taking out an expensive ($69) ad in *The New York Times*. To be honest, I saw no reason to oppose this move. But what did I know?

As the days passed and almost no one called, I observed that all the other automotive ads in *The Times* were for very expensive, "luxury" cars: our asking price was the lowest by several thousand dollars. It was also in this ad that Bob used the clever phrase, "Grandmother Car," which was mentioned by one of the few people who saw the ad and did call, although even he did not ask to see the car.

A week later, when the ad in *The Times* expired, after some gentle prompting, he took out a second, free one in *Loot*, an online marketplace that Lise told us some of her friends used. Since Bob is a big boy, I once again let him proceed unguided, although I was starting to have qualms. They quickly proved justified: unfortunately, he had failed to realize that he had placed the ad in *Loot*, Great Britain,

277

not U.S. *Loot.* That the asking-price option on the (electronic) form was in pounds, not dollars, did give him pause, but the management of *Loot* never answered his e-mail query, and the ad just appeared. Of course, there were no calls from England, Scotland or Wales, but I bet a lot of Brits were amused. I can picture them chuckling over their pies and their pints.

A week passed, during which we kept assuring each other that there was no hurry. There really wasn't. Then, at my prompting, Bob finally advertised the "Grandmother Car" where he should have in the first place, in a widely read local paper, *Newsday.* Even from that source, we initially got only a trickle of replies.

"Grandmother Car." "Mother's Curse" would have been more like it! When the car was about four or five years old, Bob, his mother, and I had been sightseeing in the Everglades a few days after a hurricane. (Lisa was visiting colleges in the Midwest with a friend and her parents.) When he was too stubborn to turn around, even after the water began lapping at the wheel tops, his mother, who had been stewing in the back seat, suddenly piped up.

"You wouldn't keep going if this was *your* car, Robert."

She was probably right. So many interesting birds and animals had taken refuge up on the road that he was oblivious to the fast-rising water. As for me, I just watched, playing the role of bemused spectator that I often played when forced to spend a few days in the company of Bob's mom. Not to speak ill of the dead, but she was a narrow-minded, penny-pinching old widow whose only redeeming feature was that she was a treasure trove of amusing malapropisms. Sorry, no examples --even I have a vestigial, superstitious respect for the dead.

Had New York City changed much over the twenty-eight years since *Buying a Car?* Of course, it had. The dance between car buyers and sellers seemed about the same, except for dollar amounts (add a zero), but, to mention only a few other obvious changes, the city had clawed its way out of its financial sinkhole, in part by becoming "wired," and had since gone through a dot-com boom and semi-bust. Mushroom millionaires had provided one basis, or pretext, for destroying the affordable housing market. There had also been a mushrooming of immigrants, making some neighborhoods as "multicultural" as any places on earth. (Did that word even exist in 1975?) The influx of these newcomers, as it turns out, has also provided me with the basis for my second career.

Has the clever reader glommed onto the fact that I'm now a social worker? About ten years ago, I fled the design rat race and went back to school for an MSW. I'm currently Assistant Director of a private agency that helps new immigrants find jobs and housing. If you wanted to be polite, you could say we "supplement" the efforts of city agencies. The truth is that we do their jobs while they sit on their you-know-what's, filling out forms and counting the years until they will be getting pensions larger than our salaries.

New car buyers, new sellers. To anticipate, Bob and I wound up selling the car to Mark, a Jewish shoemaker whose family moved here from Kazakhstan several years ago. As Bob observed after the initial telephone inquiry, a slang meaning of "mark" is "sucker." The phrase "a marked man" also occurred to me. In the interests of full disclosure, the reader should note that, to my knowledge, neither Mark nor any member of his extremely large, complicated extended family has had dealings of any kind with my agency.

"Thanks for doing this, Mom and Dad," said Lisa, after the car had been sold. We were both on the phone with her.

"Don't thank us yet, Lise," Bob replied. "This may turn into one of those central Asian blood feuds that last for generations."

"Do Kazakhstani *Jews* have blood feuds?"

"I can't imagine, dear," I chimed in, from the other line. "The 'blood feud' is your father's idea."

As even those who read solely for mindless pleasure must have inferred by now, Lisa's car was not the perfect driving machine we were claiming it was. Its single, but serious, flaw was that, ever since the Everglades escapade, it stalled in damp weather --badly. To my embarrassment, fully aware of the flaw, I let Bob talk me into sliding down the slippery slope with him. In recounting his previous automotive adventures, Bob had mentioned that the Meltzer-mobile also occasionally stalled. The difference was that she had told him and Ruth (his ex-).

"Ellie, Ellie," he said, in that tone that says it all, when I worried aloud about the stalling. "If we tell people, we'll never sell the car. Besides, it hardly ever stalls. It's such a good car, otherwise, and our price is low –below book."

"Well, yes, fifty dollars below 'book,' for this model, for this year. But their price is for a car in 'excellent' condition."

"Well, so is this one –except for the stalling."

But I can't put all the blame on him. Without fouling my own nest, have you ever noticed that, when there's dirty work to be done, even aggressive women often go limp?

Why did Bob and I sin? Just as the city was different, so were we. Maybe, we had simply changed places with the sellers of whom we had once been so wary. I can also safely say that, in the 1970's, he had no daughter, so there was no one to whom he wanted to give several thousand dollars, preferably of someone else's money. Certainly, now that we were, as Bob's mom would have said, "comfortable," our cheating —to call it by its proper name-- can only be compared hypothetically to the behavior of his earlier selves, who needed money, but did not cheat anyone.

Some things, however, had stayed very much the same over the passing decades, such as the fears about the process by which used cars and money change hands. In "Buying a Car," Bob may have been funnier about these fears, but I shared them. Of course, this time *they* would come to *us*, but where should the drop take place? Although the city had supposedly grown safer, setting the car-selling process in motion triggered all the old fears --thieves, murderers, crazies. Bob's favorite new fantasy was the use of torture (one fingernail at a time) to make us sign over the Title. Perhaps, the villains would torture each of us in the presence of the other. If they were smart, they would start with me, since I would sign the second I spotted the pincers. I'm vain about my nails.

As we prepared the *Newsday* ad, we first thought of selling the car from my brother's house, in Suffolk County, but we decided this would be an imposition on him, and inconvenient for us. Next, we thought of our own neighborhood, Greenwich Village. (How far up in the world we had moved!) But, if we opted for the Village, when prospective buyers asked to test-drive the car, the traffic might make it impossible to creep forward more than a few feet at a time. And Bob, whose job it would be, we agreed, to park and re-park the car if we tried to sell it in the Village, would be reluctant to surrender a parking space without first demanding a big deposit. (Our own car is garaged. We use it mostly when we go out of town.)

After a lot of back and forth over this detail, we finally settled on Carroll Gardens, Brooklyn, where, until her subsequent move, Lisa had been renting a small apartment on a shady street, down the block from a big, well-used park. This neighborhood is legendary for the absence of unorganized crime. "Carroll Gardens": it sounds so bucolic and old-fashioned --which, in some ways, it was. Weather permitting, in Carroll Gardens, some elderly people still sat outdoors all day, either in the park, or on ancient folding chairs in front of the brownstones, grocery stores and laundromats. It is the kind of neighborhood where a young woman like my daughter could walk the several blocks from the subway to her building in the middle of the night with (perhaps exaggerated) confidence that no harm would befall her. It was also relatively easy to park in Carroll Gardens.

What we actually decided was to advertise our phone number in Manhattan, with the intention of meeting the buyers in Carroll Gardens. Since we expected people to share our (perhaps dubious) perception of "212" locales as safer than "718" ones, was this already slightly disingenuous?

In the event, the first few *Newsday* callers all wanted to rendezvous in Manhattan, and in retrospect Bob's refusal may seem like a vestige of conscience. For ethical uprightness, you could say, he substituted logistical inflexibility.

After a few days, however, came two pairs of promising clients who were willing to rendezvous in Brooklyn. The first was a gentle Asian man named Tommy, who spoke little English, and the man who had made the call for him, his knowledgeable, English-speaking Latino friend, Name-Forgotten, who confessed to being a Toyota dealer. Nice enough guys, they were from (safe) Queens.

As we stood with them on the sidewalk on one of those lovely, golden, early June evenings, I thought that, with its new wash-and-wax job, the car looked pretty good. But, as Tommy's friend pointed out, white cars that have baked for several years in the Florida sunshine never look all that good. Even as he said this, the car's finish grew duller, and some areas of slight discoloration appeared. His point about Florida cars may have been true, and it was certainly alarming, but I also think he might just have been trying to cheapen the car. The game was on!

I confess that dealing, if not from the bottom of the deck, then at least from the middle, gave the game an edge --for both of us. My heart was beating fast. Bob's face was flushed, and he spoke even louder than usual.

Tommy cautiously drove us around the neighborhood, and, when we were back in our original parking space, his friend gave the car a pretty good going over. As he did so, I proudly remembered some of the old tricks Bob had learned from that car-buying pamphlet twenty-eight years ago, which he had subsequently shown to me: sighting along each side to detect a bent chassis (accident), inspecting the brake pedal and driver's side door handle (true mileage), noting the color of the smoke from the tail pipe (worn rings or valves), and so on. Tommy' friend checked all of the above, even sticking his middle finger up the exhaust pipe (obscene). The only thing he couldn't do was make it rain. When he had completed the once-over, he had Tommy race the still-warm engine, and claimed to hear a skip, which gave me a skip. But this was apparently just another cheapening trick, for he abruptly offered us something in the low $4000's.

"No dice," Bob replied, wearing a theatrical scowl. "Of course," he would later confide, in the privacy of our home, "there was a naughty temptation in the thought of selling this flawed vehicle to a self-proclaimed car dealer. But we should be able to get at least five." He ended the transaction by telling Tommy's friend we would call them if there were any chance of doing business. They thanked us and left.

Two days later, same time, same place, we met with a second pair, a fat, very nervous Latina clerk from some city office –Motor Vehicles, I think-- accompanied by her colleague, a frail, pleasant Latino gentleman. It was she who had made the call. They were both around forty, they seemed kind, and I took to them immediately. Was I already sorry for her? Bob acted friendly and mild toward this pair -- and calm, for him. After she had driven the car once around the block, the friend looked it over. But he did not claim to be a mechanic, and the inspection was perfunctory, as if he trusted us.

"I like this car very much," she announced, without even conferring with her friend. "But I only have forty-two hundred dollars." That sounded like a firm offer. Bob countered with forty-eight. Whoops! Why was he going so low, so fast?

As we later agreed, the quick reduction may have stemmed from a tricky combination of feelings. We had both liked the woman, wanted her to enjoy the car. But she had mentioned that she wanted it so she could drive to her evening college classes, on Staten Island. She lived in *Loisaida*, Manhattan's lower east side. Because she was asthmatic, she said, she was willing to pay what was, for her, a lot of money, for a very reliable, low-mileage car. I still thought five thou would have been generous enough --after all, this was only our second negotiation-- but maybe Bob felt two hundred dollars guiltier than I did.

When he named the price, she thought for a moment, then said, with her friend nodding encouragement, "I really want this car. This is the one." So she would go home, figure out a way to find the extra six hundred, and contact us as soon as she had it. To my surprise, Bob did not ask for a deposit, which we had agreed we would do. This was probably another sign. Nor did I pipe up about a deposit.

Later that evening, we came to a painful decision. Over dinner, we had shared a scenario in which, on a rainy night some time in the near future, she sat wheezing, slumped over the steering wheel, while a truck barreled toward the rear end of the stalled little car.

Ready now to take on some of the heavy lifting, sort of, I volunteered to make the pre-emptive call. She answered on the first ring, and after a few pleasantries, I announced, "I'm afraid I have some bad news. I'm sorry, but we just got a better offer."

"Oh, I'm sorry, too," she replied, sounding relieved. I sincerely wished her luck finding a very good car. She thanked me, and that was that.

Why had she sounded relieved? I had the feeling she did not really want to buy the car. She was the sort of woman whose feet got cold fast. At the start of our meeting, she had seemed depressed, and, again, on the phone. (I can't imagine anyone working as a city clerk very long and *not* being depressed.) I recognized this woman as a professional victim. Maybe, looking at the car had been just a pretext for a sort-of date with her colleague.

Whatever was going on, Bob and I were both glad we had not sold her the car. But we failed to draw the obvious conclusion: we should have just donated it to some charity, and told them about the problem. Once again, ethical relativism: we would not cheat people we felt sorry for —more scenery along the slippery slope.

Over the next week or so, no further car business transpired. The *Newsday* ad was still running, but Bob was out in Arizona doing some *pro bono* consulting for a college on the Navajo reservation. The alert reader may note the stark conjunction of good and bad works, possibly the symptom of a middle-aged man trying to burst the old chains of guilt --with significantly diminished arm strength. As for me, most of my waking hours were devoted to good works -- my job.

While Bob was away, Lise and I decided that, if we got any more calls, we would only show the car if it seemed absolutely safe. However, on an evening when I had an emergency at the office, she wound up showing it —alone-- in Carroll Gardens, to a pleasant young Haitian man, who gave her a $100 cash deposit, then called the next day to ask for it back. She arranged to meet him again the day after that, this time in Union Square Park, near our apartment, where, having rushed over during my lunch hour so I could act as chaperone, I watched her exchange his deposit for the receipt she had given him. The young man's expressed reason for pulling out of the deal was that he had realized he could not afford the car. A gentle, nervous soul, he must have apologized ten times.

At the risk of sounding racist, I will admit that, among the many Haitians on my caseload, there happen to be several who are emotionally unstable. Take a look at Haiti's history and current situation, and you may be less surprised by that fact. If your own liberal guilt keeps you from believing me, there are statistical studies, many of them available at the Forty-Second street library.

I admired Lisa's kindness and probity with the Haitian. To be fair, as I remembered from our own earlier car-buying experiences, and as I was rapidly re-learning from the seller's perspective, anyone can get cold feet. I'm also sure there are plenty of cheats who are expert foot warmers.

When Bob got home from Arizona, he decided to try once more to solve the stalling problem. Lise had already had the distributor cap and wires changed --twice, because of a miscommunication-- and the car had been thoroughly checked out, all to no avail. But, if at first... So, after he had taken a day or two to recover from his trip, on a Saturday morning, we brought the car back to her mechanic, the one who had changed the cap and wires.

This young man, whom Bob and I now met for the first time, looked like a punk intellectual (Granny glasses, pony tail). In his early twenties, he had a good car-side manner, and he was the manager of a very clean garage in the shadow of the Williamsburg Bridge, on the Brooklyn side, all of which made us suspect he would overcharge us.

I took the lead in this conversation, suggesting that he do everything he could to diagnose the problem, once and for all. Although he was not optimistic, he agreed to keep the car for several days. His plan was to leave it in a secure outside lot, in hopes of rain, and, if none were forthcoming, to pour water over the engine block, in hopes of catching the tricky machine in the act of stalling.

No luck: it did not rain, and buckets of water had no discernible effect. On Wednesday evening, we paid the (reasonable) bill and drove the car back to Carroll Gardens, where we immediately got another parking space.

What next? A Toyota dealer coldly informed Bob, who telephoned him, that he could probably offer us "something in the low to mid-two's." With a growing sense of frustration, I listened in on the other line as Bob, insulted, bade the dealer an abrupt goodbye. We agreed to keep trying, ourselves. I'm not sure why we still did not opt for the charity option, but I think the dealer's insult steeled us to the misdeed we seemed destined to commit. Bob did make a politically incorrect joke about donating the car to the blind --a stupid joke, since the flaw was invisible.

The next day, as agreed, he extended the *Newsday* ad for another week. At my prompting, he also substituted "Excellent Condition" for "Grandmother Car."

By now, Lise had been evicted by her greedy Carroll Gardens landlord, and had moved to her new building, the one without bicycle parking. She would still be renting a small Brooklyn apartment, but this one was on a main drag, Fourth Avenue, where traffic was fast and constant. Her new place was midway between a good neighborhood, Park Slope, and a rough one, Sunset Park. With heavy paternal humor, Bob suggested that she call her new, nameless neighborhood, "Park-Park." Actually, there was a lot of parking, and the rent was a bit lower ($600, vs. $650).

On my first visit, a Thursday evening, while Bob was logging overtime at the library, Lise pointed out the Polish delis, Polish funeral parlor, and Polish travel agency (right beneath her apartment), the old Finnish co-op down the block, and the warm, lively Mexican families passing in the street. I silently noted the almost total absence of trees, the security grill and excellent locks on the front door of her building, and the dealers waiting for the pay phone to ring in front of a nearby laundromat. I managed not to overreact to her account of how, not very late one rainy night during her very first week in the new neighborhood, she had sensed that someone was following her, as she walked home from the subway. A good, cheap dinner *a deux* at a local Mexican restaurant slightly assuaged my fears about the neighborhood.

By now, it was almost the end of June. On Saturday morning, two days after the dinner, as soon as the renewed *Newsday* ad appeared, another guy called. After a few perfunctory questions, he said he wanted to see the car. Bob, who took the call, arranged to meet him at high noon on the southeast corner of Twenty-Third Street and Fourth Avenue, a block from Lise's building. The buyer would be driving in from the south shore of Long Island, and, on Bob's advice, he would take the Belt Parkway, then come up Fourth Avenue.

When Bob told me that the guy had sounded very sluggish, maybe even stoned, I suspected another false dawn. Although I was tired from a busy week of end-of-year financial reports, I decided not to let Bob go meet the guy alone. So we grabbed the keys and papers, and hopped aboard the R. Arriving almost an hour early, we ran up to say hello to Lise, who was breakfasting late, and Bob used her bathroom. Then, we had the car washed and waxed at a bright, colorful place a few blocks from the apartment. The Mexican (Dominican?) workers were silent and unfriendly, and, despite Bob's proactive and ostentatious contribution to the *for the boys* can, they did a poor job, which he touched up, himself, with a borrowed towel, while I pointed out the places the workers had missed, and they looked on impassively.

It was still fifteen minutes early when we drove back to Twenty-Third Street and parked in front of a funeral parlor at the appointed corner. But a strung-out, filthy-looking old homeless woman junkie, who was staggering back and forth along the sidewalk, made this seem like a bad place to try to sell a car. So we drove around the block and re-parked, now on the northeast corner, in front of a cheap luncheonette. A minute later, a raggedy family group emerged from the luncheonette. The man, who looked like a stoned pimp, was lugging a big TV set. The woman seemed drunk, and there was a skinny, tag-along, little boy with a huge, filthy stuffed animal, some kind of generic marsupial or rodent.

"Mom!" screamed the son.

"I'm not going with you to your mother's p-p-p-p-place," the man announced. Nevertheless, they crossed the street and joined the junkie, who turned out to be the mother. But she was not homeless, after all for, after some arm-waving and shouting, they all went up to her apartment, which was next to the funeral parlor, two doors south of Twenty-Third Street, and a few doors north of Lise's place.

The caller, whose phone number neither Bob nor I had thought to ask, never showed. We waited forty-five minutes, moving the car from corner to corner, and driving it around the block a few more times. I was both annoyed and reflexively anxious that it might stall, even though this day, like the evenings when we had first shown it, was clear and dry. Bob was uncharacteristically silent, and I sensed his discouragement, as we waited in vain for someone to drive up and scan the corner.

Finally, we gave up, returned to Lise's apartment, and decided to take the car back to Manhattan for the weekend. The prospect of jumping into the train every time someone claimed to want to see it seemed pointlessly arduous. Lise, who was now vacuuming, while her two cats looked on warily, thanked us and wished us luck. She mentioned that she would be "seeing" a guy she liked that evening, which lifted our spirits.

On and around the Manhattan Bridge, we were punished by horrendous traffic, but when we reached the Village and headed west toward the Hudson, we immediately found an excellent parking space, good until Tuesday at eleven, and only a ten-minute walk from our building. Even the gods have some sense of fairness.

Bob's article had reached the stage where he could work at home for a few days while manning the phone. Assuming the car was not sold by the middle of the following week, the plan was for me to move it to a not-too-expensive lot near my office. That way, at least, we would not have to worry about parking it for a while.

On Sunday, we wasted a whole beautiful day waiting for calls that never came. After that, the stretch run began. Early Monday morning, as Bob would tell me when I checked in at around eleven-thirty, the phone started ringing in earnest. While I dealt with some mindless paperwork, restored to his native bubbly optimism, he regaled me with a running narrative.

"The first caller is this guy from Queens with an indeterminate accent. Asking only a few questions that make me repeat the information in the ad, he says he wants to see the car, but can't come yet. Although I tell him I may sell the car first, he says he'll call back in the afternoon. He gives me his number and asks me to let him know before I close any deal, which I promise to do --without meaning it, although he sounds like a serious customer.

"Next up is a religious Jew from Brooklyn. He says something similar, and it occurs to me that this might be a Jewish holiday – Succoth, or something. We leave it that he'll call me again when he's ready to deal. Never, I presume, and I'm reminded of that limerick your cousin Jerry told us:

There once was a rabbi from Peru,

who was vainly trying to screw,

His wife cried, "*Oy Vay*!

if you go on this way,

the Messiah will come before you."

That one is an old favorite with both of us, though presumably for different reasons. Bob continued.

"A mildly farcical episode ensues, in which a third guy calls, asks questions, and says the car sounds great. Unfortunately, he works two jobs and lives way out on Long Island —as it happens, in that town next to your brother's. (What's it called again?)

"Could you bring it out here, by any chance?' he asks.

"'No,' I reply, but do not add, 'unless I fail to sell it for several years.' "

Bob was on one of his old-fashioned rolls. I sat there at my desk, enjoying my man's raconteur-ship, laughing at the punch lines, and doing nothing to retard the flow --but still worried about selling a flawed car.

Later that day, after dinner, as we were getting ready for our usual lively evening (reading the paper and listening to music on the radio), the third guy's mother called from somewhere vaguely north of the city. Thinking it must be Lise, I picked up. With Bob eavesdropping from his easy chair, the mother proposed an improbable scheme: her daughter and son-in-law worked in Manhattan, so maybe they, or a friend of theirs, could come see the car, either during a lunch hour or some other time soon. Could we wait? She'd call them all --including the son-- right now, and call us back. I suggested that she hurry, "or the car may be gone." As if!

"You did good, Ell," said Bob, in his Godfather voice. Was I now an equal partner in this incipient crime?

Although the mother didn't call back, the phone did ring again. This time, it was a serious and well-educated-sounding Indian (Asian). While I listened in, from the bedroom, Bob took the call. The Indian asked good questions about the car, including where it was, and said he worked in Chelsea, the neighborhood directly north of the Village.

Sounding as if he were reading from a script, Bob gave him the same history of the car that we'd given, more or less, to most of the previous customers:

"My mother bought the car new in 1993. In 1997, she had to give up driving, at which time she gave it to my daughter. The mileage was only 17,000, because it had basically been a grocery-shopping car. In the three ensuing years, my daughter drove it back and forth to college, between New York and Michigan, and used it around town in Ann Arbor, bringing the mileage to about 44,000. Since graduating last year, she has been using it in Brooklyn, where she lives and works.

"The car has never been in an accident of any kind, and it has never been driven by anyone other than my mother, my daughter, and (occasionally) my wife or me. Our reason for selling it is that we have another car, and we're tired of parking and paying insurance for two cars. We're selling the newer one because it has a higher book value."

The Indian made no response to this touching family chronicle—obviously, he was an unsentimental man. After asking a few more, good, specific questions, he offered to meet Bob at 20th Street and Eighth Avenue, during his lunch hour, at twelve-twenty the next day (Tuesday). He also mentioned, perhaps to reassure Bob, that he lived in (solidly middle-class) Bayside, Queens. Although Bob sounded reluctant to give up our parking space, he promised to meet him.

Tuesday night at the dinner table, talking with his mouth full (to prime himself for a six-Rolaid night), Bob summarized the meeting. Although I reassured myself that he had always had an accurate memory, I did worry that, since he was pushing sixty, the old synapses might be starting to misfire. Even so, I'll try to stick to his words, more or less, because I think the reader may enjoy the story more that way. Will my transcript be accurate? Not that I have a phonographic memory, but after three decades of marriage, Bob's style is, shall we say, familiar. Anyway...

"So. He shows up exactly on time. Plump and neatly bearded, he's wearing a tan cardigan and brown tweed jacket with the requisite elbow patches. He might just as well have been sporting sandwich boards with the legend, *Solid Middle-Class Citizen, Kick Me.* I'm lying in wait at the southwest corner in front of a hydrant, playing Lise's wonderful Billy Holiday tape on the cassette. The music is loud, but most of the liberal passersby signal their approval with nods and smiles.

"He walks right up to the driver's side window, and offers the conventional first-name car-negotiators' Intro: 'Roger (not Raj).' I reciprocate: 'Bob, (not Robert).' His handshake is firm, and, without being asked, I turn off the music and get out so he can sniff around the car. He tries the wipers, lights, radio, heater and so on.

"'May I drive?' he asks politely. With a 'be my guest' gesture, I assume the passenger position. Taking the helm, he adjusts the seat and mirrors, and inches forward into the heavy traffic. Almost immediately, he notices that the car skips a tiny bit when it is stalled --delayed, that is-- in traffic.

"'You should get a major tune-up,' he instructs me, with the pompous, restrained sententiousness of a man who earns a lot of money and has people 'under' him. It crosses my mind that the guy wouldn't last five minutes in the classroom.

"As we turn onto the West Side Highway, that last thought prompts me to ask his profession. He is a mechanical engineer, who designs heating and cooling systems for hospitals, which may mean he understands radiators, but does not mean he has a clue about this car's problem. He does not ask what I do, so I do not tell him. He then waxes eloquent about timing belts and a few other well-known maintenance items for the healthy Camry.

"Always take it to the dealer,' he instructs me. 'It will cost you a few extra dollars, but it's well worth it. For one thing, they use proper Toyota parts.' By now, we're back on Eighth Avenue and 20th Street, where we pull up to a hydrant.

"It does not escape my notice that Roger has said *I* should go to the dealer, which suggests that *he*, himself, is not planning to do anything of the sort. This could be good (he trusts the car), or bad (no interest).

"As he hands me the keys, the interaction ends amicably enough, with an obvious little escape line on his part, about calling in the evening after he has 'thought it over.' We shake again, and he strides eastward 'for a bite before returning to the office.' I drive back to the West Village where (Glory Be!), after only a little circling, I find another parking space.

"Back in the apartment, I immediately telephone Lise's mechanic, and tell him what Roger said.

"Right,' he replies, 'people always say that. Folklore. A tune-up won't help *your* problem.' I can practically see him sneering."

In other words, as Bob and I tacitly agreed, once again over dinner, we were back at Square One.

-3-

We come now to the part of the story where we finally sell the car. Once again, I'll take the narrative helm, albeit reluctantly. Maybe, it's a genre thing, but, as I'm writing all this stuff about cars, I have a sense that I'm just being a good sport. In fact, if Bob and I were not under a very odd type of time pressure, which I will explain later, and if we were not both (possibly) in need of catharsis, I would probably not be recording these events now--or ever.

But what the heck! Recalling our marriage vows, I know that I signed a blank contract, "to be a good Jewish wife!" Besides, Bob is still down at the library in the stifling city, laboring over his footnotes, and frankly, up here in Bungalow-land, life is bo-ring.

As soon as Bob had finished his semi-amusing, semi-racist account of the meeting with the South-Asian gentleman, the phone rang again. I picked up, and he listened in. It was the man from Queens from earlier in the day, the one with the indeterminate accent. He told me his name (yes, "Mark"), and, when I did not offer mine, he asked, so I told him. Without prompting, I recited the standard history of the car, but, instead of a direct response or any specific automotive questions, he surprised me by saying that I sounded "like a good person." I inferred that he must belong to a culture in which respect for women, whether or not actually felt, must be expressed. Then, he abruptly asked where the car was located. Since he had the next two days off, still for the holiday, and since he lived in Rego Park, Queens, he could come in by subway to see the car tomorrow afternoon.

When, for whatever reason, I suggested that this would entail a long trip, he replied simply, "No, there will be enough time." He sounded like he meant business.

We arranged to meet at Twenty-Third and Sixth at two. Both from curiosity and the urge to support Bob, I decided impulsively that I would also take the day off –the holiday meant business would be slow, anyhow—and I asked Mark to call again when he reached the corner, so the three of us could walk to the car together. No more wild-goose chases or squandered parking spaces.

"Don't worry," he avowed, as if he had read my mind. "I'll be there."

To enable him to recognize us, I offered thumbnail portraits. "We're both in our fifties. Bob has a medium build. He's tall, brown hair, beard. I'm shorter, gray hair, glasses, and I'll be wearing a long light-weight brown skirt and a short-sleeved blue shirt."

Without being asked, Mark reciprocated. "I am short, with a mustache and a tan jacket. I look Asian." Since his accent didn't sound Chinese, Indian, or Pakistani, my curiosity was piqued. As I don't think I've mentioned yet, he turned out to be a Bukharin Jew from Kazakhstan.

Bob and I were excited, both of us trying not to think, "This is the one." Somehow, Monday night and Tuesday morning passed.

At 1:50 p.m., Mark called from the appointed corner, and we left the apartment to go meet him. It was a bright summer day, and we recognized each other immediately. Mark was sort of swarthy (as they used to say), in his thirties, medium build, short, thick black hair, tan windbreaker, very neat and clean-looking, but with a droopy left eyelid.

It was a fifteen-minute walk to the car. As we strolled along *en sandwich*, a sort of role reversal took place. *Mark* seemed to be reassuring *us*, as if we were the nervous buyers and he, the seller.

When we reached the parking space, for a few seconds he stood, hands on hips, silently gazing at the car, looking knowledgeable. Then, he had Bob turn the engine on and off, while he poked around under the hood. He asked Bob to gun it, to change gears, etc. After looking over the interior, without opening the trunk, which was littered with junk, he asked if the spare was a real tire or just a "doughnut." Neither Bob nor I was able to answer that, having never changed a flat on the car, but Mark said we shouldn't bother. I saw this as another expression of trust, which was confirmed when Bob offered to turn on the radio, air conditioner, heater, etc.

"If you tell me they work, Robert, I believe you," Mark said, looking Bob in the eye. I was beginning to get a sense of the culture to which he belonged, which seemed to bear a family resemblance to some of the far-flung cultures of my clients.

"Shall we go for a drive?" Bob suggested, visibly anxious to get moving.

"There is no need," Mark replied. "Why should you lose your parking space, in case I'm not going to buy the car?"

This was misleading: it sounded as if he were not going to buy the car. But he cleared the point right up.

"Look, Robert," he said.

Early on, Bob had asked Mark to call him " Bob," and it occurred to me to tell Mark that the only people who had ever called my husband "Robert," at least since I'd known him, were relatives who were now deceased.

"I trust you like my brother," he continued. "You are a good man. I can see. I am the same as you. If you say the car is good, I will believe you." I think that what he meant was that we were all in this together –i.e. Jewish. Bob and I said nothing.

"It will be a question only of agreeing about the price." He smiled at us. "Look, how much will you really take for this car? I don't want to argue about the price. Just say the lowest amount you can accept, and I will agree."

Mark's bluntness created irresistible momentum, and the deal was consummated with dizzying speed, in about ten seconds:

Bob: Forty-eight.

Mark: Forty-two.

Me: Forty-five.

Mark: I agree.

He sealed it by shaking hands warmly with us both —me, first. His hand was neither hard nor soft. I had expected a worker's hand, but his was neither callused and muscular, nor smooth and weak.

"How do you want to pay?" asked Bob. "A down payment, then come back with the rest?" That made sense to me, but not to Mark.

"No, no," he replied impatiently, "no down payment. I will pay the whole amount. In cash."

"In ... but how will you...? " I started to ask.

As Bob had once told me he learned back in 1975, selling/ buying a car involves at least two tricky logistical problems. The seller must sign over the Title and give the buyer a bill of sale, and the buyer must pay. But who goes first?

"One, two, three: you pay, I sign."

The seller then removes the license plates and scrapes the registration, but not the inspection, decal off the windshield.

The second problem is how the buyer gets the now unregistered car over to the Motor Vehicles Bureau, where the tax and registration fee must be paid, and the new decal and plates issued. The common solution is for the seller to accompany the buyer to the Bureau.

But Mark, as it turned out, had very different ideas. "Let me call my wife," he announced happily, "and tell her the good news."

We walked to the corner, where he spoke on a pay phone for a minute in a language I did not recognize. Russian? Kazakh? Yiddish? Possibly even Hebrew?

He hung up. "It's okay, forty-five hundred, as agreed. We must go together to my bank now and to my house, to get the money. I only have forty-two hundred dollars at home. Can you do this?"

"Sure," I said. "We have time." Bob nodded vigorously.

"Good. I live in Rego Park, a safe neighborhood. You don't have to be afraid. Shall I drive, or will you?"

As far as I could remember, Bob and I had never been to Rego Park, but I believed Mark. Even so, despite his warmth and reassurances, as he took the wheel and Bob gallantly hopped into the back seat, I began to feel afraid. To my shame, the fantasy of finger-removal wafted back up, which was certainly a racist response to this courtly central Asian.

Glancing across at me as he edged along the street, he seemed to read my mind. "You don't have to be afraid, Eleanor," he repeated. "Please don't worry, nothing will happen. I am a good person, just like you." This assurance triggered loud buzzing from my tiresome guilt button.

As we headed east on 23rd Street, Bob proposed a detour to our building, so we could empty the trunk, but halfway there, prompted by the buzzer, I decided this might be a mistake: I did not want Mark to see where we lived. So, as we approached our street, I said, "On second thought, let's get going before the rush hour starts." He nodded his agreement.

Ten minutes later, heading north on First Avenue, we did a brief comic shuffle about where to turn off to the tunnel, which, in fact, neither Bob nor I were certain we remembered, not having come this way in quite a while. But Bob guessed correctly, and we glided down into the tunnel, enjoying an anomalous traffic lull.

At the other end of the tunnel, Bob handed over the exact change for the toll. As we drove along the L.I.E., still in light-to-moderate traffic, Mark drifted into automobile expansiveness, telling us that he was a shoemaker with three youngish children, that his whole family had come here from Kazakhstan four years ago, that Kazakhstan was a beautiful country, but there was too much trouble, principally because of the Islamic fighters from Afghanistan, who carried their wars across the border.

"An ordinary person cannot live there now," he concluded, sadly and matter-of-factly. Bob and I made sympathetic noises.

"You're a good driver," I remarked, when he looked across to the right rear view mirror, and then waited before changing lanes.

"Thank you."

After ten more minutes, we exited onto one of the feeder roads for Queens Boulevard, where we immediately got stuck in an insane traffic jam at one of those junctions where the roads are designed to channel the flow of cars from several lanes into one, like pushing toothpaste back into the tube. Complaining with one voice, we inched forward.

"The bank is over there," Mark said, after a couple of minutes, pointing to some low white buildings.

"Should we stop?"

"No, they stay open until six today. Let's go to my house first."

This made no sense, but trusting that he knew what he was doing, Bob and I acquiesced. We finally did reach Queens Boulevard, where Mark turned onto the side road. Then, a right turn and a left, and we were on a quiet street lined with a mixture of six-story brick apartment buildings and decent, stand-alone private homes. There were only a few trees, just enough to mute the bareness of the sidewalks. Uncannily, Rego Park in 2000 reminded me of Bob's description of Maspeth in 1974, Meltzer Land, a little shabbier, perhaps, but the same basic mix and ambiance. Halfway down the block, he pointed out a parking space, which Mark took.

"I live right over there," he said, pointing to a corner apartment house about two hundred feet ahead. "Do you mind waiting in the car? I will go upstairs to get the money."

Ten minutes later, he strolled back down the street toward us, unaccompanied by two huge, unshaven thugs with their hands in the pockets of their long belted leather coats. He got back in behind the wheel.

"Here, count it, please. Forty-five hundred dollars."

He held out a slightly worn, unsealed envelope with the printed return address of a bank. A thick wad of bills bulged through the opening; there was not even a rubber band. Half-turning, and reaching back, he handed the money to Bob. Another cultural marker!

"I thought you said we had to go to the bank," Bob objected, clutching the envelope in both hands. "What happened?"

"We don't have to go. My wife went already. Haven't you seen money before, Robert? Don't worry. It's the correct amount. But count it, anyway, please."

"Of course, I've seen money," Bob snapped back. "But not forty-five hundred dollars in cash."

Fumbling, he tried to count the money, which was in twenties, fifties and hundreds, arranged in ascending order from the open side of the envelope. When he noticed in the rear-view mirror that Bob's hands were shaking, Mark laughed.

"This doesn't seem like a lot of money to you?" I protested.

"I've been handling money like this since I was ten years old. We always do business for cash."

Bob stopped counting and silently passed the envelope to me. With my own hands no steadier than his, I attempted to recount the money.

"Okay," Bob said. "But forty-five hundred dollars? I thought you said you were a shoemaker. What kind of business are you really in?" That sounded so rude that I lost count and had to start over.

Although he did not look as if he appreciated the question, Mark was a gentleman: at least, he appeared to forgive my blunt spouse. "No, no, I'm really a shoemaker," he said, with a small laugh. "Please. Stop worrying, and finish counting the money."

I started over, counting fast, and got forty-three hundred. He smiled indulgently, suggested I try again, and this time I counted more carefully and got, I think, forty-five hundred.

"Correct," I said.

After that, I sat there for a moment, holding the envelope. Bob had laid his backpack, in which we were carrying the papers and the tools to remove the plates, on the seat next to him. I handed the money over the seat, and for some reason, he opted for his inside jacket pocket, even though it had no button. I bit my tongue and hoped he would not abruptly bend over.

"What next?" he asked.

"We will go to my insurance broker," Mark announced. "It is very close to here."

"Maybe, I'd better drive now," I suggested, "since the car is still in our names." Since Mark had just driven us here from Manhattan, I realized this was irrational, but he obliged.

"Okay. As you like."

We walked around the hood and switched places. In the back seat, Bob was silent, looking thoughtful.

Mark directed me: at the corner, a right, then two blocks, and a left. Thirty seconds, and we were there. He pointed to a space at a fire hydrant, and I parallel parked in front of a couple in a dark, mid-sized American sedan. The woman, who was behind the wheel, was visibly nervous. In order to miss me by at least twenty feet before pulling out into traffic, she backed up. In our rear view mirror, I could see a sign on a storefront, in Russian and English, for a driving school and various financial and legal services.

"She missed us," I joked. Mark smiled indulgently. I backed into the vacated space, we all got out, I locked the car, and we went in, him first.

We found ourselves in a big, bare room, the walls of which were decorated with travel posters for the Caribbean, certificates from police-related groups, and pictures of very elegant vintage cars, some of which I recognized, some not: Duzendorf's, Bugatti's, ancestors to stretch Mercedes', Morgan's --that sort of thing. No Camry's.

Although, for some reason, I had never accompanied any of my clients to a place like this, I sensed there must be hundreds of such storefront businesses, in all of the neighborhoods of the city where people don't have their own lawyers or accountants, and where poverty and recent immigration make even small amounts of red tape daunting.

In the front of the room were two men of contrasting physical types, and in the back, several office machines and an expanse of empty space. It reminded me of a taxi-dispatch office. Mark shook hands with the men and introduced everyone, and the men shook with Bob and me. Like Mark, they were very courtly. The fluorescent lighting made everyone look unhealthy and mildly sinister.

The men took what seemed to be their places. Behind a big, battered wooden desk went the rat-like one, with black-rimmed glasses, thinning sandy hair, a thin tie, and a cheap, but not garish, suit. He gestured toward three molded orange plastic chairs in front of the desk, and we sat down. Mark explained, in Russian, what he needed, and the man nodded solemnly.

The second man sank into an old sprung armchair to my left, and smiled at me. A very big man with bad gold Soviet-era teeth, he was wearing a very shiny blue suit, a dirty black tee shirt, and the old-fashioned kind of white tennis shoes that used to be called "tennie runners." He dove into a newspaper with a Jewish star on the masthead, but the language, if I was not mistaken, was Russian.

Over his shoulder, I could see pages and pages of photographs of old people, and because the photographs seemed to be accompanied by loving remembrances from family and friends, I surmised that the old people were all dead. While the clerk-type began pulling official-looking forms from a desk drawer, I asked Mark about the newspaper.

"This is our paper," he explained. "There are many of us here, Jews from Kazakhstan. The paper keeps us all in touch, our community."

"Plus the news from back home?" Bob suggested.

"Of course." Then, the big man, whom I had mentally dubbed "Igor," sneezed twice.

"*Gesundheit*," I said, and he looked up and gave me a beaming smile that felt like sunshine.

"Thank you, Madame." He blew his nose into a big white handkerchief.

Out on the street in front of the door, a harassed-looking woman with a little girl was gesticulating and shouting to someone I couldn't see. "Tell him he'll have his money tomorrow! Don't worry, I'll get it." No answer. She hurried away, and the little girl clumped after her.

The clerk asked Bob for the car's Title. After examining it with exaggerated scrutiny, he had us sign it, then started filling out more forms. But, before he could get very far, a frantic, tough-looking guy rushed in, talking a mile a minute in what sounded like Russian, and waving a document. We were put on hold while the clerk climbed out from behind the desk, walked to the back, copied the document on a wheezing old machine, and returned. Without paying, the man rushed from the store, clutching his document and the copy.

Then, the clerk excused himself and disappeared into the back again, this time past the machines and empty space. A toilet flushed, and I reminded myself to remind Bob to use it before we left. Excusing himself a second time, the clerk sat back down and once again took up his pen. As he laboriously filled out what were, presumably, insurance and registration forms, he reminded me of a Soviet *apparatchik*. Although he was using a cheap ballpoint pen, he wrote with care and style. While the clerk labored at his task, Mark caught my eye, and gestured to Bob and me with what might have been admiration for the man's literacy skills. Bob nodded. I smiled.

I wondered what amount they would put on the bill of sale, since I knew it was common practice to understate prices, in order to lower the tax. When it was time for us to sign, I was surprised by the steepness of the discount: $750. I wondered if Mark had even told the clerk the real price.

"$750?' " Bob said. "Will they believe that?"

"Why not?" the clerk replied. "It is a thirteen-year old car, it could be a rusty piece of junk."

Bob turned red, and I, too, found the characterization insulting (although secretly true, in a way the clerk could not know). He returned to the forms.

"I make it easy for him," he absentmindedly remarked, as he worked away, "and he pays me for my time."

The remark made me feel even sorrier for Mark, since I guessed the man was probably exacting as much as fifty, or even a hundred, dollars for ten minutes' work, filling out three or four simple forms that anyone literate in English could have filled out. When the forms had been signed and delivered, the man wrote down a number on a piece of scrap paper, and showed it to Mark. I could see three figures, which must have represented the insurance payment, plus the fee. Mark pulled a face and said something in Russian, presumably protesting the number. With a world-weary smile, the man replied. Mark took out his checkbook and laboriously wrote a check, which was scrutinized, then secreted into a tattered wallet.

The transaction was finished. Igor and the clerk rose. Mark, Bob and I rose. Hands were re-shaken, and the three of us were soon back out on the street. I handed Mark the keys. He smiled, unlocked the car, and got in behind the wheel.

"What's this?" he asked, noticing the ignition shut-off pad, which Bob had activated for the first time before we went into the office. In the back seat again, Bob explained how it worked, and asked Mark if he wanted to write down the numbers.

"How many?"

"Four."

"I can remember."

Bob told him, and he punched in the code and started up. As he was about to accelerate, I reached across and lowered the emergency brake.

"It's in a different place on my car," he explained sheepishly. That he already owned a car surprised me, probably because he had come to Manhattan by subway.

"You already have a car?" Bob asked, again sounding suspicious. "What's this one for? You want two?"

"No, I want this one for my father, I want to give him a car."

He smiled proudly.

"How old is your father?"

"About the same age as you."

"What's next?" I asked.

"We will go to my garage. I have a space in the building. We'll take off the plates and the registration sticker, and you can remove whatever you want. I will keep the car there and move mine onto the street until I get the plates." That sounded perfectly reasonable, although of course it reawakened my tiresome fear: the time had come for him to steal back his money.

Bob's fear, too, apparently. "How do we get home with all this cash?" he asked, patting his jacket pocket.

"I will drive you home later, if you like."

"No, that's okay," replied Bob. "I don't want you to bother. Is the subway safe here?"

"Very. There are many people at this hour."

"Many pickpockets?" I half-joked. Mark did not deign to reply.

We stopped at a light. Not wanting to juggle the envelope while changing the plates, I suspect, Bob took it out of his jacket pocket.

"Where should we keep this?" he asked me.

I gestured to the backpack, still on the seat beside him, and he slipped the envelope into a zipped pocket in the small, front compartment. The tools were in the main one.

When we arrived at Mark's house, an electric eye let us into the garage and closed the door behind us. He drove straight through to an outside courtyard, where the parking, he explained, was cheaper than inside. There were about eight spaces, and he pulled into the only empty one. We all got out. He pointed to a big van in an adjacent space. Bob had brought the backpack along, and was clutching it in his arms.

"That's my car," Mark announced proudly.

We walked over to the van, which he unlocked, informing us that it was called a "Quest," a model new to me. It was unmarked, spanking clean, and dazzlingly white. Bob made an admiring face, but since I knew he hated gas-guzzlers, I doubted his sincerity.

"This man has a penchant for white cars," I thought, and I wondered if the landscape in his native Kazakhstan boasted many beautiful white features. He opened the van to show off the interior, which was also spotless, with floor mats made of a kind of Turkish-looking carpeting material.

"Wow!" exclaimed Bob.

Mark beamed, re-locked the Quest, and, as we walked back toward the Camry, made a little speech.

"I take good care of my van. I bought it from another Jew, a good man, a brother. I trusted him, and I was right. That is also why I bought your car. And I could see that your daughter has taken good care of it."

Actually, our daughter's (ex-) car had paper scraps, residues of cat litter, and so on, in the still uninspected trunk. Taking a screwdriver and wrench from the backpack, and carefully zipping it back up, Bob started to fiddle with the plates.

"Let me do it," Mark offered, and, using our tools, he had the plates off in short order.

Meanwhile, I used the Windex and a razorblade, which Bob handed me from the backpack, to remove the registration decal. I was surprised at how easily it came off --in one piece, actually—and, for some reason I carefully put it in my bag.

"You don't have to drive us home," Bob reiterated. "The traffic will be brutal by now, you'd be on the road for hours."

"Anyway, there are two of us, we'll be safe," I chimed in. Mark smiled.

"And if the subway is really safe ... " Bob perseverated.

"It is," Mark said. "But call me, anyhow, when you get home, just to let me know you have arrived."

"That's very kind of you," I remarked.

With a small bow to each of us, he recited his number to Bob (again). Skipping the trunk, we grabbed maps, papers and tapes from the glove compartment. I hoped we had not left behind any incriminating receipts. ("Check out stalling problem.") Then, we climbed into Mark's van, and he drove us straight to the subway entrance, a few blocks up Queens Boulevard. After we had shaken hands again, there was a momentary silence.

"Well, Eleanor and Robert," he smiled. "Wish me good luck with my new car."

"Good luck with it," I said, as warmly as I could, and Bob mumbled his own good wishes.

Shaking hands yet again, we said good-bye, and leaving Mark standing next to his van, Bob and I joined the flow of pedestrians into the station. As we descended the stairs, my stress level also descended, from ten to seven or eight. The train arrived almost immediately, and since we were now traveling against rush-hour traffic, it was easy to find adjoining seats. With the backpack snuggled on my lap, we shared a neatly folded newspaper someone had left behind, and enjoyed the company of our law-abiding fellow-passengers.

The ride was long, but uneventful. Up in the apartment, we locked the money into the cabinet where we keep our valuables. Hurrying out to a local restaurant, we ate an unconscious dinner (pasta, I think). Since neither of us, ironically, had brought along enough cash, we paid the bill with a credit card. Back in the apartment, there were no messages on the machine. Our simultaneous sighs of relief were deafening.

 Thinking to get it over with, Bob called Mark's number and assured his machine that we had arrived home safely. We spent a restless night, repeatedly awakened by each other's tossing and turning.

-4-

Back at my job, I spent all day Wednesday catching up on calls and paperwork. When I got home, Bob announced that, he, too, had spent a busy day, doing "the million things I've been neglecting in favor of that damned car business." But he had thoughtfully found time to grocery-shop and to prepare one of his specials, broiled chicken. After dinner, when he offered to do the dishes, I thought I caught a glimpse of the rat of guilt scurrying into a dark corner.

At around nine, Mark called. Sometime during the previous night, I realized he had never told us his last name. Picking up the extension, I hoped, of course, that he was just returning Bob's call.

"Hello, Robert. This is Mark."

"Hi, Mark," we said, in unison.

"Oh, hello there, Mrs. Robert," he replied. He sounded worried, and I hoped it was just because he had forgotten my name.

"Hi, Mark," Bob said, in his cheery-nervous voice. "We got home fine. The subway was safe, full of people. We tried..."

Mark cut him off. "Thank you, Robert, but I am not calling about that. There is a problem." Neither of us replied. "There is water in the spare-tire well, a lot of water. I am afraid this is a flood car! Such cars are worthless."

"News to me!" Bob brazenly lied. I was too frightened to say a word.

"I must check further," Mark announced, and abruptly hung up.

We spent another bad night, marginally less sleepless only because we were so exhausted. Early the next morning (as he would tell me after work), Bob called Lise's mechanic. He quoted (and I quote):

"Flood cars are found in places like Florida, where they have undergone total immersion, usually in a hurricane. Such cars have an unmistakably mildewed interior and multiple mechanical problems, including constant, incurable stalling. Insurance companies usually choose to pay the replacement cost, since repairs are futile."

At this point, Bob reported that he had mentioned the escapade in the Everglades. The mechanic's response was reassuring.

"Since the car in question is completely dry, except for the spare tire well, and since it was only up to its wheels, not immersed, it's probably not a flood car. Still, driving through the Everglades that day may account for both the water in the tire well *and* the stalling we talked about. Or else ... the water could have a different explanation. The drainage plug in that model gets clogged up a lot. But it's easy to fix: you just unclog it."

Just as I was feeling better, Bob dropped the hammer. The mechanic had had another idea.

"Of course, it could also be that the flooding caused a corroded wire somewhere. If that's the case, it's extremely tricky. In fact, the only way you might be able to find out where it is, is if you hooked the car up to a diagnostic machine when the stalling starts. But we sort of tried that already, didn't we?"

We spent the rest of the long evening, and much of the night, worrying about what could happen next. Driven by nervous energy, I managed to get through Friday, distracting myself with some intake interviews of new clients.

Over dinner (I cooked), Bob told me that Mark had, indeed, called again. Now there was a new scare, as alarming as the first one. His "cousins" (of uncertain number), who were mechanics, had checked the car out, and told him the odometer had been turned back, accounting for the unusually low mileage.

"That's ridiculous!" I said, furious. "Let's call him back right now." I grabbed the phone and dialed, Bob picked up in the bedroom, and Mark answered on the second ring.

Me: Hi, Mark. Bob told me about your call. I thought you said you trusted us.

Mark: I like your husband and you, I trust you like brother and sister. We are all Jew...

Me: Well, there are good Jews and bad Jews, like everybody else. But we didn't turn back the odometer.

Bob (characteristically piggy-backing onto my courage): Turning back an odometer is against the law, Mark. What a terrible thing to accuse us of!

Mark (sheepishly): I know, I know, I'm sorry, Robert, I still trust you. It's just, my cousins, they are mechanics, and they are the ones who are saying this. They say they are sure.

Mark was the classic man in the middle. Bob piled it on, informing him that he had gone to the trouble of calling *our* mechanic, who guaranteed that the car was not a flood car. But, before he could even get to the drainage plug, Mark said he was no longer worried about the water. The mileage was the question.

Me: Oh? So what will it be next?

Bob: You don't like a white car with blue seats? If we ever have to sell another car, God forbid, we'd better sell it to someone without any cousins.

Ha ha! The implication, of course, was, "Stop bothering us!"

And, for several weeks now, this seems to have worked: Mark has not called again. During that time, in the course of many post-mortems, although we are proud of how we fended him off, Bob and I have also been suffering from constant remorse. As usual, he has partly smothered his, in levity. Do you remember the car-buying tips he mentioned in *Buying a Car*? Based on recent experience, he has come up with a few new ones:

1. Try the car in *all* weathers, *before* buying --at least, all possible weathers at the time of year when the purchase is contemplated.

2. Take it to your mechanic *before* you buy it.

3. Don't use up your complaints on false accusations.

During that conversation with Lise about blood feuds, I summarized the odometer business.

"So that's how you shut him up? Very clever." Children are so often their parents' annoying consciences.

"And is taking his money without telling him the car only runs in dry weather against the law, too?" I riposted. By then, she had gratefully accepted the $4500.

"It might be; it's misrepresentation," she replied, missing or ignoring my irony. Anyway, what does she know? She's not a lawyer.

Bob is much more thin-skinned than I am. In fact, even with the jokes, he has recently incurred three unusual maladies: sleeplessness, atypical migraines, and benign vertigo. (He would also shuffle around the apartment cryptically muttering, "Queens bureaucrats, Bokharin shoemakers.")

Sleeplessness, of course, is common enough, but, before we sold the car to Mark, it had been unusual for Bob. Atypical migraines: twice, upon awakening, my poor husband's entire visual field was broken up into those shifting diamonds used on TV to cover people's private parts, or the faces of alleged criminals.

"We call them 'atypical migraines,'" pronounced our eye doctor, when we visited his office. "Contrary to popular belief, migraines are not headaches, *per se*, but spasms in blood vessels of the brain. They may affect pain centers (headache) or other areas, such as the visual cortex" (diamonds).

In fact, he confided that he had once experienced a visual migraine, himself, while he was out jogging. "The cause is unknown," he explained helpfully, "but the malady is not serious unless it becomes frequent." Since the first two episodes, Bob's VM's have not recurred. I think the cause was acute stress --from which, of course, he is still suffering.

Interestingly, after years of macular degeneration, when my mother-in-law was becoming blind, she, too, would "see" things, like trees in the air and hundreds of little American flags. When we took her to a neurologist, a wise, kindly Indian-American woman, she suggested that Dave's mom might have been drawing on stored memories in the visual cortex to compensate for her failing vision.

Coincidentally, this sounds something like recovered memory, which has been diagnosed in some of my clients by expert witnesses at trials, when those among the new immigrants who are quick studies in American culture have tried to sue people. Litigiousness, alas, is a frequent concomitant of paranoia.

Turning to poor Bob's third malady, the same eye doctor told us that "benign vertigo is dizziness when you lie down, get up, or jerk your head." When we realized that the dizziness seemed to follow hard on the heels of the diamonds, we called the doctor back, and his assistant informed us that such dizziness is unrelated to atypical migraines. She suggested that Bob drink a lot of water and stop worrying. We sought a second opinion.

As a friend's ear doctor (also on the phone, this being the age of HMO's and time-consuming referral procedures for all office visits) explained, "Benign vertigo is caused by 'debris' in the inner ear, a frequent side effect of bad colds." A few months before the car selling began, Bob had suffered from such a cold.

Since neither of us can figure out how to work the fax on our printer, this doctor was unable to send us his exercises for the condition. (I don't know why he couldn't just drop them in the mail.) Instead, he suggested that Dave roll around on the floor and, generally, try to be as active as possible. Lo and behold, after two hours at the gym, where he had not set foot for more than a month, having been preoccupied with you-know-what, his dizziness vanished.

-5-

The city has changed. We have changed. There has also been significant meteorological change. According to recent science, one of the signs of global warming is said to be prolonged and extreme weather patterns. As of this writing, it has not rained in New York City for over a month. But today is cloudy, and the forecast for the next few days is for steady rain.

I mentioned that Bob has a deadline for his article; it looms. Up here in bungalow-land, I, too, have a "deadline." I'm hurrying to complete this story before the rain and attendant humidity finally move into our region. When they do, there is a strong chance that the phone will start ringing again.

Here is a sidebar story, also involving modes of transportation. I recently heard at my office that a colleague (Jewish) was driven to the airport by a fanatical Muslim cab driver from Egypt. While they were stuck in numerous traffic jams, the fanatic regaled him with advice about his soul. Stupidly, the colleague, a softhearted gay man of forty, disclosed his name. (It must have been one of those cases where, at the last minute, the driver held out his hand, stated his own name, and asked.) Anyway, ten years having passed, my colleague has recently started getting phone calls from the driver, exhorting him to come to the mosque with him to "meet my teacher."

"Meet my teacher,' indeed!" scoffs the victim. "More like, 'meet your maker!' "

Bob and I have concocted a response to *our* anticipated "Call." When Mark complains about the stalling, we will begin by acting surprised. When he persists, we will point out that he has owned the car for several months, so what does he expect us to do? But he may still persist.

If he does, we will say (with a sigh), "Okay, get it fixed, and send us a copy of the bill. Depending on our mechanic's advice, we may agree to pay part, or all, of it." And who knows? *His* mechanics (the cousins) may be better than ours; they may actually solve the problem.

Alas, we have little faith in the above. No, we agree that we should anticipate the extreme scenario: a demand for a full refund. When that happens, any reader who is still interested may look forward to Part Three of this saga.

But *Buying Back a Car* will be Bob's party.

Flagman

Manhattan & Staten Island, 2014

I must of seen this guy hundreds of times, but I still can't believe him. First of all, he isn't a dwarf or a midget (I think there's a difference), but no way he's over four-foot-something --closer to four than five. And he's not bulked up, or anything, but sturdy, a fireplug. What could he weigh, one-ten, one-twenty? Gray hair, thick, definitely not a rug. Age, forty-five, fifty? Till maybe a month ago, clean-shaven, but then (I shit you not) he grows himself a little pussy tickler, also gray! Not to toot my own horn, but I notice stuff like that.

Another thing I also can't believe is, he seems to wear practically the same uniform every single day of the year, throughout the four seasons. I guess the garage pays the dry cleaning, and they give him several sets of uniforms: white shirt, black pants, shoes, red tie, all tiny. In the warmer months, the shirt has short sleeves, in colder, long. In spring and fall, they add a black cap and windbreaker, and in winter, gloves, hat (with ear flaps) and parka, also black. The shirt, coat, jacket, cap and hat all have a red logo in large squiggly letters: "ATLAS PARKING," the name of the garage. And, finally, they provide the guy with a big red flag that looks like it's attached to his hand. He waves the flag so hard I can't understand why it does not shred or why the stick does not break. No, he doesn't "wave it," he *snaps* it. They must replace the flag at least once a month, it always looks new. And he never shouts to would-be customers, just tries to snap them down to the garage (underground). Since the traffic on that particular block usually crawls, those drivers seeking one of the non-existent parking spots on the street have plenty of time to decide to end their misery by springing for the garage.

Who is this strange-looking little dude? Until a couple months ago, his guyrations with the flag made me think it could be a mistake to try and chat him up (although I sometimes do converse with strangers). Because, frankly, he looked like a nutcase! Plus the foot traffic on the sidewalk in front of the ramp down to the garage is so heavy you feel like you better plunge your car right into any opening before the pushy pedestrians clog it up again. ("He who hesitates...") And, on my way back up the ramp, I'm usually anxious to get to the worksite, since I'm usually late.

You see, I was in possession of a monthly parking pass for this place, which is why I seen the guy so much —every day for ten, eleven months. The space set me back three-and-a-half c's per month, which (I shit you not) is a real bargain for this area. Anyways, I make good money, and I'll pay anything to avoid the fuckin' subway ride back and forth to my home in Bay Ridge, Brooklyn – "BR." Why do I hate the subway so much? Don't ask! But I'll tell you this much, it takes maybe an hour each way --on *good* days.

Recently, however, I finally decided to stop for a mo' on the way back up the ramp, after handing over my keys to one of the "African-Americans" who park the cars —and collect the tips. See, I overslept that day, so I didn't reach the city till ten, ten-thirty. To my surprise, however, when I come trudging back up the ramp, the flagman was temporarily idle. He looked like he was maybe waiting for the next wave of cars. Or else by then, all the cars that were coming in were in already, and he was just waiting to be informed that his morning's work was over and he could go home to, I assume, his little house and little family for five, six hours (depending on where he lives), till it was time for the cars to be flagged back out and carry their drivers off to their own homes (which I notice a lot of them are in Jersey).

Anyways, last month, my chinwag with the flagman finally occurred, on Monday, July 14th, to be exact, the day after the World Cup final (Germany 1, Argentina 0). Since the Cup was a ready-made topic of conversation, and since I was already late and he was free, I decided to engage him in a brief exchange of views. Actually, I did it just to hear what the guy who had been flagging me in and out of the garage all those days, weeks, and months sounded like. It makes me uncomfortable to see some person three hundred times without so much as a "Hey, how you doin'?" (Not that I am ignorant of what curiosity done to the cat.)

"Some game yesterday, eh?"

"Wass no good. Who care? Was shit game!"

Well, well. His voice was high-pitched and nasal, with an accent I couldn't place, maybe Latino. Was he a Mex or *Platano* (i.e. Dominican)? Probably not an Argentine, however. I say this because men from Argentina, at least judging from the Cup, seem to mostly range from medium to tall. Or maybe he was from Eastern Europe, one of those former Commie shitholes.

"Well, the Germans played great," I replied, determining to pull his chain a little. "Too bad Messi had such a bad day." I heard it said that Lionel Messi, who may be the world's best player (and five-seven), was seen puking before the final. I don't know if this is a fact, or maybe he pukes before every game, but Lionel did look "peeked," or something, without his usual amazing flash. Anyways, as I was saying all this crap to the flagger, I could see from his face that he didn't know what the hell I was talking about. We could of been from different planets.

He just kept shaking his head, with the big flag drooped next to his right knee. By now, his face was a blank, but still with undertones of anger. As I said, although he was obviously p.o.'d at the outcome of the game, I didn't think he was an Argentinian. (I hear a lot of people from the other --excuse me-- spic nations hate the Argentines.) Who knows, maybe he dropped a few shekels on the game. Anyways, I said no more, I just walked away, waving back over my shoulder as I headed for the worksite —another new luxury condo building, my third in the past three years.

In case you're wondering, my specific job entails grunt work -- hauling cement and other shit, hosing down the site, whatever. To tell the truth, I don't have any real skills. My only asset is my strength, which, however (if I may say so, myself), is considerable. As the end of a shift approaches, in mid-afternoon, I'll still be hopping on and off the truck beds, while the college boys are bent over clasping their knees and sucking wind. (I refer to the summer employees, many of who are the boss's relations.)

Actually, to tell the truth, I was sucking wind myself that day, because I was still half-wasted from the World Cup bash the day before. Which was like a wake, anyways, since by then the U.S. was history. I wonder if there are studies indicating who drinks and eats more, fans whose teams are still alive, or those who are not. Anyways, in the two, three hours the final took (counting the two fifteen-minute overtime periods), I must of put away a whole package single-handed ("Sadder, But Wiser"), plus maybe five pounds of food: cold cuts, bread, potato salad, pie, cake, candy, chips, and so forth. But let's not go there, my heartburn will recur.

Three days after my chitchat with the flagman —it was Thursday, by then-- I was eating lunch with the boys on the stoop adjacent to the worksite. This stoop belongs to a very fancy building, a four-story brick townhouse. The only time we ever see the owners is around 8:30, when we would be having our ten-minute, stand-up, first coffee break out in front of the site. Most days, two young suits carrying computer bags, both of them males, come hopping down the steps, not making eye contact, or anything. Since they never lock the gate behind them, later on, at half-past eleven, we seat ourselves in our "reserved lunchroom" –their stoop-- although I, for one, would guess these guys are the type who might get snippy if they knew we ate lunch on their property every day.

I will say that we leave no litter, however –not a single bit. Have you ever noticed how construction grunts never leave litter? If I was to hazard a guess as to "why," it would be because, after we work like a bitch erecting a new structure, we want the work area to remain pristine --at least until the job is finished and our backs are turned! In fact, when I see a person spitting out their gum on a sidewalk our men have recently laid, I have to stop myself from charging after the person and cold-cocking him. (Of course, I would not cold-cock a female, I'm not *that* big an asshole.)

I wonder if the guy couple we see every morning own the whole building or are just renters. My guess is the former, since that building does not have the look of being broken up into separate units. I can't put my finger on the exact difference, but there is one. (I tried to check for doorbells once, but the vestibule was locked.)

Anyways, I was on the stoop with the boys enjoying my usual, which on Thursdays is a hot Meatball Parmigian with a chilled Coke (liter bottle, but I save some for the drive home). As usual, we were shooting the usual shit about the job, the foreman, and so forth, and making our usual pig comments about the passing honeys, of which there are many in this particular 'hood, as well as side-of-the-mouth cracks about all the mutton (of both sexes) pretending to be lamb, of which there is also plenty around here.

During one of our numerous conversational silences, broken only by the sounds of five men glugging, chewing, grunting, sighing, and occasionally breaking wind (from both ends), don't ask me why, but my thoughts turned to the flagman. Since I was aware that at least a couple other dudes on the site also use that garage, I thought I'd ask if anyone happened to know the little guy. But, as I like to do, I came at the question indirectly, from the side, so to speak.

"Say, boys, any of you park your car at that place over on Fourteenth just west of the Square? I think it's called 'Atlas,' or something." Don't ask me why I said that, I *know* it's called Atlas. And, as I might of guessed, it was Jock, the runty Frenchman, who responded, by cracking wise.

"Let me guess why you are asking us this question, John," he said, in his faintly Frog accent. You could see the ears of the other three get big as they awaited for the inevitable Jockie-ism. "You are going to tell us, 'Sorry, but the place has just burned down,' or 'There was a big crash there this morning.' Or something similar [seem-oo-lah.]. Is this not correct, John?"

That speech was one of Jock's weaker efforts, and it got the exact response it deserved –none. Except from me.

"Very funny, Jockie Boy," I said, "except nobody's laughing. Actually, I was going to ask you guys a specific question, but I better direct it specifically to the other three of you, rather than to this moron Frog."

That got a chuckle. Jock placed his sandwich and coffee container delicately on the stoop next to him. Springing to his feet and hopping down the three steps, he assumed the pugilist position.

"Let us go, John," he said, "let us go right now. Nobody calls me 'Moron'!" By now, he had stopped reacting to "Frog."

I could see that the Jockie was genuinely pissed, but so what? Placing my own food and beverage on the stoop, I coolly stood up, trotted down the steps, and got in his face. But I left my hands hanging at my sides. Since Jock is about a foot shorter than me, the boys all roared. My plan, if necessary, was to bear hug him.

"Suppose I was to apologize, Jock," I ventured. "I take it back, you're not a moron."

"Very well, then, accepted," he said, sounding relieved. He hopped back up the steps and reached for his sandwich.

"No," I said, standing right where I was. "You maybe *used to* be a moron, but since you got that *gavoon* haircut last week, *now* you look like an idiot!" The boys, of course, all roared.

"Asshole!" Jock contented himself with, probably because he didn't want to put the sandwich down and challenge me again, just to get laughed at again.

Returning to my place, I also resumed my meal. But after a few bites and a slug of Coke, I spoke up again. "So. I'll ask my question once more. Is that okay with you, Jock?" He avoided eye contact and did not reply. "So. Any of you bozos happen to know the parking attendant with the red flag in front of the Atlas garage?" Out of consideration for Jock, I did not add, "the little guy."

Well, Jamie did know him. "Jamie" is really "Jaime," pronounced "Hymie" (but no Jewish connection). A young Cuban dude, very good worker, well liked, a carpenter. Plus he can take a joke. For instance, a while ago, one of the other guys told this racist riddle: "What did the Latino fireman name his two sons?" "Hose A and Hose B." Jamie laughed like everyone else, no problem.

Actually, the guy who told that joke, George, is from Uruguay, which will go down in history because their player actually *bit* an Italian player. (And didn't the Aztecs play soccer, or polo, or something, using a skull for the ball?) George is a decent guy, however, quiet, a hard worker.

Anyways, as I now learned, Jaime's grandfather knew the grandfather of the flagman. The flagman's name, also according to Jaime, is "Raimundo." Back in the day, shortly after that asshole Castro took power, Raimundo's grandpa brought the whole family over to the good old U.S. of A. I think Cuba is the last remaining Commie power on earth. A bunch of fucking ostriches!

Anyways, Jaime told me that much, which satisfied my interest in the flagman, since in light of Jaime's story, the little guy's sour reply to my conversational gamble now made perfect sense. His daddy was probably one of those bitter old *Cubanos* who still hang out in Miami, playing dominoes and chomping on non-Cuban cigars while they swap lies about returning to the homeland. The apple don't fall far from the tree.

Well, a few weeks later, even if I had still wanted to chat up the little flagman again (which I didn't), the window of opportunity slammed shut: that is, the garage closed. And how! You see, a catastrophe occurred.

What actually happened was this. As usual, I was driving in. A Tuesday morning, early August it was, by then. But just before seven, when I hit the F.D.R., I run into the worst traffic jam I ever experienced. (Which is saying something.)

The night before, as usual, I fell asleep on the couch in the middle of a ballgame. Marie had gotten pissed, as usual, and gone up to bed alone, muttering her usual suggestion that I perform the sex act upon myself. Well, that wouldn't of mattered —what else is new?-- only we both missed the evening news.

Which I realized was a very bad thing, when I became embedded in the cement-like traffic the next morning. What I learned after getting off the Drive and parking the car in a rip-off day garage ($25.33, plus 18.375% tax, total $30), and taking the subway up to the job (same site), was that, in the middle of the night, a 100-year-old water main burst, half a block west of Atlas. I first learned this from Jock, actually, while we were hauling sheet rock. The deluge resulting from the break caused big-time damage. Three nearby apartment houses had already rented temporary boilers, because theirs got flooded out. The water was completely shut off in dozens of buildings, and landlines were down for a radius of three, four blocks. (We were lucky --we use cells on the job, and our water comes through a different pipe.) As for the Atlas, it was totally submerged.

What I also heard, later on, from another co-worker who used to park down there once in a while, is that every single one of the vehicles, maybe fifty or more, many of which are really expensive rides --Mercs, Jags, Beamers, high-end SUV's, and E.T.C.-- were completely buried in mud! Actually, the guy who told me this saw the cars being towed up the ramp, one by one, a few days later, on his way to the site from the subway. He said it was unreal, just like a disaster movie. And this mess was going to be at least a six-month nightmare for the insurance agents and the vehicle owners and all others making claims. By the way, did you know that elevators which have their works in the basement and get flooded out are not eligible for coverage? I was told this about the elevators by Peter, our foreman, a knowledgeable guy (but a prick).

Several thoughts entered my head at the time. One: it was lucky *my* car wasn't down there. Two: would I even be able to find a space now, since the other nearby facilities might also be closed? And, if not, they would certainly not miss this opportunity to gouge the hell out of all the unlucky dislocated parking slobs. For me, personally, it was going to mean months of subway hell.

And then I thought of what's his name, Raimundo. What would the catastrophic event mean to his job? Oh, well, that was his problem, why should I care? But a few days ago, during a lunchtime lull, I did think of the little flagman again. So I asked Jaime, who said he heard Ray (as he calls him) got re-assigned to one of Atlas's places out in Queens --Forest Hills, he thought, or Kew Gardens.

"But what do you care what happens to Ray, John? It's no skin off your ass."

I ignored that. "Good for him," I said, my tone indicating that I didn't give a shit. Jaime gave me a "Well, you asked" shrug.

Which I didn't (give a shit), actually, since I am facing some big new problems of my own. First of all, Marie and I recently underwent another nuclear incident. This one was over her horrible cooking, for which I blame my ulcers on. When she started in with the old crap about my "hereditary disposition," I completely lost it, and flung the offending dish (a big bowl of what she calls "goulash") against the newly painted white wall of our dining tomb, right next to her prize plug-ugly China cabinet. Off to the parental dwelling she stormed, a postwar split-level in Babylon, L.I. –accompanied, of course, by *my* three kids!

By now, I'm just sad about this incident, which happened three, four weeks ago. And I been on my own ever since. Which means TV dinners and lots of take-out, both of which really fuck with my poor guts. It also means coming home (by subway) to an empty house, no kids. But a peaceful house, however, because no Marie to pull my chain every minute. Silver lining, right? Well...

As if all of that ain't bad enough, the big job near Union Square has finally been completed. Ta-ra! A ten-story condo building, one spectacular unit per floor, at two mill a pop. Actually, we did a beautiful job, if I may say so myself, although truthfulness makes me add (in case you're thinking of purchasing a unit) that by the time of the water main break, it was too late for us move the boiler up to the roof. How does that saying go, "*Caviar emptat*"? ("Watch out, Buyer!")

So for me and fifty-three other grunts, it's *sayonara*, back to h.q. to await for the next job. Which isn't so bad, however, when you think of it, since they mostly seem to have several projects in the pipeline. Or, if not, maybe a month or two of Unemployment bennies till the next job call. But still, however, a major hit to my income stream.

And, you might ask, will the city now replace all the rest of the hundred-year old water mains before more of them blow? Are you kidding? Political suicide! And, unless they're indicted, most pols are not the kind of gees who normally fall on their own swords!

Does that last point sound like I'm getting a little cynical, or even morbid? Well, maybe I am. Because, besides all of the aforementioned misfortunes, my own vehicle (how ironic!) is starting to show early warning signs of needing a new tranny (sluggish in first and in reverse, 3.5 K). Plus, I have to get ready to fork over significant spondoolicks for a mega property tax hike, because the city is finally going to replace the ancient sewers in B.R. (also ironic!)

I know, you're asking, "Which of the pols have fallen on their swords, after all?" Do I really know? Maybe our 86-year-old Councilman is among them, finally ready to step back from the trough after eleven terms, and transfer his heroic efforts on behalf of John Q. to a full-time gig out on the links.

Oh, and of course, Marie's salary doesn't cover the kids' school and camp expenses, plus that "certain amount" she feels obliged to fork over to her parents for filling the hungry mouths of three growing kids, plus her own big fat gut!

At any rate, after all this, do I really have to explain why I don't give a flying you-know-what about poor little Raimundo? (Remember him?) He's probably still out there in Queens, waving his red flag. And if not, for all I care, he could be on his way back to Cuba in a leaky rubber raft with an outboard motor, accompanied by eight other stiffs, each of them armed with an antiquated weapon.

***

Stop the Press! It's not even ten a.m., and two major events have already transpired today. First, I leave the house (no new job calls) to go get the paper, and I'm blindsided by a huge headline:

OBAMA TO FIDEL: LET'S MAKE NICE!

Well, fuck me! A "thaw!" Does that mean we can forget about poor little Ray in his leaky raft? Then, I get home, and, just as I'm pouring my second cuppa, the phone rings. It's my baby sister, calling to cry on my shoulder because Billy, her son, has decided to become her daughter! Whoa! Maybe, it's time for Y.T. to sell the house and move to a new planet.

Stop the Press (#2)! And get this! The new administration says the *Cubanos* are poisoning our diplomats. So it's "poor little Refugee-Ray," after all!

Acknowledgments

The Rented Pet--Piker Press, Kindle Select, Akorin* Books, all 2012
*Akorin Books is the author's imprint.

Norman's Cousin--*nth position online magazine*, 2007
Voir, Dear--*sage of consciousness*, 2008
Flagman--*Adelaide Literary Review*, 2018

About the Author

Ron Singer, b.1941, has been both a lifelong resident of New York City, and one who has traveled to, lived in, and written about the wider world. For forty-four years, Singer was a teacher and writer. Singer's life and writing have both featured political activism. For instance, while he was in South Africa working on a book, he was invited to read poetry at a memorial for activist/poet Dennis Brutus. The book is *Uhuru Revisited: Interviews with Pro-Democracy Leaders* (Africa World Press, Red Sea Press, 2015). It can be found in libraries around the world. *Norman's Cousin & Other Writings* is Singer's 21st published book.

About the Press

Unsolicited Press based out of Portland, Oregon and focuses on the works of the unsung and underrepresented. As a womxn-owned, all-volunteer small publisher that doesn't worry about profits as much as championing exceptional literature, we have the privilege of partnering with authors skirting the fringes of the lit world. We've worked with emerging and award-winning authors such as Shann Ray, Amy Shimshon-Santo, Brook Bhagat, Kris Amos, and John W. Bateman.

Learn more at unsolicitedpress.com. Find us on twitter and instagram